"I have to get back to work."

"Wait." Kid held up a hand. "I'd like to talk about oil leases."

"What?" Lucky eased back into her chair.

"Shilah Oil would like to lease your land for oil and gas."

She wanted to laugh and without realizing it, she did. She had something Kid wanted. This was going to be fun.

"No," she replied without having to think about it.

"Come on, Lucky. This could be good for you." He glanced around. "Maybe you could get out of this beer joint."

That did it.

"The land is not for lease."

"Why not?"

"I'm not leasing to a Hardin."

He drew back as if she'd hit him. "Come on, Lucky."

Come on, Lucky. That and his I-live-for-you smile were his trademarks. *Come on, Lucky.* He'd kiss her cheek. *Come on, Lucky.* He'd stroke her hair. *Come on, Lucky.* And she'd do anything he wanted.

But not anymore.

Dear Reader,

The Texan's Christmas is the last book in The Hardin Boys miniseries. I've lived with these characters for almost two years and it's sad to let them go, but I'm going to end the series with a bang—with tears and laughter. The best way!

If you've read the other two books, *The Texan's Secret* and *The Texan's Bride,* you're well acquainted with Cisco "Kid" Hardin, the middle brother. If you haven't, that's okay. You'll still love Kid, the charmer, the ladies' man. He has a devil-may-care attitude and nothing in life fazes him much. Until he has to face his past—his first love, Lucinda "Lucky" Littlefield.

You probably know someone who has the gift of gab. Who never meets a stranger. Who's the life of the party and always makes you laugh. My younger brother, Paul, is like that. He keeps everyone in stitches at family gatherings and is fun to be around.

Kid Hardin has some of those traits, and it was a challenge to see what it would take to make him serious. Kid and Lucky have a love story that has kept me on the edge of my seat and I hope you enjoy these characters as much as I've enjoyed creating them. So it's goodbye to the Hardins, but I hope they live on in your mind.

With love and thanks,

Linda Warren

P.S.—It's always a pleasure to hear from readers. You can email me at Lw1508@aol.com or write me at P.O. Box 5182, Bryan, TX 77805. Visit my website at www.lindawarren.net
or www.facebook.com/authorlindawarren. I will answer your letters as soon as I can.

The Texan's Christmas

Linda Warren

TORONTO NEW YORK LONDON
AMSTERDAM PARIS SYDNEY HAMBURG
STOCKHOLM ATHENS TOKYO MILAN MADRID
PRAGUE WARSAW BUDAPEST AUCKLAND

If you purchased this book without a cover you should be aware that this book is stolen property. It was reported as "unsold and destroyed" to the publisher, and neither the author nor the publisher has received any payment for this "stripped book."

Recycling programs
for this product may
not exist in your area.

ISBN-13: 978-0-373-71747-7

THE TEXAN'S CHRISTMAS

Copyright © 2011 by Linda Warren

All rights reserved. Except for use in any review, the reproduction or utilization of this work in whole or in part in any form by any electronic, mechanical or other means, now known or hereafter invented, including xerography, photocopying and recording, or in any information storage or retrieval system, is forbidden without the written permission of the publisher, Harlequin Enterprises Limited, 225 Duncan Mill Road, Don Mills, Ontario, Canada M3B 3K9.

This is a work of fiction. Names, characters, places and incidents are either the product of the author's imagination or are used fictitiously, and any resemblance to actual persons, living or dead, business establishments, events or locales is entirely coincidental.

This edition published by arrangement with Harlequin Books S.A.

For questions and comments about the quality of this book please contact us at Customer_eCare@Harlequin.ca.

® and TM are trademarks of the publisher. Trademarks indicated with ® are registered in the United States Patent and Trademark Office, the Canadian Trade Marks Office and in other countries.

www.Harlequin.com

Printed in U.S.A.

ABOUT THE AUTHOR

RITA® Award-nominated and award-winning author Linda Warren has written thirty books for Harlequin, including stories for the Superromance, American Romance and Everlasting Love series. Drawing upon her years of growing up on a farm/ranch in Texas, she writes about sexy heroes, feisty heroines and broken families with an emotional punch, all set against the backdrop of Texas. When she's not writing or at the mall, she's sitting on her patio with her husband watching the wildlife and plotting her next book. Visit her website at www.LindaWarren.net.

Books by Linda Warren

HARLEQUIN SUPERROMANCE

1167—A BABY BY CHRISTMAS
1221—THE RIGHT WOMAN
1250—FORGOTTEN SON
1314—ALL ROADS LEAD TO TEXAS
1354—SON OF TEXAS
1375—THE BAD SON
1440—ADOPTED SON
1470—TEXAS BLUFF
1499—ALWAYS A MOTHER
1574—CAITLYN'S PRIZE *
1592—MADISON'S CHILDREN *
1610—SKYLAR'S OUTLAW *
1723—THE TEXAN'S SECRET**
1735—THE TEXAN'S BRIDE**

HARLEQUIN AMERICAN ROMANCE

1042—THE CHRISTMAS CRADLE
1089—CHRISTMAS, TEXAS STYLE
"Merry Texmas"
1102—THE COWBOY'S RETURN
1151—ONCE A COWBOY
1226—TEXAS HEIR
1249—THE SHERIFF OF HORSESHOE, TEXAS
1333—HER CHRISTMAS HERO

*The Belles Of Texas
**The Hardin Boys

Other titles by this author available in ebook.

I dedicate this book to my brother,
Paul William—you'll always be the life of the party.

I would like to thank all the patient and understanding people who answered my endless questions about the oil industry, trains and cattle rustling. All errors are strictly mine.

CHAPTER ONE

LUCINDA LITTLEFIELD.

The name evoked a torrent of high school memories—heavenly blue eyes, kissing in the bleachers, making out in his old pickup…and a whole lot of regret.

Cisco Hardin shifted restlessly in his truck as he sped down the road in High Cotton, Texas. Everyone in school had called her Lucky, and they'd dubbed him Kid. Somehow he knew they'd meet again, but he never dreamed it would be like this.

In his mind their eyes would lock across a crowded room. She'd smile that smile that turned him inside out and all the promises he'd broken would be forgotten. Chickens wearing high heels might be a more likely scenario, he mused. Lucky wasn't going to forget what he'd done. It was time to roll the dice and see if twenty years had mellowed the cockles of Lucky's heart.

As he pulled into the parking area of the one beer joint in the small town, his cell jangled to the tune of "Ain't Going Down ('Til the Sun Comes Up)." Turning off the ignition, he reached for the phone on his belt.

"Hey, Cadde." His brother was the CEO of Shilah Oil. Kid and Chance, their other brother, had a vested interest in the company, too. The Hardin boys were in the oil business.

"Did you get Lucky to sign the lease?" Cadde always came straight to the point.

"I just reached The Joint."

"What took so long?"

"Well—" he tapped his fingers on the steering wheel "—I wanted to see Aunt Etta and Uncle Rufus and then I went to Chance's, but the baby was asleep so I stopped at your house to play with Jacob. He's crawling everywhere and pulling up to his feet by himself."

"He'll be walking soon. Jessie and I can hardly keep up with him." There was a long sigh. "Kid, you're stalling."

"Maybe." He had to admit this wasn't easy for him.

"You were only a boy when you promised to call and come back after you left for Lubbock and Texas Tech, but you didn't. That was years ago. You've both moved on."

"I know. I can't figure out what she's doing in High Cotton running her dad's bar."

"Don't worry about her life, just get the lease signed. I've already purchased our drilling contract from Anadarko and it didn't come cheap. Since Bud transferred the land and mineral rights to Lucky, we need her fifty acres to complete the desired acreage to drill the oil well. We have a personal stake in this because our property left to us by our parents is a major part of the tract."

"I'm well aware of that, big brother."

"Do you want me to talk to Lucky?"

"Hell, no. Leasing is my department and I'll handle it."

"You'll have to get out of your truck to do that."

Kid looked around. "Are you watching me?"

There was a laugh on the other end. "No, but I know you and, believe me, this is a first—Kid Hardin afraid to talk to a woman."

"Lucky's not any woman."

"You might want to analyze that statement and why this is so hard for you."

He'd rather not. "You always said my past was going to come back and haunt me. I can feel the ol' Ghost-busters chomping at my butt."

"If you don't want to see her, Chance or I will do it."

"Like hell."

"Then get out of your truck."

Kid clicked off before the curse words could leave his mouth. Grabbing his hat from the passenger's seat, he got out. The parking lot was graveled as it had been years ago and it crunched beneath his boots like corn-flakes. The weatherworn siding and tin roof with the rusty spots were the same, too. An iron rail ran across the front. Bud had put it up after a drunk had plowed through his building one night. "The Beer Joint" blinked from a neon sign. Bud hadn't used much cre-ativity in naming the place. Besides Kid's truck, three more were nosed up to the rail and it was only five o'clock on a hot September afternoon.

Opening the heavy door, he stepped into the dimly

lit bar and just like that, twenty years smacked him in the face. They were seventeen years old and he'd fixed up an old Ford pickup to drive to school. After classes, The Beer Joint was the first place they'd stop. Lucky would go in the side door and sneak out two beers. Then they'd cruise the back roads, stopping at the old abandoned Potter place beneath an overgrown entrance. He'd drink his beer and then hers because she'd only take a couple of sips. The rest of the afternoon they'd spend making out when they should have been studying.

He was her first and he'd thought he would love her forever.

After his eyes adjusted, he saw the inside was the same, too; the back wall had a row of red booths that now looked more orange than red. Wooden tables were scattered in the center, the old jukebox that probably held records from the 1980s occupied another wall, and to the left was the mahogany bar Bud had built. It shone like glass. A couple huddled together in a booth, two guys sat at a table and three cowboys were bellied up to the bar talking to a waitress.

He didn't see Lucky.

Straddling a faded red bar stool, he looked around, his eyes falling on the waitress. She made no move to serve him. One cowboy said something and she laughed. His mind reeled. Oh, my God! He knew that soft, seductive chuckle. It visited him often in his dreams. Could she be…?

His eyes roamed over her slim yet curvy figure dressed in tight jeans. Her breasts pushed against a blue fitted blouse and the first button was undone. That he noticed, but her hair drew his attention. Lucky's blond hair was long and flowing. This woman's was short, kind of chic, *wobberjawed* is what he'd call the style. It looked damn good on her, though.

Lucky.

What have you done to your hair?

Just when he was about to fall off his bar stool from shock, she turned and walked over to him.

"Can I get you anything?"

The soft lilting voice was the same but there was no recognition in the blue eyes—the eyes that used to sparkle for him. Now they just stared at him with irritation.

He wanted to say, "It's me, Kid," but somehow the words got tangled up in the past of his misdeeds. What he said was, "Beer. Miller Lite."

"Can or bottle?"

"Bottle."

Behind her was a large cooler filled with numerous kinds of beer. She opened the door and grabbed one. After placing it in front of him on a napkin, she laid a ticket on the bar. He pulled out his wallet and placed a five on top of it.

"Keep the change."

Without a word, she put the ticket and money in the cash register. She slammed it shut and went back to the cowboys, ignoring him as if he were invisible.

That was cold.

But she was beautiful and sexy, just like he'd remembered. The classic lines of her face were now mature as was her body. And her breasts—were they always that full? They used to fit the palm of his hand perfectly.

She didn't recognize him! That took a moment to digest. Getting her to sign a lease was going to be so much easier now. He'd worried for nothing.

Looking down, he saw the bottle still had the cap on it. He knew it was a twist-off, but just to niggle her, he called, "Miss?"

She glanced his way.

"Aren't you supposed to remove the cap?"

"Oh." She moved over to him, her blue eyes narrowed. "I thought you could flick it off with your thumb."

He frowned. Was she joshing him? He used to brag about that in high school. Not that he could, but it didn't keep him from boasting.

Taking the bottle, she gave it a quick twist and placed it in front of him on the napkin. Foam oozed from the top and spilled onto the side. Did she shake it?

Again, without a word she walked away.

He needed another napkin, but decided against asking. He took a cold sip.

A man came through the door on the right, carrying a case of beer. Bubba Joe Grisley. In school, he'd had a big head and his body had finally caught up. The man was huge. Did he work here? From the apron he wore, Kid figured he did. Bubba Joe used to have a crush on Lucky. Had they hooked up? Chance had said that Lucky wasn't married, but that didn't mean a thing.

Bubba Joe unloaded the case into the cooler and

turned, his eyes catching Kid's. "Well, if it ain't Crisco Hardin."

Kid ran his thumb over the frosty bottle. "If you call me *Crisco* one more time, I'm going to jump across this bar and show you how strong I've gotten in twenty years."

Bubba Joe laughed, a sound that rumbled through his large chest. "Hey, Kid. I'm joking."

"I didn't like it when you called me that in third grade and I don't like it now."

"Hell, Kid, you got all the looks and charm and all I got was a big head. I had to have some fun." Bubba Joe rubbed his balding head. "I think I still have knots that you put there."

"I didn't hit you that hard."

"Life was good back then, huh?" Before Kid could answer, Bubba Joe shouted to Lucky. "Hey, Kid Hardin's back in town."

"I know. I served him a beer," she said without any emotion, and without looking his way.

That was even colder.

She remembered. On that thought came another. After all these years she was still pissed and madder than a bear caught in a trap. He knew Lucky and her stubborn pride. She wasn't ever going to forgive him. Forgiveness wasn't something he needed—too many years had passed for that. But he was sorry he'd hurt her.

After his parents' tragic deaths, his mind was all messed up and Lucky was there to comfort him in a way no one else could. They were friends a long time before their relationship had become intimate.

"Are you moving back to High Cotton like your brothers?" Bubba Joe asked, leaning on the bar.

"Nah." Kid took a swallow. "I'm staying in Houston. I've gotten used to the bright lights."

"Yeah. I bet." Bubba Joe snickered in that I-know-what-you-mean sort of way.

Kid just drank his beer, but every now and then he could feel Lucky's heavenly baby blues on him. But now there was nothing divine about them. Instead, they gave off more of a fire and brimstone feel.

"Chance built a huge roping pen back of his house. I see him out there roping most weekends. His little girl, too. Sometimes Tyler Jakes ropes with him. He's a roping champion."

Kid brought his attention back to Bubba Joe. "Tyler's a rodeo guy and he and Chance will always be cowboys." Tyler was younger than the Hardin boys but his rodeo success was well-known.

"Chance's wife just had a baby."

"Yeah." Kid twisted the bottle. "A little boy named Cody."

"His wife teaches at the school. My cousin has her for a teacher and he has a big crush on her—a beautiful blonde. Who wouldn't?"

"Shay's a real nice lady and Chance is lucky to have met her." But the relationship almost disintegrated on its own when Chance had found out the truth about Shay's past.

Chance had been asleep in the backseat the night their parents had crashed into a tree and died. Loud voices had awakened him. Seemed their father was leaving his family for another woman. That was the horrible secret Chance had kept, never telling anyone until about three years ago when he'd finally told his brothers.

No one knew who the other woman was until Shay literally crashed into Chance's life. The other woman was her mother.

Kid gulped the cold beer. That news had been hard to take, but they'd gotten through it as brothers. Their father had been a big part of their lives, so much so they'd followed him into the oil business. Chuck Hardin had roughnecked most of his life. He'd told his sons that they'd do better than him. They'd get an education and move up the ladder into a position of power. Everything their father had taught them felt tarnished by his betrayal.

"We all knew Cadde was going to succeed," Bubba Joe was saying. "He had that drive, even back then. Who knew he'd marry the boss's daughter."

"Yeah, who knew?" Kid swirled the beer around in the bottle. The marriage of convenience had turned into something special. Nothing much distracted Cadde from the oil business, except Jessie. When they'd lost their first child, Kid feared Cadde was never going to make it back from the edge. But he'd heard love had the power to heal. Kid didn't know much about that, though.

"I see his wife every now and then at Walker's General Store. She pushes the baby around in a stroller looking at everything in there like she's at Neiman Marcus. Her dog is in the stroller, too. It's a weird thing without any ears and if you get anywhere near that baby it growls and barks. Jessie, I think her name is, always apologizes. Man, she's a looker, and pregnant again. You Hardin boys are going to keep the name alive."

"Yeah," was all he said. His brothers had found something rare and he was happy for them. But he would always be the uncle and he was comfortable in that role.

"How about you, Kid. You married?"

"Nah. How about you?" Kid drained his beer.

"I still live with my momma. Every time I try to leave she gets sick."

Kid wanted to laugh. "Big-headed momma's boy" is what they used to call Bubba Joe. He didn't quite understand why kids had to be so cruel. In third grade Billy Ray Tarvel couldn't say "Cisco" so he'd called Kid "Crisco" because that's what his mom used to make pies. Kid had to forcibly hold Billy Ray down one day to make him say "Kid." After that no one but Bubba Joe called him that twice. Bubba Joe never did it in a cruel way. It was fun and he wanted to be Kid's buddy. Kid put knots on his head anyway.

Mostly, he had good memories about school, especially high school, and Lucky was a big part of that.

"Nice talking to you, Kid," Bubba Joe said. "I have to get back to work. Stop in again when you're in town."

"Thanks." He nodded and glanced toward Lucky. She was still talking to the cowboys as if they were her very best friends and giving them a very good view of her breasts. This wasn't the shy, demure girl he'd once known. It didn't matter. He was here on business and he had to get the job done.

"Lucky?"

She glanced at him, said something to the guys and came his way.

"You want another beer?" Her voice was so cold a chill ran up his spine.

"No. I…uh…I'd like to talk." Damn! He sounded like he was sixteen asking her for a date. But he'd never been this nervous. Talking to women came naturally to him. Why wasn't it easy to talk to Lucky?

"Talk," she replied, keeping the temperature subzero.

He stood and motioned toward a table. "In private."

He thought she was going to refuse, but she walked around the bar and sat down on a faded chair. He joined her. The air-conditioning was cool but he could feel the heat building between them. And it wasn't a good heat.

Removing his hat, he placed it on the table and looked into her cold, cold eyes. "You look great."

Lucky clasped her hands in her lap. What was she supposed to say to that? *You lying cheating bastard* came to mind. But she wouldn't sink to his level.

"I'm thirty-eight years old and I left looking good behind in my twenties."

"Come on, Lucky, you're still a knockout."

So are you.

This was where his deep sexy voice and sincere brown eyes always broke any resolve about not letting

Kid get to her. He had a way of making a woman feel special, as if she was beautiful and the only woman in the world for him. As a teenager she had fallen for his smooth-talking lies. As a mature woman she could hardly believe she'd been so naive—so naive that she'd actually believed a popular boy like Kid loved the barkeeper's daughter.

Due to her father's occupation the kids in school tended to look down on her. But Kid took her to school parties and dances and the shy girl finally fit in for the first time in her life.

Because Kid Hardin loved her.

Briefly.

Why couldn't he have loved her the way she'd loved him?

From the rumor mill in High Cotton she'd heard that many women had filled her shoes since. That hurt.

"What do you want, Kid?"

His warm glance slid over her face, and she felt a weakening deep in her stomach. The years had been kind to him. His hair was dark with just a hint of gray, and his chiseled features, strong chin, devil-may-care attitude and twinkle in his eyes could melt the coldest heart. The five o'clock shadow added to his sex appeal.

Don't let him get to you.

"Why did you cut your hair?"

"Excuse me?"

"Your hair." He waved a hand toward her. "It used to be long and gorgeous."

She looked him straight in the eye. "I'm not eighteen anymore."

"Ah, Lucky, I think we'll always be eighteen." That *you're special* gaze in his eyes did a number on her senses. She felt like that young girl who believed in fairy-tale endings—who believed in Kid. The thought stiffened her backbone.

"I'm not going down memory lane with you."

As if she hadn't spoken, he said, "What are you doing running your dad's beer joint? What happened to your plans of being a nurse?"

What happened?

Her stomach clenched tight. The day Kid had left for Texas Tech played vividly in her mind as if it were yesterday. It was mid-August and hot, much the same as today. Kid had driven to her house in his new red Chevy pickup that Dane Belle had bought him. After his parents' deaths, the Hardin boys lived on the High Five ranch, owned by Dane, with their aunt and uncle. Dane became the father figure they'd lost. All the boys loved and respected him.

That day they'd leaned against his truck saying goodbye.

"I wish your dad had sprung for you going to nursing school in Lubbock, and then we could have been together."

"It's too far away and I'm all he's got." She stroked his chest. "I wish Dane hadn't insisted you go to Tech."

"It's where Cadde is and Dane feels we need to stay close as brothers."

"But I'm going to miss you."

"I'll call and write," Kid said, running his fingers through her long hair.

She pressed into him, not knowing how she was going to exist without Kid. He kissed her long and deep.

"When are you leaving for Austin?" he asked against her lips.

"In about two weeks."

He tucked her hair behind her ears, his eyes dark and serious. "You're not going to forget me, are you?"

"I'll never forget you," she whispered.

"I love you, Lucky." His voice cracked when he said her name. "I will always love you."

"There'll never be anyone else for me."

"I'll call as soon as I get there," he promised.

They'd held on to each other for a long time and then Kid had driven away. She'd waved until she couldn't see him anymore. Every day she'd waited for that call. At the end of two weeks she finally had to admit to herself that he wasn't ever going to call or come back for her.

She'd left for Austin with a broken heart.

Kid Hardin was a liar and a cheat.

Why was she even talking to him?

"Lucky?"

She quickly got her emotions under control. "What do you want, Kid?"

"My brothers and I are in the oil business."

"I'm aware of that. I don't live under a rock. Cadde and Chance have moved back home and I see their wives all the time."

"You know Shay and Jessie?"

"Yes." Why did he seem so shocked? She supposed he thought the barkeeper's daughter wasn't good enough to socialize with the Hardins. She immediately pushed all that resentment away. "Darcy's the only kid I know who would come into a bar to sell Girl Scout Cookies."

"Shay let her do that?"

There was that note of concern again. In that moment she knew what she'd probably known for the past twenty years. That Kid had used her like all the other boys in school had tried. But he'd done it with words of *I love you* and *forever*. And she'd fallen for his lies like a child tottering on a cliff.

"Don't worry, Kid, Shay was waiting outside. Chance had said that Darcy had to sell the cookies herself and she was determined to sell the most in her troop."

"Yeah. I bought two cases. I munched on those things for months."

She took a long breath, not wanting to get into a family discussion. That was too easy, too familiar.

"I have to get back to work."

"Wait." He held up a hand. "I'd like to talk about oil leases."

"What?" She eased back into her chair.

"Shilah Oil would like to lease your land for oil and gas."

She wanted to laugh and without realizing it she did. She had something Kid wanted. This was going to be fun.

"No," she replied without having to think about it.

"Come on, Lucky. This could be good for you." He glanced around. "Maybe you could get out of this place."

That did it.

"The land is not for lease."

"Why not?"

"I'm not leasing to a Hardin."

He drew back as if she'd hit him. "Come on, Lucky."

Come on, Lucky. That and his I-live-for-you smile were his trademarks. *Come on, Lucky.* He'd kiss her cheek. *Come on, Lucky.* He'd stroke her hair. *Come on, Lucky.* And she'd do anything he wanted.

But not anymore.

CHAPTER TWO

KID SANK INTO A COMFY CHAIR in Cadde's den, feeling out of breath and sucker punched by a blue-eyed, short-haired blonde.

The land is not for lease. To a Hardin.

After that, Lucky put the lid on anything else he had to say. It was the first time in his life that his smile, his words, had failed, but it wasn't over. Lucky just thought it was.

His chest tightened and he focused on Jessie playing on the floor with Jacob. The moment the baby saw him he fell to all fours and crawled over, pulling up on Kid's jeans.

"Hey, partner." Kid lifted the nine-month-old baby onto his lap. Jacob bounced up and down, smiling, showing off his two lower teeth. Kid had always thought he didn't want kids, but the moment Jacob was born something changed in him. Instead of going on a date, he'd play with Jacob. He didn't understand that. Maybe it had something to do with his thirty-eight-plus years, which he'd been reminded of more than once today.

The whirl of a helicopter sounded above. Before Roscoe Murdock, Jessie's father, had died, he'd purchased a top-of-the-line helicopter for Shilah Oil so they could save time when traveling to oil wells. It was also an easy way for Cadde and Chance to go to work in Houston. Jacob's eyes opened wide and his mouth formed an O. Quickly he scooted from Kid's lap and crawled to his mother.

Jessie clapped her hands. "Daddy's home."

Excited, Jacob bounced up and down again on his butt. All he had on was a diaper and a T-shirt.

"What door does Daddy come in?" Jessie asked.

Jacob's mouth formed another O. "Da, da, da, da," Jacob babbled. Mirry, Jessie's dog, barked and trotted to the back door. The baby zoomed after her.

"He's understanding a lot," Kid said.

"Yes, he does," Jessie replied. "We read to him all the time and he loves animals."

"Wonder where he gets that from?" Jessie had an affinity for animals. Besides Mirry, she had a one-eyed donkey, a ram with no horns, five abused horses that were now healthy and a fawn she'd raised from a bottle. She'd set the doe free, but she always came back for feed and pampering.

When he'd first met Jessie, she was standoffish, but a looker, like Bubba Joe had said, with dark tumbling hair and black eyes. Her father protected and sheltered her all her life. On his deathbed, the man had made a deal with Cadde—marry my daughter and keep her safe and I'll give you my shares in Shilah Oil.

For ten years Cadde had worked his ass off for Roscoe. He'd earned everything he'd inherited, but Roscoe forgot to mention that Jessie received the largest part of Shilah. That set up the biggest test of wills Kid had ever seen. It had brought his strong brother to his knees and Jessie almost lost her sanity. But through it all they found the magic formula—love.

Love—what the hell was it?

"You look a little down," Jessie remarked, picking up a toy.

Kid clasped his hands between his knees. "I just had to face my past and it was a little unsettling."

"Cadde said you were trying to lease a piece of land from an old girlfriend."

"Yeah. My high school sweetheart, Lucky Littlefield."

"Oh." Jessie paused in stacking Jacob's toys on the coffee table. "I've met her."

"That right?"

"Yes, at Walker's General Store. I was browsing so long at the old neat stuff that Jacob grew fussy. He threw his stuffed dog out of the stroller. Lucky handed it back to him. Mirry didn't bark or growl like she usually does if anyone gets near him. Mirry's a very good judge of character. Lucky introduced herself and I liked her. She's very pretty with a stylish haircut."

"Yeah."

"Why are you frowning?"

Was he? He hadn't realized that.

"Don't you like her hair?"

He shrugged. "It used to be long."

"And you liked it that way?"

He looked into Jessie's teasing eyes. "Could we change the subject?"

She picked up another toy as if he hadn't spoken. "Cadde said she was the owner of The Beer Joint. When he said 'beer joint,' I had this vision of an older woman with yellowish bleached blond hair, tight-fitting clothes, a cigarette dangling from her lip and someone who had lived a rougher-than-rough lifestyle. Lucky wasn't like that at all. It's all about how we perceive people and most of the time it's wrong."

He stared down at his locked hands. "Kids in school looked down on her because her dad ran The Beer Joint."

"Did you?"

"What?"

"Did you look down on Lucky because of her circumstances?"

Did he?

"No," he answered his own question. "We were close since about the seventh grade. I didn't care what her father did for a living."

"That's a long time to know someone."

"Yeah." He rubbed his hands together. He remembered the first time she'd smiled at him and his heart had almost pounded out of his chest. He remembered the first time he'd kissed her. He remembered…

The back door opened and childish squeals of delight echoed from the hallway. Cadde walked in with Jacob in his arms, Mirry at his feet, barking, as if to alert everyone that Cadde was home.

Jessie placed her hand on the coffee table and tried to stand, but at seven months pregnant she was having difficulty.

Cadde kissed his son's cheek. "Go play with Uncle Kid. Daddy has to help Mommy."

Jacob shook his head vigorously and clung to Cadde. Reaching down, Cadde lifted Jessie with one arm while still holding Jacob. Nestling into his side, Jessie kissed him, her eyes sparkling.

"I think this baby is going to weigh ten pounds," she said, rubbing her stomach. She stroked Jacob's head. "You get a little territorial when Daddy comes home."

Jacob made a whimpering sound and Jessie laughed. "I'm going to check on supper. Kid, you're welcome to stay."

"I didn't know you cooked."

Her eyes darkened and he knew that was the wrong thing to say. Trying to rectify the blunder he quickly added, "Thanks, Jessie, but I'm eating at Aunt Etta's."

"Rosa does not do all the cooking at our house," she told him. Rosa and Felix Delgado had raised Jessie since she was seven. They now lived next door in a house that Cadde had built for them. They were Jessie's protectors. Her family. When Roscoe's niece had been kidnapped and murdered, he made sure that no one could get to his daughter. Roscoe was more than paranoid about her safety. But that was all behind them and he knew how important it was for Jessie to have a life. A family. He should have kept his mouth shut.

"I'm sorry, Jessie. I've had a rough day."

She walked over and kissed his cheek. "You're forgiven."

After Jessie left, Cadde sat on the sofa with Jacob resting against him, his legs locked around Cadde's waist.

"Stop aggravating my wife."

"I seem to be pissing off everyone today—without even trying."

Cadde rubbed his son's back, kissing his fat cheek.

As Kid watched his brother with his son, he felt a blow to his chest. This was what he wanted; a child rushing to the door in excitement to greet him, a woman who had eyes only for him. He wanted his own family.

"From the look on your face I'd say that you managed to piss off Lucky."

It took a moment for him to focus. He shifted in his chair. "She'd rather tar and feather me and then set fire to me before leasing to Shilah."

"I'll talk to her."

"No. I just need to regroup."

He could feel Cadde's eyes on him. "Maybe you need to start with an apology."

"It's been twenty years. What do I have to apologize for?" He stood in an angry movement. "We didn't even know what love was."

"Do you now?"

"Hell, no."

"The Kid I know would have sweet-talked his way through this, but somehow Lucky is a stumbling block for you. Why?"

"I don't know. All these memories seem to crowd in on me."

"Guilt, maybe?"

Kid ignored that. "I just can't figure out why she's running her dad's place."

"Why does it matter?"

"I'm going down to Chance's to talk to him." He was going to kiss Jacob but saw he was asleep.

"Kid," Cadde called as his brother walked away.

He glanced back.

"Let me or Chance handle this. We need the lease signed."

"I said I'd do it and I will."

In less than a minute Kid was in his truck and headed down the road to Chance's. He had stayed in High Cotton longer than any of the brothers. He probably knew more about Lucky than anyone, and Kid planned to be prepared the next time he saw her. Today she'd knocked him for a loop. That wasn't going to happen again.

Cadde had built a big two-story house to the right of their parents' old house. To the left was Chance and Shay's house, a sprawling one story with a barn and a corral. Because of Jessie's animals Cadde also had a barn and pens. The Hardin boys had come home in a big way.

Pulling over to the side of the road, he gazed at the old home place for a moment. The decaying white frame house sat on Kid's part of the land. Some day soon they'd have to do something about the house. For years they'd been putting it off. They might be grown men but they were afraid to open the door and face the demons of their youth. Or maybe it was the memories they didn't want to face. Memories that were perfect in their minds, but maybe in reality they weren't.

Whatever it was, Kid decided he had enough demons to face. One in particular was Lucinda Littlefield.

Kid saw Chance and Darcy at the roping pen so he drove there. Darcy was throwing a rope at a dummy calf while Chance leaned on the fence watching her and giving instructions. Tiny, Darcy's Chihuahua, sat at Chance's feet.

"Twirl it," Chance shouted to his daughter. "Use your wrist."

Eleven-year-old Darcy flung the rope toward the dummy and it missed by an inch. "Shoot." She stomped her foot.

"Try again," Chance said.

Kid joined his younger brother at the pipe fence. "Are we having a rodeo or something?"

"Nah. Just showing Darcy a little extra attention. Everyone makes a fuss over the baby and I don't want her to feel left out."

Darcy was adopted, but no one would ever guess that by the way Chance doted on her.

"Hey, Uncle Kid." Darcy waved. "Watch me."

"Hey, hotshot." He waved back. Hotshot was Chance's nickname for her. Now everyone called her that. It fit. The girl was spunky and didn't have a shy bone in her body.

She swung the rope and it landed in a perfect loop

over the dummy. "Daddy, Daddy, did you see?" Darcy jumped up and down.

"That's my girl."

Darcy ran and jumped on the fence. Chance lifted his daughter over the top.

"I'm good, huh, Daddy?" Darcy pushed her glasses up the bridge of her nose.

"You're the best." Chance hugged her and kissed the top of her head.

"Here comes Mommy." Darcy drew away and dashed to meet Shay who was walking across the lawn, holding baby Cody. Wearing denim shorts and a tank top, Shay looked beautiful, as always.

"He was asleep earlier," Shay said, handing the baby dressed in a blue outfit and cap to him. "Now he wants to see his uncle Kid."

Kid stared down at the three-month-old baby. Cody moved his head around, his greenish-brown eyes wide-open as he flailed his hands and legs.

"I just nursed him and he wants more."

Chance kissed his son's forehead. "Enough, buddy."

"Can I hold him, Mommy?" Darcy wanted to know.

"When we get back to the house."

"Does anyone notice how much Cody looks like Jacob?" he asked, studying the chubby cheeks and cap of brown hair.

"Yeah," Chance replied, "except Jacob has Jessie's black eyes. Cody's will probably be brown like mine."

Kid cradled the baby in the crook of his arm and there it was again. That feeling. Suddenly he could put a name to it. Loneliness. His brothers, his running partners, were married and settled with families. He was the odd one out—alone and unattached. Holding their children filled that loneliness inside him. But it wasn't enough. The thought startled him.

"Shay."

Shay's cousin, Nettie, strolled toward them. The woman wore a long full skirt and a gypsy blouse with her long gray hair flowing down her back. A purple scarf was tied around her head. Beads of every color were around her neck and on her wrists. She professed to be a gypsy-witch and took some getting used to. But she and Kid were now friends.

From the start, Shay had wanted Nettie to move in with them because Nettie had raised her and Shay didn't want her to be alone. Nettie, not wanting to horn in on newlyweds, refused. She liked her independence. When Shay became pregnant, Nettie changed her mind. She moved in about four months ago and took care of Cody while Shay taught school.

"It's too hot out here for the baby," Nettie said.

"The sun's going down and it's only for a few minutes," Shay told her, glancing at her son. "He's asleep so you can put him down. How's that?"

"I know I'm a little overprotective." Nettie's beads jangled as she talked.

"A little?" Chance laughed.

Kid handed off the precious bundle to Nettie, who immediately pulled the cap over Cody's forehead.

"Hey, Nettie, how about telling my future?" Nettie read palms and Kid thought he could use some help.

"It's right in front of your face."

"What? You haven't even looked at my palm."

"I don't need to. Your life line is long and leads to home, but it will not be a pleasant journey."

Kid frowned. "Are you yanking my chain?"

Nettie smiled and walked toward the house with Cody.

Darcy waved a hand in front of his face. "Can you see anything, Uncle Kid?"

"Don't be a smart..."

Chance cleared his throat.

"...butt," he finished.

Darcy giggled and darted after Nettie, Tiny trailing behind her. "I'm gonna help with Cody."

Standing on tiptoes, Shay reached up and kissed Chance. "Supper's in about thirty minutes. And we have ice cream."

Chance smiled and kept smiling.

"Kid, you're welcome to stay," Shay said, looking at him.

"Thanks, but Aunt Etta's waiting." What was it with the cooking? The women he knew didn't know how to use a stove.

"I can't beat that."

Shay followed the others and Kid noticed Chance was still smiling.

"Is *ice cream* a secret code or something?"

"What? Oh. Just memories of when we were dating." Chance turned to him. "How'd it go with Lucky?"

Kid placed his boot on the bottom pipe of the fence. "Like sticking a needle in my eye for pleasure."

"Ouch."

"She's mad and refused to sign a lease. No." He rested his elbow on the fence. "She's angry as hell—at me. After all these damn years, she's still angry. I don't get it."

"Do you want me to hold a mirror up to your face?"

"What?"

"Nettie said your future is in front of you. Maybe you have to confront your past before you can see the future."

"Is the heat making you loony?"

Chance sighed. "Kid, back away from this and I'll talk to Lucky in the morning."

"No." Kid pointed a finger at his brother. "Cadde said the same thing, but neither one of you is taking over my job."

"Okay. Okay." Chance held up his hands. "I'm not going to mention how important it is to lease Lucky's land. Everything else is leased up. Without that piece of property, we're not drilling a well."

Kid removed his boot and leaned his back against the pipe. He knew all the risks and he never saw a problem until today. There had to be a way around his shady past.

"How long has Lucky been home?"

Chance shrugged. "Five or six years. Why?"

"You've talked to her, right?"

"Lots of times."

"Did she ever ask about me?"

"No."

"Never?"

"Never." Chance sighed again. "She didn't bring up your name and I didn't, either. Why is this so important to you?"

"Why did she come back?"

Chance leaned heavily on the fence and Kid got the impression he wanted to bump his head against it. "We were kids, but I know you remember the time two guys tried to rob The Beer Joint."

"Yeah. It's the only crime ever committed in High Cotton. Some stealing, family squabbles and speeding tickets, but no big crimes like the attempted robbery. As I recall two guys came in after closing with guns drawn demanding all the money. They just didn't count on Bud having a .45 pistol in the cash register. He shot both of them before they could blink. When he walked around the bar, one of them squeezed off a shot and hit Bud in the hip."

"That's about it. One winter he slipped on some ice and injured the hip pretty bad again. Lucky came home to take care of him and she never left."

"So she got a nursing degree?"

Chance shook his head. "I don't think so, but I've never asked."

Kid kicked at the dry September grass. "Why is she slinging beer?"

"That bothers you?"

"For some reason it does, and if you mention something about a mirror again I'm going to hit you."

Chance shook his head. "Okay. But the bottom line is that Cadde's not going to let this slide. It's too important for Shilah. And it's too important to us as a family."

Kid headed for his truck. "I know. Talk to you later."

No one had to tell him what signing that lease meant. They'd researched it thoroughly and the land around Giddings was rich in oil and gas. Through sheer tenacity Cadde had managed to secure several leases from other oil companies. That didn't happen overnight. It took a lot of hours of negotiating.

The only holdout was the Littlefield tract. Bud had leased the land many years ago but the contract had expired without the property being included in a well. His research showed that ten years ago Bud had transferred the title of the land and all mineral rights to Lucky.

As someone who had leased many tracts of land for Shilah, he wondered about that. Why would someone in this economy refuse money? He couldn't leave it alone so he dug deeper, calling some old friends who worked for other oil companies. The response he got was the daughter was harder to deal with than the father and it wasn't worth the trouble for those fifty acres.

So maybe it wasn't about not leasing to a Hardin.

Maybe it was something else.

AFTER KID LEFT, LUCKY SPOKE with Mr. Harvey, who had leased his land to Shilah. He was excited about the deal. She wasn't and she'd just as soon never see Kid again. She tried to act normal, but her nerves were shaky, her stomach queasy. Hurrying to the storeroom, she sank onto a couple of cases of beer and took several deep breaths.

How could he waltz in here as if they'd never been lovers, never planned a future together? And how could she keep holding on to that pain? She bent forward, sucking air into her lungs. Oh, God, she hated herself for this weakness. She'd gotten over Kid a long time ago, she told herself. It was just seeing him so suddenly that had wiped out years of perfecting a cool facade. She hoped none of her inner turmoil showed.

Her nerves subsided and she forced herself to relax. As always, he was cool, collected and charming. That hadn't changed, but when she looked at his handsome face all she could feel was the pain he'd caused her—the pain was a permanent reminder of their teenage relationship.

Her hand went to her hair. He used to love her long tresses, but that wasn't the reason she'd had it cut. The style was easier in her line of work and it drew less attention. She took another breath. Running her hands through the thick layers, she wondered how different she looked to him.

Stop it!

Her cell buzzed and she eagerly reached for it, anything to keep Kid out of her head. It was her boss, Travis Coffman, and they set up a time to meet. She didn't like working in The Beer Joint any more than Kid liked it, but it was part of her job, which meant a lot to her. It gave her validation and purpose she desperately needed.

As she slipped her phone into her pocket, Bubba Joe walked in. "It was great seeing Kid, huh?"

"I know you like him, Bubba, but I'd rather he didn't come in here anymore."

"Oh." That blew Bubba's mind. Everybody liked Kid.

"Listen." She got to her feet. "I have to go out for a little while. Can you handle things?"

"Is Thelma Lou coming in?"

"No. It's a weekday and it won't be that busy." She hated to douse Bubba's obvious enthusiasm. He and Thelma had something going and she didn't want to know about it. Thelma's husband had left her with four kids and Lucky thought Bubba was getting in over his head. But then, what did she know about relationships? "I won't be long."

Going through the side door, she felt a rush of energy. This was the job she loved and she did it well, even if she had to run The Beer Joint as a cover.

Fortunately, Kid would never know about her secret life. And that was fine with her.

CHAPTER THREE

LUCKY HURRIED THROUGH the back door of her home, wanting to check on her father before meeting Travis. She found him in the living room in his recliner watching *Wheel of Fortune*—a double-barrel shotgun lay across his lap. Ever since he was wounded in an attempted robbery years ago, the gun was never far from him. Faithful as always, Ollie, his black-and-white border collie, lay by the chair, also watching the TV as if he understood every word.

"Hey, girl, what're you doing home so early?"

"I wanted to check on you and make sure you had supper."

Her father's fall about six years ago had injured an already bad hip. Now it was stiff and cumbersome and he walked with a cane. He was the only family she had. She didn't even remember her mother, who'd died when she was small. Her grandmother helped raise her, but her father was always in charge. No matter what, she would be here for him like he'd been there for her.

"I had a bowl of soup. I'm not too hungry."

"Dad, you have to eat." She worried about him. He'd gotten so thin in the past few years and it took effort to get him moving around. The cattle on the property were his only interest. Every now and then she could coax him into coming into The Joint so he could visit and talk to people.

"Girl, you get on my nerves sometimes."

"That's what daughters are for."

"Humph."

She went into the kitchen, cut cheddar cheese into wedges, grabbed crackers, a clump of grapes and a Dr Pepper, his favorite drink besides beer. Placing them on the TV tray by his chair, she said, "Something for you to nibble on."

Ollie looked up at her, wagging his tail.

"Okay, I'll get you some bacon strips."

Once Ollie had his treat, she glanced at her father, who was trying to look around her to see the TV.

"I saw Kid Hardin today."

"What?" She suddenly had her dad's full attention.

"I tried to maintain my cool." She wrinkled her nose. "I think I failed a couple of times, but I didn't get my gun and shoot him. It was on my mind, though. He strolled in bigger than Dallas expecting me to forgive and forget. Not that he asked for forgiveness. He just wanted the past swept under the rug, like it had never happened."

She took a deep breath. "He…uh…looks as good as ever. He's gotten older, of course, but even that's appealing with a couple of gray hairs and a Hollywood five o'clock shadow. On most men the look seems as if they need a bath, but Kid has it perfected. His body isn't as lean as it was, either. He's filled out with a lot of muscle."

"Sounds as if you looked at him pretty good."

Maybe too good.

"I was trying to figure out where to put the bullet."

Her father laughed and it felt good to hear that robust sound. He didn't laugh enough.

"After all these years, did he have a reason to stop by?"

"Oh, yeah. He wants to lease our land for oil and gas."

"That son of a bitch!"

"Mmm. When he left, I talked to Mr. Harvey. The rumor is that since the oil well on the Hardin property isn't producing, Cadde acquired the drilling contract from another company, as well as another tract, for a pretty penny. But they need our land to complete the desired acreage for a horizontal well or whatever."

"So, now Kid wants a favor?"

"That's about it."

Her father's eyes narrowed. "What was your answer?"

"Hell, no." She looked down at her fingernails. One she'd bitten down to the quick since this afternoon. Damn Kid! She'd wondered for years what her reaction would be if she ever saw him again. *Hi. How you doing?* They would be polite, or maybe just indifferent. She just didn't expect all the hurt and pain to still be there, and be so vivid.

"Lucky." Her father noticed her hesitation, her inner struggle. She could never keep anything from him.

"I'm okay." She brushed it away. "It was just a shock seeing him after all these years." She reached down and scratched Ollie's head. "I've got to go. I have to meet Travis in a few minutes."

"Lucky."

"Dad, I really don't want to talk about Kid."

"I'm not worried about Kid. It's Travis. I want you to get out of this job."

"It's what I do and I'm very good at it."

"It's dangerous."

She sighed at this same old conversation. "I'm well trained and can take care of myself."

"You're a woman and cattle rustling is a man's game."

Her job was top secret and she knew her father would never tell anyone. It would endanger her life. She worked as an undercover agent to a special ranger for the Texas and Southwestern Cattle Raisers Association. Cattle rustling was on the upswing because of the economy. Not only cattle, but tractors, ATVs, farm equipment, saddles and tack—anything that could be sold. She spent most of her day selling beer and listening for tidbits of information. Sometimes it paid off and they could shut down an operation or a petty thief eager to make a fast buck.

"Don't worry." She kissed her dad's cheek and headed for the door before he could get in another plea.

In her Chevy pickup she sped toward an old dirt road

that was rarely used. She tried to push thoughts of Kid away, but he was always there in the hidden corners of her mind. So many wasted years of regret. She wished she could erase him like a recording and all that would be left would be a blank tape—a place to rewrite, a place to start over.

She spotted Travis's truck. Parking behind him, she pushed a button and the window slid down. The heat of the late afternoon was still oppressive, or maybe it was just the warring thoughts inside her.

A tall lean man with sandy-blond hair and blue eyes walked toward her. At the lowest point in her life she'd found a friend—a true friend who wanted nothing but to help her.

When her dream of having a nursing career had fallen apart, she'd had to search for work. No way could she come home with her tail between her legs. The old biddies in High Cotton said she would never amount to anything. How could she? She was practically raised in a bar. The Bible-touting women did little for her self-esteem, but Kid had restored her confidence in herself, in life.

And then he'd destroyed it.

She'd fought the memory like she'd fought for so many things. After years of menial jobs, she was hired as a gopher for a big convention center in Austin. It was still a menial job, but it was interesting. That's how she'd met Travis. The Texas and Southwestern Cattle Raisers Association was having a big meeting and

Travis was the keynote speaker, educating people on how to keep their cattle and their equipment safe.

He'd arrived early as she and another lady were setting up microphones, video equipment, tables with water and every little thing that had been requested. One of her jobs was to make the guests comfortable with coffee, water or whatever. She liked Travis and he was easy to talk to. Before she knew it she was telling him about High Cotton, her dad, The Beer Joint.

It was a one-meeting-type thing, or so she'd thought. He'd called the next day and asked if she was interested in a job. When he'd told her what he needed, she was shocked and told him she had no experience. His answer was she'd have to be trained. She went to seminars at the police academy in Austin, took self-defense classes and learned to use a gun.

It was exciting compared to her ho-hum life. While they were working a case, she'd asked him why he'd picked her without any qualifications for an undercover agent. His answer was simple—he'd liked her character and she knew her way around a bar. Surprisingly, that didn't hurt her feelings. Beer and rustling seemed to go together.

She'd worked several counties with Travis where rustling was the strongest. Her cover was always in beer joints in small, out-of-the-way towns. Then her dad had fallen and that had given her the courage to return home. She was still the barkeep's daughter, but ironically it didn't matter anymore. Even though no one knew her real job, she felt good about herself. And that's all it took—belief in herself.

Like Kid had once made her feel.

As Travis stopped at her window, she wondered why she'd never fallen for him. He was handsome, personable and trustworthy, but the passion, that special chemistry, wasn't there.

She feared she'd used it all up on a man who hadn't deserved it.

"Got anything?" he asked, tilting his hat. Sweat peppered his forehead. For the first week in September, it was still hot.

They usually met once a month if they were working a big case, but most of their contact was through the phone and text messages. She was careful to delete everything from Travis in case someone managed to get her phone. His name wasn't even on her cell. His number was under a fake name. They were very cautious.

"No," she replied. "The three cowboys came in, but they didn't let anything slip. They only stayed about thirty minutes and were more interested in flirting with me."

"Lucky, be careful. These guys are no good." Concern coated every word.

"I'm always careful. You know that."

"Yeah. You throw yourself into these cases and sometimes I feel guilty. You should be married with babies."

Her heart stopped and for a moment she couldn't

breathe. He was right. At thirty-eight she should be married.

I'll love you forever, Lucky.

But Kid hadn't loved her at all. Why couldn't a starry-eyed teenager see that? Because she wanted to believe.

"Nine cows and six calves were stolen from the Hopper place last night," Travis was saying. She blinked and forced her thoughts back to the conversation.

"The Hoppers are in their seventies and they use the money from calf sales to supplement their Social Security. Now it's gone—" Travis snapped his fingers "—just like that. I preach infrared digital game cameras to ranchers all the time. They're relatively cheap at a sporting goods store, but I have a hell of a time getting anyone to use them until something is stolen."

Lucky had installed two on their property in trees overlooking their corral and the fence line. They were battery operated and snapped photos of anything that moved, even at night. Her father had also used calf sales to supplement their income. He usually sold calves around Christmastime so Lucky could have a good Christmas. One year rustlers wiped out his herd and Christmas was very lean at their house. Lucky always remembered how hurt her father had been. Maybe that's why she was in this business. She didn't want anyone else to go through that. Or maybe she enjoyed doing something meaningful for the community. It boosted her self-worth and confidence.

"It's always an afterthought," she said, running her hand along the steering wheel.

Travis reached for his cell and showed her several photos. "There's the Hopper brand that's on the cattle. And here's a silver inlaid saddle Mr. Hopper was going to give to his great-grandson."

She studied the pictures. "The Hoppers are really nice people." She didn't know them personally, but they were big in the church and spoke to Lucky whenever they saw her. Most of the holier-than-thou people turned their heads without acknowledging her presence.

"Yeah. My guess is the cowboys will try to move the saddle quickly. If they come back in tonight, they'll probably have a lot of cash."

"I'll watch for the signs."

Travis patted the window opening. "Just be careful. I'll be patrolling the back roads tonight. Call if you need anything."

He strolled to his truck and she started her engine. She'd be on the alert. If the cowboys had stolen the cows, they'd be flashing cash and the more they drank the more they wouldn't be able to resist bragging. That was usually a rustler's downfall—the urge to brag to his friends.

Now if she could just keep Kid out of her life, but she knew he'd be back. Good thing she was licensed to carry a gun.

AFTER SUPPER, KID TOSSED and turned on the bunk he'd slept on as a kid. Thank God Chance had installed heat-ing and air-conditioning years ago or he wouldn't be able to sleep at all. Chance was the homebody, always there for their aunt and uncle. Now that Chance was married with a family Kid decided he needed to help out more. It was the very least he could do.

He flipped onto his side. The room was small, cramped, and Aunt Etta hadn't changed a thing about it in almost twenty-five years—the night their parents had died.

A twin and a bunk bed filled the room. A closet was on the left and a dresser on the right. They barely had space to get into their beds, but they didn't care. It was a place for the brothers to be together. A place to grieve.

But Dane Belle hadn't let them grieve long. He kept them busy on the High Five ranch. A man was what they had needed in their lives and Dane had fit the bill. He was the most assertive, strong and loving man Kid had ever known. He made the orphaned Hardin boys part of the Belle family.

Aunt Etta was the housekeeper for High Five and Uncle Ru cowboyed for Dane. They lived in a small house not far from the Belle residence. Actually, in their backyard.

Dane was a ladies' man and had three daughters by three different wives. Caitlyn, the oldest, lived on the ranch because her mother had died in childbirth. Madison and Skylar lived with their mothers, but they spent every summer on the ranch. They had great summers with the sisters. Through the laughter and fun, their grief had slowly eased.

The sisters were all settled now and living in High Cotton. Caitlyn had married a neighboring rancher, Judd Calhoun. For years, he'd been her arch enemy, mainly because Cait had broken their youthful engagement without an explanation. Somehow they'd worked out their differences and now had twin sons. Maddie, the sweet sister, had fallen in love with Walker, the constable, and they had three children. Dane's wild child, Skylar, owned High Five with her husband, Cooper Yates. Kid would have bet money that Sky would never live in this homey town. Now she was a mother of two, living in wedded bliss. If Sky was cooking, he might have a heart attack. What was it about this place that drew everyone back? What made them rethink their lives and settle for the best of the best?

Kid sat up on the edge of the bed and bumped his head on the top bunk. Damn it! He'd done that so many times when he was a boy and he suddenly realized the bed wasn't suitable for a grown man. His feet hung over the end. The cot was harder than he remembered, too. Back then they were just boys and they didn't care about much of anything besides sports and trucks.

Chance had been twelve, he was fourteen and Cadde had turned sixteen—young boys just starting to discover life…and girls. They weren't ready to face the death of their parents and later they certainly weren't ready to face the truth about their father—an adulterer—who was willing to leave his wife and young sons for another woman.

Oh, God. Why was he thinking about it? To keep

from analyzing his own feelings, his own actions. Why hadn't he called Lucky? Why hadn't he come back for her?

He meant to call her that first night after he'd reached Lubbock, but there was a party going on and they drank way into the wee hours of the morning. A hangover kept him in bed for two days. Then there was another party. When he finally sobered up, it was time to start classes. He still avoided the call because he knew she was going to be so mad.

And there were all those Texas Tech beauties smiling at him. He was young, wild and a whole lot of crazy. One day turned into another and the call was never made. He was having too much fun. After that he didn't have the nerve to call. The miles and the different environment drove them apart. It was his fault. He was very aware of that.

Dane had insisted he come home for Christmas that year and he had, along with Cadde. The next morning they'd left again for Lubbock. After that first year in college, he decided sitting in a classroom wasn't for him. He and a friend headed for the Alaskan oil fields to get a hands-on job and to learn the business from roughnecking. The freezing weather almost got him, but he stayed for two years.

Every time he talked to Dane, he'd asked Kid to come home. Aunt Etta and Uncle Ru had asked, too. For some reason he couldn't do that. It was the first time he'd done anything without Dane's approval.

Another guilt mark on his soul.

When he'd returned to Texas, Chance was at the university and the Hardin boys partied all night. But soon Kid left for the East Texas oil fields. And then south Texas. He roughnecked just about everywhere.

Cadde had graduated with a petroleum engineering degree and was working his way up the corporate ladder. Chance wavered between the oil business and cowboying, but he was never far from home. On the other hand, Kid couldn't seem to get far enough away.

Until he got the call.

Dane Belle had passed away.

Kid's return was painful and heartbreaking. He'd looked for Lucky at the funeral, but she wasn't there. When he tried to talk to Bud, he'd walked away and Kid knew he wasn't welcome in High Cotton.

The strip of guilt got wider.

But he never let it show.

He ran his hands over his face and got up, turning on the light. Cadde was right. He had to start with an apology and now was as good a time as any. Reaching for his jeans on Cadde's bed, he noticed something on the wall by his bunk. It couldn't be. He bent down to take a closer look. It was a heart he'd drawn with a Magic Marker. Inside he'd printed Kid Loves Lucky, and underneath that was Lucky and the Kid. Damn! Aunt Etta had never removed it.

All those feelings of first love blindsided him. He sat on the bed with a thud. Maybe he'd been trying to outrun them. Maybe that's why it was so hard to come home. Maybe it was Lucky.

He quickly dressed and searched for a pen and paper in the dresser drawer. Some of their high school books were still there. Did Aunt Etta never throw out anything? Scribbling a note he tiptoed into the living and kitchen area and placed it on the table. Suddenly the lights came on. Aunt Etta stood in the doorway in a flowered cotton robe, her gray hair sticking out in all directions.

"I'm sorry. I didn't mean to wake you."

"Who sleeps?" Aunt Etta went to the refrigerator and pulled out a carton of milk. "I thought you went to bed."

"I did, but I'm going out again and I was leaving you a note."

"A note?" Aunt Etta paused in reaching for a pot.

"So you wouldn't worry."

"Ah." She grabbed the pot and poured milk into it. "It comes with the territory. And if an old aunt might be so bold, where are you going this time of night? It's almost twelve."

"I need to talk to Lucky."

Aunt Etta turned from the stove. "Now, Kid, I think the time for talking to Lucky has long passed."

"I screwed up." He finally had to admit the truth.

She nodded. "Yeah. You've done that a time or two. You've always had this urge for freedom and you and Lucky got too serious too quick. I think you're a lot like your father."

No, no! Don't say that!

"I'm not like him, am I?" Suddenly that was very, very important.

Aunt Etta bristled. "Why wouldn't you want to be like him? He was your flesh and blood."

He collected himself quickly. Aunt Etta didn't know about her brother's infidelity and Kid couldn't tell her. At this late date, he couldn't break her heart.

Giving her a peck on the cheek, he swung toward the door. "I'll see you later."

He'd dodged a bullet, but he thought about it all the way to The Beer Joint. He liked women. It was a fact he couldn't deny, but he never cheated on anyone. Well, that wasn't quite true. At Tech, he'd dated two girls at the same time. There was no commitment, though. Just fun. He never crossed that line of committing to forever, except with Lucky. He'd promised her as soon as he had a good job, they'd get married. They'd be together. No… oh, God!

He *was* just like his father.

WHEN HE REACHED THE BEER JOINT, he parked on the left side, away from the glare of the big spotlight Bud had installed. Three trucks were on the right so someone had to still be here. He slipped out of his vehicle. Before he could take a step, Bubba Joe came out, head down, and quickly drove away in the little Nissan. Did he leave Lucky by herself?

Suddenly, three cowboys half staggered to the Dodge pickup, the ones he'd seen earlier talking to Lucky, but they didn't get in. They stood there talking, but Kid couldn't make out what they were saying. His eyes centered on the door as Lucky came out, a purse over her shoulder, keys in her hand. She locked the door and made her way to the Chevy truck.

Unlocking it, she opened the door as one cowboy came around the front and the other two around the back to confront her. How he wished he had something besides his fists because this wasn't good.

"Hey, Lucky," one of them shouted, "why don't we continue this party somewhere else?"

"You're drunk, Clyde. Go home." She looked at the other two. "That includes you, too, Earl and Melvin."

"You've been teasing us all evening," the one called Earl said.

"Yeah. Now it's time to ante up," Melvin, the heavy-set guy added.

Clyde grabbed her arm and she knocked it away. "Don't touch me or you'll regret it."

"Hot damn, she's got a temper." Clyde and the other two closed in.

Kid stepped into the light. "Get away from the lady."

All three cowboys swung around.

"Who the hell are you, mister?" Clyde asked.

"Someone who's going to kick your ass if you don't get out of here."

Earl snickered. "You think you can take us?"

"In a heartbeat."

Melvin pulled a switchblade knife from his pocket, the silver catching the light with a startling eeriness. "Can you take this?"

Before Kid could reply, the other two jumped him. They went down into the gravel, fists flying. Kid slammed a right into Clyde's stomach and he rolled away, moaning. He didn't have time to think as a blow connected with his chin. Kicking out with his boot, he knocked Earl over the rail and he landed against the building. His body slithered down like a snake. Kid immediately jumped to his feet to face Melvin who was coming toward him with the knife.

"I'm gonna cut you six ways from Sunday, mister."

Suddenly, a gunshot ripped through the September night. Lucky had a gun. Where in the hell did she get a gun?

"Party's over, boys," she said in a voice he'd never heard before. "Now get out of here."

"What…?"

She pointed the gun at him. "Shut up."

With grunts and moans, the cowboys lumbered to their feet. Melvin looked at him one more time before they got in the Dodge and left.

Lucky reached with her left hand into her purse for her cell and poked in a number. The gun was still pointed at him and he found that a little disturbing.

"Walker, this is Lucky. Three drunken cowboys just left my place. They're headed east in a black Dodge Ram. You might want to alert the highway patrol. Yeah. I'm okay." Deftly she slipped the phone back into her purse, her eyes and the gun focused on him. "I want you out of my life for good. Don't come back here or to my house. You got it?"

"That's cold for someone who saved you from a fate worse than death."

"You didn't save me from anything!" she shouted. "I had the situation under control. I knew they were waiting for me and..."

"What!" He had no idea what she was talking about.

"Get in your truck and leave. Now!"

He could feel anger emanating from her in waves of white heat, much like the simmering night. "Put the gun down, Lucky, and let's talk."

"I'm not talking to you."

He stepped closer, going on a hunch that she wouldn't shoot him. "Why are you so angry?"

At the question, she took several deep breaths as if to calm herself.

"I'm worried about you," he said when she remained silent, hoping to find a chink in that solid wall of steel she'd built around herself.

She laughed, a sound that curdled his insides. "Worried about me? That's rich."

He knew what she was talking about now. He didn't have to ask—the past.

"Okay. I screwed up. I'm..."

"Don't say the words and make a mockery of my intelligence. Just don't say them."

She was full of anger and all of it was directed at him. "I know you're upset, but it's been twenty years."

"And I've lived every moment of it."

There was a lot of emotion behind those words that he didn't understand. "What are you talking about?"

"Just stay the hell out of my life."

She made to get in the pickup, but he held the door,

very aware she still had the gun in her hand. "Come on, Lucky."

The supposed magical words didn't have the old effect they used to. She eased back against the truck, her eyes as hard as he'd ever seen them.

"I'm going to give you a good reason to stay out of my life."

"I know..."

"You know nothing." She waved the gun. "Do you remember saying 'I love you, Lucky'? 'We'll get married. I'll call. I'll write. We'll be together, I promise.'"

"Yeah." He swallowed hard. "I said all that and I meant it."

"Unfortunately, I thought you meant it, too."

"Lucky..."

She raised the gun. "I'm not through talking. I waited every day for you to call, but you didn't. When I left for Austin, I told Dad to contact me the moment you phoned. Stupid me, I actually believed you still would. I was so stressed out with you leaving and then not calling I didn't realize I'd missed my period. Twice. I prayed I wasn't pregnant, but I was—three months."

What! The ground beneath his feet moved.

"I couldn't call my dad or come home because I was ashamed and couldn't face anyone. I had to drop out of school because they didn't accept pregnant girls in the program because you have to work long hours on your feet. It was a liability thing. I'm sure it's different today. They refunded my money and I lived on that until I got a job at Walmart to put food in my mouth. I couldn't afford a doctor so I had to go to a free clinic. I wanted my baby to be born healthy so I tried to do everything I was supposed to. I started having contractions a month early so I drove myself to an indigent hospital. They said I wasn't far enough along and to come back when the contractions were closer together. When I reached my apartment, the pain became severe and I asked my neighbor to drive me to the hospital again. She couldn't stay because she had kids. By the time they saw me the placenta had separated from the baby and he was deprived of oxygen. He was dead. He died..."

"Luc-ky."

"Shut up. I'm not through." She pointed the gun at his face. "He was a beautiful baby boy and I got to hold him for a few minutes. I was in a room with three other women, but I was all alone. They had families. I had no one. I dealt with the gut-wrenching pain alone while you were in Lubbock County trying to lay every woman in sight. I feel the pain of his death every day. I feel the pain of your betrayal every day. So don't talk to me about anger because I'd just as soon shoot you, you low-down bastard."

She jumped into her truck and tore out of the parking lot, spewing gravel across his chest.

Oh, my God! His knees gave way and he sank into the rocks as a pain like he'd never known before slashed through him. The spotlight was clearly on him and his sins, but it wasn't the one in the parking lot. It was from above, exposing the guilt that had haunted him for years.

They'd had a child. A son.

He'd let Lucky down and, God help him, he'd let their baby down.

How did he live with that?

CHAPTER FOUR

LUCKY DROVE STEADILY HOME, breathing heavily.

A tear slipped from her eye and she slapped it away.

She wouldn't cry.

Kid Hardin would not make her cry.

Lights flashed behind her and she pulled over. She knew it was Travis because she'd called him about the cowboys before she'd gone outside to confront them. Turning off the engine, she wiped her face with the back of her hands. Why was it wet? She wasn't crying.

Drawing a deep breath, she got out of the pickup. The moon was bright and she could see Travis strolling toward her.

"There's a man kneeling in the gravel back there. What happened?"

"The cowboys were waiting for me. They flirted and drank most of the evening. No big amounts of cash, though. I gave you time and then I went to my truck. They were there, but Kid Hardin interrupted."

"Of the oil Hardins?"

"Yes." Her stomach clenched.

"What was he doing there? Is he hurt?"

"I supposed he came to see me. I didn't know he was

there until Clyde grabbed my arm and they got into a fight."

She could feel his eyes boring into her. "There's a lot more to this story than you're telling me."

"Kid and I have a past, but he won't be coming back."

There was silence for a moment and the warmth of the night seemed to calm her shattered nerves.

"I knew there was someone," he said, startling her, "but I sense you didn't want to talk about it."

"No." That was the last thing she wanted. Kid was out of her life for good now.

"I'm worried about you. You're taking risks that you shouldn't. You're not *ever* to confront the criminals, especially alone."

"I knew you were on the way."

"That's not the point. It's not worth you getting hurt."

"Okay, I screwed up, but I didn't want them coming back inside. They were too drunk to drive so I called Walker, the constable, and he notified the highway patrol. They're probably being arrested as we speak. There might be some evidence in their truck."

"I'll follow up on it. Your safety is my main concern and I don't want a repeat of what happened tonight."

"Okay, Travis, I get the message."

He sighed. "Lucky, you're so consumed with your job that it worries me. Do you even have a private life?"

"Of course." She was lying. She didn't even know what a private life was anymore.

"Lucky."

By the soft tone of his voice she knew the conversation was headed in a personal direction—one she wasn't ready for and she didn't know if she would ever be. Once burned, a lifetime shy was her motto.

"I better check on my dad. He won't go to bed until I'm home."

"I'll see if Hardin is hurt." He moved toward his truck. "Talk to you in the morning."

She slipped into her pickup and wondered what was wrong with her. Travis was a good man and with just some encouragement from her they could have a relationship. But something held her back. Maybe the past had crippled her emotionally and she wasn't ever going to love like that again.

When she went through the back door of the house, she heard the TV. Her dad was asleep in his chair, snoring. Picking up the remote control, she turned it off. He immediately woke up.

"Lucky, girl, you're late."

"Busy night." She sank down by his chair and laid her head on the arm.

"What's wrong?" he asked, sitting up.

"I told Kid about our son tonight."

"Holy cow, girl, why did you go and do that? You said you never would."

"I don't know. He kept asking why I was so angry and the words just came spewing out like all this venom I had inside me." She took a breath. "I saw the hurt on his face and the pain in his eyes and I wanted to feel some kind of victory. But I didn't. Where's my victory,

Dad? I wanted to shatter his big ego, but all I felt was his agony."

"Oh, Lucky. Sometimes we think we want something and we really don't. It's just human nature."

Unable to stop them, tears flowed from her eyes. "I hurt him, Dad, and I feel more empty now than ever."

"Shh." He stroked her hair. "It will be different tomorrow."

"I don't think so." She was always going to see that tortured look in Kid's eyes. Ollie whined and she wrapped her arms around the dog. "I've asked myself a million times why I didn't come home when I found out I was pregnant. Why did the town's opinion matter so much to me? If I'd been stronger, I'd have my son today."

"That's my fault. When you kept making excuses not to come home, I should have gone to Austin to see you. But I thought you were building a new life, getting over that Hardin boy. I never dreamed you weren't in school and going through such turmoil on your own. It's my fault for not keeping tabs on you."

"No, Dad, what happened is all because of me and my insecurities and my self-doubts."

"I should have choked the life out of old lady Farley and Mrs. Axelwood a long time ago. Nothing but vicious gossipers with narrow minds."

It wasn't their fault, either. All of it lay squarely on her shoulders. She'd stood up to three drunken cowboys tonight. Why hadn't she had that strength years ago? She'd been weak, but now she was strong and no one was going to take her pride again. Not even Kid.

Her father continued to stroke her hair. "You know Kid will be back."

"Why?"

"Remember when he was about fourteen, Chuck told him he couldn't come over here on your birthday 'cause it was a school night? After Chuck and Carol went to bed, he cranked up the tractor and came anyway."

"Yeah. He brought me flowers from his mother's garden."

"Damn fool woke us up."

"Only Kid does things like that," she murmured.

"Chuck grounded him for a month."

"I never liked Chuck Hardin." When she was a teenager, she'd seen the man with more than one woman at The Beer Joint, about a mile from where he lived with his wife. She never understood how Chuck could do that.

"Did you ever tell Kid what you knew?"

"No. I couldn't. He looked up to his father, held him on a pedestal."

"It was mighty hard for ol' Chuck to maintain his balance up there."

She rubbed Ollie's head. "I'm glad Carol never had to know."

"Mmm."

The year Kid's parents had died had been sad. He'd cried in her arms several times and they'd bonded closer. From then on it was Lucky and the Kid. She'd thought nothing would ever come between them. He was more like his father than she'd ever imagined.

KID LIFTED HIS HEAD FROM the steering wheel and saw he was parked in front of the Shilah offices in downtown Houston and it was morning. He wasn't sure how he'd gotten here. All he remembered were Lucky's words: *Our son died while you were trying to lay every woman in Lubbock County.*

They'd had a son. He'd died because of Kid's selfish, womanizing ways. How could he? He moaned and slipped out of the truck. Unlocking the back door, he took the elevator up to the top floor. For some reason he went to Cadde's office. Sitting in the dark, he let the pain eat away at him. He deserved it.

Suddenly the light came on. He blinked and tried to focus on his brothers. They glanced at each other and then back to him.

"What happened to you?" Chance asked. "Your face is blue on one side."

"And you look like hell," Cadde said, sitting in his chair at the big desk.

He could tell them. They'd understand and support him. Yet his actions were so horrible he couldn't say the words. There were a lot of ways to excuse his behavior. Then again, none came to mind—none that would ease his conscience.

"I gotta go." He rose to his feet, but before he could reach the door Chance kicked it shut.

"You're not going anywhere until you tell us what's wrong with you. Are you drunk?"

"No, but I wish I were stoned out of my mind. I think I'll go down the hall to the apartment and accomplish that feat."

"Sit down, Kid," Cadde ordered. "Have you been fighting in a bar again?"

"Outside a bar, actually."

"When the hell are you going to grow up?"

Kid sank into a leather chair and buried his face in his hands. "I grew up last night."

"What do you mean?" Chance asked.

"I talked to Lucky."

"And she hit you?" Chance was clearly shocked.

"No. I waited until the bar closed so we could talk, but then three guys accosted her. Let's just say they didn't leave easily."

"You took on three guys?" Chance asked.

"Yeah. I wasn't going to let them hurt Lucky."

Cadde shook his head. "Was she grateful enough to sign the lease?"

"Damn it, Cadde. I don't give a flying pig's ass about the lease."

His brother frowned. "Isn't that why you talked to her?"

Kid jammed his hands through his hair and wanted to pull it out by the roots, pull until there was nothing left but the pain. He drew a calming breath. "It started out that way, but she was angry and I couldn't figure out why. So I asked and she told me in a colder-than-ice voice I'll never forget."

"What did she say?" Chance took the seat next to him.

Kid had to swallow several times. "Soon after I left for Tech she found out she was pregnant."

"What!" echoed around the room.

"Kid." Chance spoke up. "Lucky doesn't have a child. I'm positive of that."

He had trouble breathing and he gulped a breath. "He...he died."

Silence followed those two words.

"How?" Cadde was the first to speak.

"Lucky had to drop out of nursing school because of the pregnancy and she had very little money. She had to go to a free clinic. When she went into labor, she went to an indigent hospital and they sent her home. The baby wasn't due for another month. But the pains wouldn't go away so she went back. It was too late. The placenta had separated and the baby was deprived of oxygen. Lucky dealt with all that alone."

"Why didn't she call her father?" Chance wanted to know.

"She was ashamed."

"She could have called Aunt Etta and she would have gotten in touch with you."

Kid jumped to his feet. "Don't you dare blame Lucky or I'll knock you out of that chair."

"Calm down," Chance said. "Placing blame isn't going to change what happened. Somehow you have to make this right with Lucky and talk without all the anger."

He knew that. He just didn't know how.

He slid into his chair, his hands clasped between his knees. "If the baby had lived, I'd have a twenty-year-old son. That's mind-boggling."

"Where's he buried?"

He looked at Cadde. "What?"

"When Jessie had the miscarriage, we buried the fetus so I'm sure Lucky buried a full-term baby."

"I hadn't thought of that." He was on his feet again. "I have to go and talk to Lucky."

"Kid." Cadde stopped him at the door. "Chance or I will handle the lease from here."

"Don't you go anywhere near her!"

"This is important."

"So is my life. I supported you two when you were going through hell with Jessie and Shay. I expect the same consideration."

"This is about Shilah, too."

"Screw Shilah." Kid pointed a finger at his brother. "If you talk to Lucky about leasing her land, I'm outta here."

"This is a multimillion dollar deal and I can't just sweep it under the rug." Cadde stood as his voice grew angry.

"I busted my ass on those Louisiana leases and the wells made a lot of money for Shilah so don't tell me about the big bucks or the bottom line or I'll..."

"Everybody calm down." Chance intervened and

looked at Cadde. "I'm sure Shilah can wait until you get your emotions sorted out."

Cadde threw up his hands and sat down.

"I'm sorry, Kid," Chance went on. "I hope you and Lucky can get through all the bad stuff."

Kid nodded but didn't say anything. It was going to take a bulldozer to get through all of his bad behavior.

"Kid."

He paused at the door.

"Take all the time you need," Cadde said. "I'm sorry I lost my temper. Losing a child is not an easy thing."

Kid walked out and went to his truck. He wasn't upset with his brothers. They were always honest with each other and he understood Cadde's concern for Shilah. He'd worked hard to make the company a success. Kid's focus now was on his sanity. He had to be able to look himself in the mirror every morning and know he was a good person.

Or as close as he was ever going to get.

He refused to think beyond that as he drove to his apartment, showered and changed clothes. Then he collapsed into his recliner and let his thoughts take him to the gates of hell. He tried to remember the faces of the women he'd been with over the years, but all he could see were the tears in Lucky's blue eyes the day he'd left for college.

She'd been pregnant. In the months that followed he'd never thought of that, not once. They always used protection so why would he? Why would he not? Condoms weren't a hundred percent sure thing. The thought of her alone in Austin after the birth was almost more than he could bear. He should have been there.

But he was eighteen years old and knew nothing about kids. After the crippling pain of losing his parents, he was eager to get away and enjoy life without a reminder of that tragic day. Freedom was like a shot of Kentucky bourbon. The more he tasted, the more he wanted. And then there were the girls who were like the roses in his mother's garden. Each one had their own stunning appeal. He couldn't seem to get enough. What did that make him? The biggest cad who had ever lived.

He never forgot Lucky, though. She was always there at the back of his mind and on his conscience. The strip on his soul was completely black now.

Running his hands over his face, he wondered what he needed to do. Apologize? Grovel? Beg?

Cadde had always said Kid's past would catch up with him. He'd been right. But Kid couldn't continue to dwell on his misdeeds. There had to be a way to redeem himself, his conscience.

And it started with an apology.

He stood and winced. Damn! His chest hurt and his back ached, not to mention his jaw. His body didn't bounce back as quick as it used to. A little rest and he'd be good as new. Walking into the bedroom, he yawned and fell across his king-size bed.

They'd had a son. He couldn't get that thought out of his head.

LUCKY SAT ON THE FRONT STOOP enjoying some free time before getting ready for the day. A freshness mingled with the morning air, a hint that fall wasn't far away. Since she didn't go into the bar until about four, she did the housework and cooked lunch for her dad. Now she was just relaxing, trying not to think about what had happened. Last night she'd cried herself to sleep. She'd said she would not cry one more tear over Kid Hardin, but she'd lied. Her pillow was soaked with regrets. She should never have let her anger get the best of her. Telling Kid served no purpose now but to hurt him. And to her dismay, she'd found it wasn't something she really needed to do.

Twenty years was a long time to carry around a heartache. She could now see that she had to shoulder a lot of blame. She'd made all the wrong choices to save her pride. It had cost her everything. Today she was wiser, more mature and she intended to never get caught in that trap again. She'd stand up for herself and her dad without sinking to a level of self-destruction.

Her cell buzzed and she fished it out of her jeans pocket.

"Lucky, are you all right?" Travis asked.

"Yeah."

"When I went back last night, the Hardin man was walking to his truck. I asked if he was okay, but he didn't answer. He didn't appear to be injured." She closed her eyes and could see Clyde and Earl hitting Kid hard. She was sure he wasn't okay. And then she had added to his pain.

"The highway patrol stopped the black Dodge last night and arrested the cowboys," Travis was saying. "No evidence was found in the truck and they'll probably be out on bail by the end of the day. Could you please not go to work today? I'm afraid they'll come looking for you."

"Yeah. They're not going to be pleased about me pulling a gun on them and Kid showing up. But they don't know I had anything to do with their arrest and if I don't go in, that will look even worse, don't you think?"

There was a long pause. "Hmm. Could you please not close up then?"

"I'll make sure Bubba Joe stays with me. Does that make you feel better?"

"I don't want anything to happen to you." There was that tone in his voice again.

"I'll be very careful."

"Lucky…"

Please, Travis, don't get personal.

"I'll be close by so call if anything goes awry."

"I will."

She clicked off, so glad he hadn't said something they both would regret.

A new goldish-tan fancy-looking truck was coming up the lane, dust billowing behind it. There was only one person it could be—Kid.

She went inside to prepare herself.

CHAPTER FIVE

KID DROVE UP TO THE OLD farmhouse, his palms sweaty on the steering wheel. That hadn't happened since the first time he'd come here, when he and Chance had fixed up an ancient Ford and the only place he'd wanted to go was to see Lucky. Bud wasn't known to be the friendliest person in the world and any thoughts that he'd mellowed would be ludicrous.

The white house with the long porch across the front was the same, as were the two rockers and the wind chimes tinkling in the warm breeze. A barn and corral were to the right. It seemed as if nothing had changed in the intervening years. But that wasn't true. Back then he and Lucky were kids exploring life in the only way they knew. Today they were adults and he hoped they could talk like grown-ups without getting sidetracked by all the emotions of youth.

He got out of his truck and walked to the front door. It opened before he could knock. Lucky's beautiful face was tight with worry, and her eyes guarded. She made no move to undo the latch on the screen door. Cool air wafted through from the air-conditioning.

"What do you want, Kid?"

He removed his hat. "Could we talk, please?"

"We've said enough."

Bud walked up behind her, leaning heavily on a cane. Kid did a double take. Bud had changed considerably. His hair was now white, his frame thin and stooped. The strong man who could make people flinch just by the tone of his voice was long gone.

"You better leave, Kid. I may be old and crippled but I can still use my shotgun." Maybe not completely gone. Kid wanted to take a step backward, but he stood his ground.

"It's okay, Dad," Lucky assured her father. "I can handle it."

"You sure?" Bud's shaggy eyebrows knotted together.

"Yes." She unlatched the screen door and stepped out.

"Thanks," he said, twisting his hat. "I'd like to talk about the baby."

She sighed and sank into one of the rockers. "Why?"

He pulled the other rocker forward and sat close to her, placing his hat on the floor. "I…uh…I'd like to know something about him. I don't deserve to but…"

"There's nothing to tell, Kid. I held him for a few minutes and that was it."

"Did he have hair?"

"Yes. It was brown like a cap on his head."

He swallowed. "And his eyes?"

She gripped her hands in her lap. "I…I opened his eyes and they were blue."

"Like yours?"

"I don't know!" she shouted. "And I'm not answering any more questions."

He gave her a minute. "I'm sorry, Lucky, I wasn't there. I'm sorry I let you down."

She chewed on her lower lip, something she always did when she was upset. "I'm…I'm sorry I told you like I did. I shouldn't have done that, but you made me so angry."

"You should have gotten in touch with me long ago." The words were out before he could stop them.

Her eyes darkened. "If you had called or had been within a hundred-mile radius, I would have."

Even the hurt in her voice couldn't stop the words in his throat. "Aunt Etta had my number. You could have contacted her."

"I wasn't using the baby as a way to get you back, but, oh, I kept hoping right up until the end. With each contraction I kept thinking Kid will come. He'll make everything right. I kept believing until I held our dead baby. I knew then that you were never coming back. You made your choices so don't sit there and tell me what I should have done."

Silence followed her words.

He couldn't seem to let it go. "Why didn't you call your father?" The questions that Cadde and Chance had posed were in his head and he had to ask them, even it they made her angry, even if they made him angry.

"I couldn't," she murmured. "He was paying for my apartment and thought I was in nursing school. I didn't know how to tell him. I was eighteen years old and trying to come to grips with the fact that I was pregnant and the man I loved was a liar."

Her barbed words hit his heart like a sledgehammer, but he sucked in a breath and let the pain pass. "When did you call Bud?"

She looked down at her clenched hands. "When they took the baby from me, I lost it and had to talk to someone. Dad brought me home and I cried for a solid month. Then I picked myself up and got on with my life. I worked in Austin until Dad fell. I've been here ever since."

"I'm sorry, Lucky."

She stood. "That doesn't change a thing."

He got to his feet, too, standing inches from her. The scent of strawberries reached him. She still washed her hair with strawberry fragrant shampoo. Maybe some things never changed.

"Aren't you curious about my life?"

She shook her head. "No. I hear all I need to from the rumor mill in High Cotton, especially from Mrs. Farley and Mrs. Axelwood. If I'm in earshot at the convenience store or Walker's General Store, they make sure I hear of all your exploits with your numerous women and how fortunate you are to have escaped the clutches of that tramp Lucinda Littlefield."

He frowned. "How do they know anything about me?"

"You're like Brad Pitt to them, movie star status."

"I can't believe they'd be so cruel to you. Mrs. Farley

is big in the church in the center of town and so is Mrs. Axelwood."

"Kind of scary, isn't it?"

What was wrong with people? He was a sinner. No one knew that better than him. Sometimes people's minds were so narrow it stopped the blood supply to their brains. It had certainly hampered the Christian Bible-touting women of this town. If they were holding him up as an example of manly virtues, then their tiny minds must have exploded.

"Lucky…"

"It's over, Kid. Let's leave it that way."

She was probably right, but once again he couldn't let go. "May I ask you another question?"

She sighed. "Kid…"

"Where's our son buried?"

"Why do you need to know that?"

"For my own peace of mind."

"You don't have to worry. I take very good care of our son's grave. It's always mowed and I keep flowers on it."

"Is he buried in Austin?"

She looked off to the hilly landscape, her body stiff with irritation. "No. When Dad picked me up, we also brought the baby home to bury. I had to sign papers to do that. He was in a small sealed box. Daddy dug a grave and we buried him on the hill next to my mother and grandparents."

"So he's here?"

"Yes."

Kid jumped off the porch and strolled toward the small cemetery.

"Kid!" she shouted after him, but he kept walking.

He opened the gate on the chain-link fence that enclosed the graves and went inside. The area was neat and mowed like she'd said. An arrangement of plastic flowers was at the base of each tombstone. He squatted by the small grave on the end. White roses were nestled in a basket, along with an angel and booties. It was anchored to the ground with steel rods so it wouldn't blow away.

The headstone grabbed his attention. *Baby Franklin Cisco Littlefield.* His son didn't have his last name. He felt as if a bullet just pierced his heart. It took a moment for him to catch his breath.

Lucky stopped beside him.

"You named him after your father."

"Yes."

"Why isn't my last name on there?"

"You had no interest in me at the time so I did what I thought was best for myself and my son."

He let the angst in her voice slide over him and he wanted to understand, but he didn't. "I want him to have my name. He's a Hardin." Anger was building to the surface and he was trying to keep it under control.

"It's too late for that."

He stood and faced her. "I want the headstone changed."

"After all this time, not likely. And you don't have a say in this."

"I'm getting it changed." He was determined.

"You come onto this property and go anywhere near my son's grave, I will have you arrested."

He poked a finger in his chest. "He's my son, too."

"It's a little late to think about that."

"All right, I screwed up, but don't do this to me." He touched her hair. "Come on, Lucky."

The bright sun bore down on their heads and for a moment he thought she was going to weaken. Suddenly, she stepped back. "Sorry, I don't feel in a mood to grant you favors."

"It will be changed, Lucky. You can count on that." He strolled down the hill, anger eating at him once again. He had no rights. He had no say. But if it was the last thing he did, his name would be on that headstone, even if he had to do it in the dead of night.

LUCKY KNELT IN THE DRIED GRASS and straightened the angel and booties in the basket. "You met your father today. He's really not an angry person. He's fun-loving, a jokester and a teaser. It takes a lot to get him mad. I think you would have been a lot like him."

Maybe she was being pigheaded about the name. Adding *Hardin* wasn't going to change a thing, though. The past was over and they had to let it go. Besides, they had different, separate lives now. Kid was in Houston chasing dreams. She would always be here, close to home, close to her son.

Her hand went to her hair where he had touched it. For a moment she wanted to give in. *Come on, Lucky,* and that look in his dark eyes still had the power to get to her. But, as she kept telling herself, she was now stronger. More mature. And knew Kid's charm and appeal. She would not weaken.

She got to her feet and walked down the hill to the house. She had other things to think about—like her job. If the cowboys came in tonight, she had to be prepared with a story. They'd certainly ask about Kid and what he was doing there. She'd have to have a good answer.

As she stepped up on the porch, she saw Kid's hat. He'd been so angry he'd left without it. She picked up the hat and carried it into the house.

"What've you got?" her dad asked, sipping on a Dr Pepper.

"Kid forgot his hat. I'm sure he will be back for it."

She laid the Stetson on an end table. Ollie sniffed it and went back to his spot by her dad's feet.

"I saw y'all at the cemetery. You showed him the grave?"

"He insisted. He's upset his name isn't on the headstone."

"That boy has a lot of nerve."

She sank onto the sofa. "I don't know what to do. I can see his point, and then on the other hand I get angry he even has me thinking about his point of view."

"Ignore him. He'll get bored and go back to Houston." He set his glass on the TV tray. "Did he say anything about the lease?"

"No. He didn't bring it up."

"He will. Cadde Hardin is a driven man, though I've

heard he's softened since his marriage, but he'll pressure Kid to get the lease signed. I was talking to Wilma—"

"You've been talking to Bubba Joe's mother?" Lucky was shocked. She didn't think her dad talked with anyone.

"Yeah. She's worried about Bubba Joe and I'm worried about you."

"Dad, Bubba Joe weighs at least three hundred pounds and he can take care of himself. So can I."

"You'll forgive me if I'm not bowled over with comfort by that statement."

"Dad, please don't be like Wilma. She comes into The Joint in that black, god-awful wig and sits at the end of the bar nursing a Coors and watching her son like he's going to disappear if someone breathes on him."

"Wilma's a little paranoid."

"That's putting it nicely, but I'm glad you're talking to someone. Maybe you could invite her over here to watch a movie or something."

His wrinkled brow knotted so deep his hair folded into his eyebrows. "You mean like a date?"

She shrugged. "Whatever you want to call it."

"I have one foot in the grave and another on a banana peel and I ain't wasting any of my TV time on Wilma. She'd drive me nuts, and you've sidetracked me. I was talking about Cadde. Wilma said he's planning on drilling a well on the Hardin property."

"I told you that."

"You did? I forgot." He waved a hand. "It doesn't

matter. What I'm trying to tell you is that Kid will be back. That lease is important to the Hardin family."

She stood and kissed his cheek. "I know that, too. Now I have to get ready for work. I left a plate of roast and veggies in the refrigerator. Please eat it."

"Ah. I'm gonna check on my cows and then watch a John Wayne movie. I probably won't be hungry."

"I'll call Wilma to come keep you company then. I bet she can get you to eat."

"Don't you dare."

Lucky smiled all the way to her bedroom. But her father was right. Kid would come calling again, probably with a chisel in one hand to etch his name on the headstone and the lease in the other. Any way she looked at it, she was going to see Kid one more time. Her insides didn't cramp up at the thought. She was actually looking forward to it.

KID DROVE TO THE ONE PLACE that gave him comfort when he was a boy—his aunt and uncle's house on the High Five ranch. Everything was quiet as he passed the Belle residence. Cooper and Uncle Ru were busy on the ranch and sometimes Sky helped. He got out and went inside the old log cabin. It wasn't locked. He sat on his bunk in the room they shared as boys. His eyes kept going to the heart on the wall.

He hadn't meant to lose his temper with Lucky, but his son deserved his name. Before he did anything drastic, his usual modus operandi, he'd talk to her again.

"Kid," Aunt Etta said from the doorway. "What's wrong?"

"Nothing. Everything."

"Oh, your face."

"I'm okay," he tried to reassure her.

Aunt Etta sat on Cadde's bunk, facing him. "Since you didn't come home, I thought you went back to Houston."

"I'm sorry. I should have called." He was a selfish bastard.

"You're not a teenager anymore so I didn't worry, but maybe I should."

"Nah. Just got into a fight. Nothing unusual for me."

"Kid…"

"Thanks for all the years you put up with my inconsiderate ways."

Etta wiped her hands on her apron. "You're scaring me. Tell me what has you so down and why you're fighting."

"You don't want to know. It would change your opinion of me." God, he sounded whiny.

"I don't think so. I was there the day you were born. I changed your diapers, watched you grow, grieve and fight back. I also saw you hide all your pain behind laughter. I know you inside and out and there's nothing you can say or do that would ever change my love for you."

He ran his hands down the thigh of his jeans. "I screwed up…bad."

"What'd you do?"

From somewhere deep inside him he found the strength to tell her about Lucky and the baby. She moved to sit beside him and gave him a hug.

"I'm so sorry, Cisco." She touched his bruised face. "Did Lucky hit you?"

Oh, no. When she called him by his given name he knew a lecture was coming so he braced himself.

"Ah…no. I made a nuisance of myself at The Beer Joint."

"Cisco!"

"I know I'm too old to fight and I should leave Lucky alone."

She hugged him again. "I always felt I should have put a stop to that relationship. You were too young to get that serious."

She wouldn't be Aunt Etta if she didn't take the blame for his selfish behavior. She was always protecting her nephews. "It wasn't your fault. I would have found a way to be with Lucky."

"Uh-huh. What happened to those feelings once you reached Lubbock?"

He ran his hands over his face. "I don't know. I just felt free from all the sadness that lingered here. It was a whole new life and I liked it. I wanted to call Lucky but I kept saying I would call her tomorrow—tomorrow became a week, a month, a year and then I knew it was too late."

"And another girl took her place." Aunt Etta rubbed his shoulder to ease the impact of her words. "You were always too handsome for your own good."

"I never forgot Lucky."

"That's little solace for her now." She shook her head. "Why didn't she call me? I would have taken her and the baby in. This is too sad."

"It's my fault. Not Lucky's."

"It's not a time to place blame. It's time to get on with your lives."

He clenched his hands between his knees. "The baby is buried at the Littlefield place and Lucky didn't put my last name on the headstone. I can't get beyond that. I don't have any rights, but…"

"Now, Cisco. I know that tone of voice. Do not do anything stupid."

"I'm putting my name where it should be," he said with force.

She clutched his arm. "Listen to me. Talk to Lucky and work this out. You used to be able to talk her into anything."

"She's changed."

"You haven't. You've always been determined to get your way just like…"

He looked into his aunt's startled, gray eyes. "…Dad."

"Yes."

Something in her expression drew his attention. "You thought so much of him."

"Not always. He had his faults like everyone else."

"Like what?" Could she possibly know the truth?

"We're not talking about Chuck. We're talking about you."

"Oh, no. You know something about Dad and I'm old enough to hear it."

"Leave it alone, Kid."

"No, we're not keeping any more secrets in this family."

"Kid."

"I'm a womanizer, a liar and a cheat just like Dad."

"Oh." His aunt visibly paled.

"I'm sorry, but that's the truth."

She smoothed her apron. "Yes."

"You knew Dad was leaving us, didn't you?"

"It was so long ago."

"It seems like yesterday. Just tell me the truth."

His aunt paused. "Yes, I knew he was leaving Carol for another woman. He asked me to look out for her and you boys. I did everything I could to talk him out of it, but nothing worked. He was besotted with that…"

"Finish it, Aunt Etta."

"With that woman, Blanche Dumont."

"You knew who the other woman was?"

"Yes, but—" she frowned "—how do you know? He was going to tell Carol the day after the big championship game. They had the wreck and I was relieved he hadn't broken up the family."

"He told her on the way back from Austin. Chance wasn't asleep like he'd told the highway patrol and he heard everything except the woman's name. Mom started hitting and demanding he tell her. That's how he lost control of the car. Chance has known all these years and he finally revealed his secret to Cadde and me when he joined us in Houston." He scooted to face her. "When Chance married Shay, you knew her mother was Dad's lover?"

"Yes."

"How did that make you feel?"

"Sad. But once I met Shay I liked her and saw no reason to dredge up your father's sordid past." She suddenly hit his shoulder, which was like a feather brushing his arm. "How could you boys keep that from me?"

"We knew how much you loved Dad and we didn't want to hurt you."

Aunt Etta's demeanor crumpled. "My poor, sweet Chance. What a burden he's carried. I have to talk to him."

Kid hugged her and smiled into her worried face. "Please let me give them a heads-up. If they're going to kill me, I'd like to have a running start."

His aunt smiled slightly. "I'm sorry I said you were like Chuck. You have his adventurous spirit, but you have Carol's sensitive side, her willingness to compromise, to smile and to work things out. Chuck never compromised on anything. I loved him, but he was stubborn as a mule."

She hugged him again and he hugged her back. "Thank you. I needed to hear I have some good qualities." He made to stand and forgot where he was and bumped his head on the top bunk. "Damn." He rubbed his noggin.

Aunt Etta laughed and he laughed with her.

She touched his cheek. "You've always made us laugh. Never stop laughing, Kid."

CHAPTER SIX

AS KID DROVE TO CADDE'S, he remembered Aunt Etta's words, but he had a feeling his brothers weren't going to be laughing. He pushed Lucky to the furthest corner of his mind. There were just so many regrets he could take in one day.

He went in through the back door, which was unlocked. No one seemed to lock their doors around here. Jessie was in the kitchen, stirring something in a pot with Jacob on hip. When Jacob saw him, he held out his arms and Kid gathered him close. Again, all the baby had on was a diaper and a T-shirt.

He stared into that adorable face and wondered if his son would have looked like Jacob. His gut twisted at the thought.

A helicopter sounded overhead and Jacob wiggled to get down. Mirry barked and trotted to the back door. Jacob took off after her.

"Is this a daily occurrence?"

Jessie leaned against the counter in denim shorts and a white maternity top. "Jacob's asleep when Cadde leaves and when he wakes up, he searches for him all day. He gets so excited when he hears the chopper. He knows Daddy's home." She paused for a second, her dark eyes on him. "Cadde told me about Lucky and the baby. I'm sorry, Kid."

"Does Cadde tell you everything?"

"Yes." She smiled.

"I feel like I've been hit by an eighteen-wheeler going about ninety."

"I hope you and Lucky get a chance to talk."

"Aren't you going to berate me for being a heartless bastard?"

"No." She turned toward the bubbling pot. "I think you can do that all on your own."

Loud barks and excited baby jabber echoed from the hall.

"I have to break up my two children," Jessie said. "Jacob pulls up and tries to reach the door handle. Mirry gets frantic that he's going to open the door and get out."

"He can't open it, can he?"

"No, but it won't be long. Cadde's putting a latch higher up so he can't." Jessie walked toward the noise.

"Do you mind if I talk to Cadde alone for a minute?"

One dark eyebrow lifted. "Is there going to be yelling?"

"Probably."

She made a face but didn't say anything. As she left, he reached for his cell and called Chance. "Can you come over to Cadde's?"

"Kid, I've been gone all day and I want to see my wife and kids."

"It's important and it won't take long."

"Have you done something stupid?"

"Not yet." Why did they always ask that?

He heard a curse word as he disconnected.

In less than two minutes his brothers strolled into the den. Angry wails could be heard from the kitchen.

"Kid, what's so important that you have to interrupt my family time?" Cadde was clearly upset.

"It's about Aunt Etta."

"What?" Chance was immediately alert. "I just saw her yesterday and nothing was wrong."

Kid shifted in his seat. "I went to tell her about Lucky and we got to talking. She said I'm a lot like Dad. Not something I wanted to hear, but the way she spoke I sensed she knew a lot more than she was saying." He raised his eyes to face his brothers' wrath. "She knows Dad was leaving us for another woman. He asked her to look out for Mom and us. She also knew the woman was Blanche Dumont."

Cadde plopped into his chair. "Why couldn't you have left well enough alone?"

"Because I'm tired of secrets. How many are there in this family?"

"I've always felt Aunt Etta knew something," Chance said. "I just never pushed her, but we should get everything out into the open."

"She wants to see you," Kid told him.

"Shay and I will talk to her after supper."

Jacob crawled in, his hands and knees carrying him just as fast as they could, straight to his father.

"Sorry, he got away from me," Jessie called.

"It's okay, honey." Cadde picked up Jacob and cradled him against his chest. "Daddy's here."

Kid thought it was time for him to leave. "One more thing. If Walker or the sheriff calls that I've been arrested, don't worry about it."

"What are you up to?" Cadde rubbed Jacob's back, his eyes not too friendly.

He shrugged. "Lucky didn't put my name on the baby's headstone. No matter what I did, my son deserves my name and I'm going to have it put on there even if I have to chisel it myself."

"Oh, hell." He heard Cadde's words as he walked out.

Chance followed him all the way to his truck. "Kid, think about this. Don't do something crazy."

"He's my son," he snapped, opening his door.

Chance grabbed the door. "Okay. Take a deep breath and think like a rational person. Can you do that?"

He did as Chance asked and then leaned against the truck, trying to dislodge the outrage in him. What was he doing? Acting like a man who had a right to issue orders. He had no rights. He'd thrown them away in the same self-centered mindset Chuck Hardin had. Oh, God. The truth was as blinding as the September sun.

"I take it Lucky said no about the name."

For a moment he'd lost track of the conversation. "Yep. No discussion. Nothing. Just no."

"Give her time. I know that's hard for you, but if you do something behind her back and illegal you'll never find a middle ground with Lucky. For your son, take some time."

"I hate it when you do that."

"What?"

"Make me see reason. I don't like this grown-up crap." He stared off into the warm afternoon and wondered if his life could get any more complicated. "I'm sorry if Shay's going to be upset about Aunt Etta."

"She'll be fine. We were talking about telling her, but we never found the right time. Aunt Etta loves her and Shay will be happy that she knows the truth."

"Oh, crap."

"What?"

"Here comes Cadde. He's going to hammer on my poor aching head some more."

Cadde stopped beside Chance. "Have you talked some sense into him?"

"Yeah," Chance replied.

"Good." His older brother looked at him. "Please make better judgment calls than you did in your twenties."

Kid climbed into his truck. "I'll have to look up the description for *better*."

As he started the engine, Cadde asked, "Are you coming in to work tomorrow?"

"Probably not."

"Kid…"

He backed out staring at his brothers' expressions—the one that said "God protect the world from Kid Hardin." He might be a loose cannon, but he did it with a smile. Like Aunt Etta had said, he wasn't ever going to stop laughing, even if his heart was breaking.

HE HAD NO CLUE WHERE HE was going. Seeing Lucky was out of the question. She was at work anyway and he couldn't talk to her there. Swiping a hand through his hair, he realized he didn't have his hat. Where in the hell had he left it? At Lucky's.

Turning toward the Littlefield place, he decided to retrieve it. He just hoped Bud was in a friendlier mood. When he drove up, he saw the man sitting on the front porch in one of the rockers. His cane rested against his leg and a shotgun lay across his lap. Great. He had to face another Littlefield with a gun.

He got out and strolled toward the steps. A black-and-white border collie barked.

"Boy, you better have a good reason for coming back here."

He took the steps slowly. "Bud, I'm not a boy anymore."

"Humph."

He sat in the other rocker. "I came to get my hat."

"What you sitting for then? It's in the house near the sofa."

"Is Lucky okay?"

"Hell, no. Seeing you is like a slap in the face and if you think you're getting anywhere near the grave, you'd better think again. I'll fill you with so many holes we'll be able to use you as a sprinkler."

Old Bud had a dry wit, but Kid didn't think for a second that he didn't mean what he'd said. "I get the message."

"You sure you don't have a Magic Marker in your pocket?"

Kid drew back. "I wouldn't deface my son's headstone."

"But you want your name on it?"

"Yes, but I wouldn't do anything stupid." Not now. Adult reasoning was testing his brain and it wasn't a good feeling.

"Aren't you the same boy who used a red Magic Marker to draw a heart on my wall with Kid Loves Lucky inside?"

"Yeah, I did that."

"Aren't you the same boy who talked Lucky into stealing beer from my store?"

"Yeah, I did that, too, but I'm older now and...well, to be honest, the truth is age hasn't changed me much. I planned to put my name on it when Lucky was away. But I can see now that isn't a wise idea."

Bud squinted at him. "Who are you?"

"Come on, Bud, give me a break."

"Over your head maybe. You hurt my daughter and I'll never forget that."

"I'm sorry for all the pain I caused her."

"Then go back to Houston and leave her alone."

He took a long breath. For the first time he realized the past was over and there was no way to go back. Not even his name on his son's grave would change that. He just got blindsided by all the pain. He had to leave Lucky in peace and he had to find a way to live with himself. And that was about as grown-up as he could get.

Something else bothered him. "Aren't you worried about Lucky working in that bar?"

"All the time." Bud squinted at him again. "Somebody hit you. There's a bruise on your left jaw."

He touched the sore spot. "That happened last night when those guys tried to accost Lucky."

"What guys?"

He frowned. "Didn't Lucky tell you?"

"No. She didn't mention a thing."

How did he get out of this? Clearly Lucky didn't want her father to know. But for once he used that better judgment thing Cadde was talking about.

"I got into a fight with three cowboys and Lucky had to separate us with her gun."

Bud stared at him for several seconds. "Boy, you don't lie very good."

"Okay, Bud, it wasn't a pretty scene, but Lucky had everything handled."

"That girl is into something dangerous and I can't stop her. She's hell-bent on—"

"What do you mean 'something dangerous'?"

"What?" Bud had a blank look. "Nothing. I'm just an old man rambling."

"No, you're not. What's Lucky into?"

"Get your hat, boy, and leave." Bud clammed up fast and Kid knew he wasn't going to say another word.

He'd let it be for now and walked into the house. Inside everything had changed. New furniture, bigger

TV and a brightly patterned area rug covered the hardwood floor in the living room. A fresh cream color covered the walls and completely obliterated the heart he'd drawn over the sofa. They'd been fooling around that day, just the two of them as it often was. He drew hearts on her homework and she got mad. Then he'd drawn a big one on the wall. She giggled and said he was crazy. Her father was going to kill him. Bud was pissed. He'd called Aunt Etta and Kid was grounded for a week. He offered to paint over the heart but Lucky wouldn't let him.

He guessed she finally had. Probably when she'd discovered Kid Hardin wasn't worth the ink that was wasted on the wall. He took a long breath and picked up his hat. What he and Lucky had was over, but a whole lot of memories remained.

LUCKY SERVED BEER WITH ONE EYE on the door, watching for the cowboys, but so far they hadn't showed. It was just as well. She had enough on her plate with Kid threatening to change the headstone. Why couldn't he leave? He had no problem doing so years ago.

The place was busy and she didn't have time to dwell on Kid and his unpredictable behavior.

Luther Farley slid onto a bar stool. "Coors. Can."

She disliked the man to the point of wanting to cringe. He was a big, boastful, egotistical idiot with a spare tire around his middle. His mother believed drinking was a sin, so Lucky didn't know why he kept coming in here. Guess the rules didn't apply to the Farley family.

Placing the can in front of him, she asked, "Anything else?"

He popped the top and winked at her. "You sure are looking fine tonight, Lucky."

"I'll remember to tell your wife that."

"She doesn't talk to women like you."

Lucky's hands curled into fists. *Stay calm.* "Must be nice living in that righteous world. Does she know you're in here?"

"Hell, no. A man has to have some fun." He leaned over and whispered, "You and I could have a lot of fun."

She turned on her heel and marched into the back room before she hit him. Suddenly she heard a familiar voice. It couldn't be. She peeped around the corner. Kid was sitting next to Luther. Why couldn't he just leave?

"Hey, Kid," Luther was saying. "Long time no see."

"Been sort of busy."

"Yeah, you Hardin boys are in the oil business."

"It's a dirty job but someone has to do it."

Luther's laugh was an obnoxious sound. "What are you doing in here? Getting reacquainted with Lucky?"

"No. It's hot and I wanted a beer."

"Yeah, right." Luther snickered and then shouted, "Hey, Lucky, bring some beers to the back table for the guys and me."

"You're going that way," Kid butted in. "Why don't you carry them yourself?"

"Because that's what she does—wait on men."

Kid turned on the stool. "I don't like the way you said that."

"Who cares what you like, Hardin? Lucky's a tramp and you ought to know that better than anyone."

That's when Kid's fist connected with Luther's jaw and he went flying into another time zone—almost. He landed against the jukebox and an old Waylon Jennings song came on. "I've always been crazy…"

How fitting could that be?

The room became completely quiet and she motioned to Bubba Joe. Luther moaned and Bubba helped him to his feet as Luther's friends gathered round.

"Time to go," Bubba Joe said.

At the door, Luther turned back, rubbing his jaw. "This ain't over, Hardin."

"I'm right here, Luther."

"Fun's over," Bubba Joe announced and everyone went back to their drinking.

"What are you doing?" Lucky snarled at Kid.

Kid twisted his fist and sat on the stool again. "Breaking my hand, I think."

"I want you to leave."

"I didn't like what he said."

"So? You're not my protector. Who do you think comes in here? A Bible study group? It's men with loud mouths, dirty ideas and bad attitudes."

"Then why in the hell are you doing this?"

She exhaled a hot breath. "I want you to leave—now."

"All right, I was wrong—once again and…"

"Don't you dare say you're sorry because sorry doesn't even start to cover the multitude of your sins."

He winced. "Can I have a beer, please?"

"No."

He held up his hands in defeat. "I'll leave if you'll tell me what those guys were doing here last night."

"You're not in a position to make deals. And it's none of your business."

"Are you into something illegal?" he persisted.

She stomped her foot, went into the storeroom and sat on several cases of beer. Bubba Joe stood in the doorway and she nodded.

"Lucky."

"Do it."

She got up and listened near the doorjamb.

"Kid, you have to go," Bubba Joe said. "Lucky wants you out of here."

"Yeah, I got that impression."

"Just leave. I don't want to fight with you."

"I think I'll go put some ice on my hand and maybe my head. I seem to make all the wrong decisions. Look out for Lucky."

"I always do."

Lucky leaned against the wall and wondered how long she could keep this up. A part of her was happy that he'd taken up for her, the other part was angry. She knew what the people of High Cotton thought of her, but it cut deep to hear it said in front of Kid. Hating him got her through many days and seeing him after twenty years was doing a number on her resolve to never let Kid get to her again.

He would leave and her life would get back to normal. She prayed it would be soon.

CHAPTER SEVEN

UNABLE TO STOP HIMSELF, Kid waited outside until closing. When Lucky and Bubba Joe walked out he knew she was okay and drove away. Trying to maintain his adult dignity, and at times that was hard to find, he made the trip to Houston and his apartment. He called Aunt Etta to let her know where he was.

After stripping out of his clothes, he found ice in the freezer for his hand and jaw and fell into bed. Before sleep claimed him, he saw Lucky's blue eyes and wondered if she'd ever smile for him again. Why was that so important to him?

He woke up groaning. Every muscle in his body ached, especially his hand. He had to stop fighting in bars or it was going to kill him. Literally.

The ice had melted and the bed was damp. He didn't bother with it. The maid would change the sheets. He winced all the way to the bathroom. He had a Jacuzzi but he never used it unless he had female company. After filling it with water, he slipped in and let the hot, swirling water relax him.

Afterward, he felt much better and was ready for the day. He dressed and headed for Shilah. The company was located in the Murdock Building in downtown

Houston. It was twelve stories high with a huge sculpture of an oil derrick out front surrounded by a flower bed of blooming plants that the gardening crew kept looking spiffy. He parked in his spot and got out. At the back door, he realized he didn't have his keys. Damn! He'd left them at the apartment.

He strolled to the front entrance. Carlos, the maintenance guy, opened the front doors early. He went through the large lobby where Stephanie, the receptionist, was settling in at her desk. When she saw him, she tottered around it on four-inch platform heels until she was almost touching him with her body. The low-cut tight-fitting knit dress left little to the imagination. It was exactly the way he liked his women. Why wasn't he liking it now?

"Hey, Kid, I haven't seen you in a while." She smiled in that seductive way he knew well.

He took a step back. "I've been busy." He dated her a few times, but she was a little young and over-the-top, even for him. A complete airhead, the only thing Stephanie saw or cared about was her reflection in a mirror. He wasn't sure what that said about him and his taste in women, but then again he did. He was an airhead, too.

She fluttered the fake eyelashes. "Wanna have some fun tonight?"

"I..."

"My friend's in town so maybe you could ask your brother and we could make it a foursome."

He frowned. "My brother? Which one?"

"Not the CEO. He's much too intense, but the other one is nice."

"You mean Chance?" He could feel his face setting into one big frown like a plaster-of-Paris mold.

"Yeah."

"He's married with kids and if the world was coming to an end he wouldn't cheat on his wife."

"Oh. I just thought he'd like to have some fun."

"Fun to Chance is seeing his wife after a long day, hugging his daughter and holding his newborn son."

She rolled her eyes. "B-o-ring."

"It's called integrity, honor and until death do us part."

Placing a hand on his chest, she murmured, "We can make it a threesome."

He removed her hand. "I'm not into that."

"Since when?"

"Since forever," he flung over his shoulder as he walked to the elevator.

He kept the steamed up emotions inside until he fell into his chair in his office. Why had Cadde and Chance inherited good qualities? While he had received the short end of the stick on morals and values from good ol' Dad?

He'd once told Chance that people are shaped by the ones around them. Genes and environment play a factor. As does free will when we mature. He'd learned that in Bible study as a kid. So maybe he needed to stop blaming his father and look inward. He'd had choices and no one had made them but him.

In school, he'd loved Lucky. He'd never cheated on her and he could have, many times. So what had made him into the selfish bastard he was today? The answer was simple. He had. And only him.

His head was starting to hurt so he grabbed his briefcase and went to work. With the leases in a folder, he walked down to Cadde's office. As usual, Cadde was at his desk. He was a permanent fixture.

His brother looked up. "I thought you weren't coming in today."

He laid the folder in front of him. "There're the leases for those tracts in south Texas. It'll have to be a smaller well because the rest of the land is leased up."

Cadde glanced through the folder. "Good. I'll have Barbara take it to bookkeeping." He leaned back. "What about Lucky's land?"

"I told you that's off the table and I'm serious."

"Kid..."

Chance walked in, interrupting them. "Have you... Oh, Kid, I didn't think you were coming in today."

He could feel Cadde watching him. "What's wrong with your hand? You're holding it funny."

"I did something stupid...again." He flexed his fingers.

Chance gasped. "You didn't! You said you'd take some time and think."

"I didn't do anything to the headstone so pull your eyeballs back into your head."

"What did you do?" Cadde asked.

"Well, I went to The Beer Joint and Luther Farley

said something I didn't like about Lucky so I decked him. Didn't even think about it. Just bam—knocked him clear across the room right into the jukebox."

Chance sank into a chair with a long sigh.

Cadde stared straight at him. "What did Lucky think about this?"

"Let's just say she wasn't happy and asked me to leave."

"Listen, Kid." Cadde used his "board meeting" voice—a rough growl that made everyone pay attention and for once Kid was listening. "If you feel anything for Lucky, stop fighting, especially in her bar. If you don't care for her, then get the hell out of her life."

"I've already figured that out myself. I don't know what I'm feeling at the moment so I'm taking some time off to get my head straight. All my work is updated so I'm outta here."

"Where're you going?" Chance asked.

He shrugged. "Not sure. Probably spend some time with Aunt Etta and try to talk to Lucky in a nonconfrontational way."

"Please leave the headstone alone," Chance begged, "until Lucky is ready to change it."

With his hand on the doorknob, he couldn't resist teasing his honorable, upright brother. "Oh, Chance, I forgot my key this morning. When I came through the front, Stephanie stopped me and asked if I wanted to go out tonight. She requested that you come along. Her friend is in town and they'd like to do a foursome. I told her I'm busy, but she could certainly call you."

"You didn't! Kid!"

He took the stairwell and laughed all the way down at the shocked look on Chance's face. What the hell was wrong with laughter?

LUCKY SAT ON THE STOOP, having her early morning coffee and talking to Travis on her cell.

"The cowboys didn't come in," she told him.

"I know. I drove by several times."

She gripped the phone. "Travis, don't you trust me to do my job?"

"Sure, but when it gets dangerous, I'm going to be there."

In a way it was nice he was looking out for her. With Kid around, she might need his help, but she didn't want it to come with any emotional strings.

"Thanks," she muttered, giving in a little.

"Anyway, the rustlers are on the move. Three registered Brahma cows were taken from the Southern Cross ranch last night."

"From Judd Calhoun?" She was shocked. Southern Cross and High Five were the biggest ranches in High Cotton.

"Yep, and he's fighting mad."

"I bet. The rustlers are getting stupid. To go onto a ranch that size takes nerve. How did they do it?"

"The east side of the property borders an old county road that closed many years ago. They came down it with a trailer, cut the fence, threw up portable pens and coaxed the cows into it with feed. I'm at the site gathering evidence. The rustling will be in the limelight now because Judd will make it that way."

"I know Judd and he's not going to stand for it."

"By my calculations the rustlers have a big herd stashed somewhere in a back wooded area and they'll try to move it soon."

Lucky chewed on her lip. "Tomorrow is Saturday and it's always a busy night at the bar. I'm sure the stolen Brahmas will be the topic of conversation. I'll keep my eyes and ears opened."

"Good. Call if anything comes up and I'll drive by the bar later."

She sighed. "If you have to."

"I'll be busy here most of the day trying to pacify Judd. Not one damn surveillance camera on this big ranch."

"Well, Travis, with armed cowboys I don't guess he saw the need."

"He does now."

Lucky clicked off. The rustlers weren't some petty thieves. This was an established ring of skillfully planned robberies. She had to be extra careful and watch her backside. But most of the time her concentration was on Kid. Any minute she expected him to come flying up the lane in that fancy truck demanding she put his name on the headstone.

She got up, coffee cup in her hand and glanced toward the hill. Her childhood was buried there, as were all her foolish dreams of first love lasting forever. She didn't know how to go forward without looking back. Twenty years and she still didn't know how to do that.

SATURDAY NIGHT WAS BUSY and Lucky was run off her feet. Thelma Lou came in to help out. After serving a table of six with beer, pretzels and peanuts, Lucky froze. The three cowboys walked in and pushed their way to the bar. She motioned to Bubba Joe who moved closer to them. She'd told him things had gotten out of hand the other night so he'd be prepared. But before either of them could do a thing Kid strolled through the door.

She didn't need this tonight.

With his devil-may-care attitude, he went right up to them, leaning on the bar beside Melvin.

What was he doing?

"Hey, guys, I'm glad I ran into you," he said in his smooth-as-butter voice. "I'm sorry about the other night. I was drunk and thought y'all were ganging up on a woman. When I sobered up, I realized that wasn't true and I'd just misread the signals. Actually, I'm known for that—making a fool out of myself. The name's Kid Hardin. How about if I buy y'all a round of drinks? Hell, I'll buy you two just to prove I'm sincere."

"I could have cut you, man," Melvin snarled.

"Don't I know it? That's how drunk I was. I don't make good sense when I'm inebriated. Hell, most people would say I don't make good sense when I'm sober, either."

The cowboys laughed.

"We all get drunk," Clyde said. "But you came close to getting killed."

"Yeah. I still have aches and pains."

"Are you getting us a beer or what?" Earl asked.

What was he doing? Making friends?

Kid looked around. "It's busy as a hornet's nest in here. I'll get it since Lucky and Bubba Joe are busy." His eyes met hers and he winked.

He winked!

As bold as a rattlesnake he walked around the bar, opened the cooler and pulled out four longnecks. Bubba Joe met him before he could move any farther. They whispered something and then Kid twisted off the tops, setting them in front of the cowboys. After that he yanked out his wallet and handed Bubba some bills.

"What's he doing?" she asked Bubba.

"Being Kid. Who knows?"

"He's not licensed to serve beer."

"Well, that's a minor technicality. I say let's just leave it alone. He gave me five twenties so they're set for a while. I'll watch it closely."

And if the night couldn't get any worse Luther Farley and Frank Gibbons walked in.

"Damn. This is going to get bad," Bubba said.

"Make sure your shotgun is handy." She moved to the register where her gun was stashed.

"Hey, Lucky," a guy called from a back booth, "we need beer."

"I'll get it," Thelma Lou said. As she grabbed beer

out of the cooler, she noticed Kid on the wrong side of the bar. “Hey, who’s the hunk?”

“Kid Hardin, and he’s fixing to leave.”

“Damn. I’d like working with that kind of eye candy.”

“You’re married…and remember Bubba Joe.”

“So? I’m not dead.”

Lucky let that pass. She had more important things on her mind. Like how to get Kid out of here without causing a scene. Her stomach roiled with a sick feeling but she ignored it.

Luther pushed Fred Carter off his bar stool. Fred came up with his fists in the air. “Get another spot,” Luther said.

“Uh…Luther, I didn’t know it was you.” Since Fred was of a small stature, Luther could pulverize him like a piece of steak. Fred worked for Luther, so he picked up his hat and joined a group at another table.

Luther eased his big frame onto the stool facing Kid. Lucky edged closer to her gun. No one was fighting in here tonight. She just wished her stomach would settle down.

“Hey, Luther.” Kid jumped right in. “I’m sorry I hit you last night. I lost my temper. You know I was always doing that in high school.”

“You never knew how to fight fair.”

“Hell, man, you were big as an ox and picking on poor Bubba Joe. I had to do something.”

“You didn’t have to pull down my pants in front of Betty Simmons.”

"You married her so I don't see a problem. Maybe she got a glimpse of what she really wanted."

A rumble of laughter followed.

"You're insane, Hardin." Luther was trying hard not to smile. "You've always been insane."

Kid rubbed his hand. "I think I broke my wrist on your steel jaw."

"Maybe that'll teach you to think before you swing."

"Yep. Learned a lesson." He glanced toward Bubba Joe who was standing in the doorway to the storeroom, close to his shotgun in case a fight broke out. "Bet you don't pick on big Bubba anymore."

"Hell, no. He can bench-press me without any effort." Luther's eyes narrowed. "You working for Lucky now?"

"No. I was apologizing to these guys for making an ass out of myself." He thumbed to the cowboys. "How about if I buy everybody a round?"

"Sounds good," Luther replied.

This time Lucky met him at the cooler, placing her hand on the handle. "What are you doing?"

"Now don't get upset." His brown eyes twinkled like she remembered and her heart fluttered crazily.

"Too late."

"Just give me a few minutes and I'll be out of here." He touched her hand and she jerked it away.

"Don't touch me." She took a long breath, knowing she was fighting a losing battle with her emotions. "You have a few minutes and then I want you to be invisible."

"Come on, Lucky, invisible is really hard to do." He

shot her a cocky grin and not hitting him was even harder not to do.

"Do it." She grabbed the beers and handed them to him, careful that their hands didn't touch.

He winked...again! She gritted her teeth.

"Where y'all from?" Luther was asking the cowboys and she forced her attention there.

"Around Cameron," Clyde replied. "We work cattle for people."

Kid placed the beers in front of them, but the conversation didn't stop.

"Ain't much money in that," Luther remarked, taking a swig from the bottle.

"We get by."

Frank slid in beside Luther. "Did y'all hear that rustlers took three of Judd Calhoun's prized cows?"

"You shitting me." Clearly Luther hadn't heard.

"Who's Judd Calhoun?" Clyde asked.

"Owner of the Southern Cross ranch, a big spread," Luther told him.

"Is rustling big around here?" Kid joined the conversation.

"It has been lately." Frank motioned for a beer and Bubba served him. "But they'd been targeting small places until last night. Hitting the Southern Cross was a bold move."

"Only an idiot would make that kind of mistake." Kid leaned on the counter, talking as if they were good friends.

"Are you sure you're not involved, Hardin?" Luther tipped up his bottle.

"Like I got time to rustle cattle. And this is High Cotton. What happened to our sleepy little town?"

"It's the economy," Frank said. "Everybody needs money. I was down at the general store picking up barbed wire and Nell said a special ranger for the Texas and Southwestern Cattle Raisers Association is here talking to Judd. Things will get lively now. Cops will be all over the place."

Lucky pretended to wipe the counter, listening with both ears, but there were people chattering in the background and it was hard to hear everything.

"Boys, I've enjoyed talking to you, but the big city awaits." Kid pushed away from the counter. "Bubba Joe, give the guys another round on me."

"You're a pretty decent guy." Melvin reached for a bottle. "But don't mess with us again."

Kid nodded and walked toward Lucky, stopping at her side. "I'm going to find out what you're up to," he whispered. His breath fanned her cheek and her knees wobbled. Damn him!

Weaving his way through the crowd, he left with a smug expression on his face.

Now she knew what he was doing here—screwing up her life.

CHAPTER EIGHT

KID DROVE TO AUNT ETTA'S and ate supper. Afterward, he and Uncle Ru watched a rodeo on TV. Soon Ru fell asleep, snoring in his chair. His aunt dozed on and off.

He got up and whispered, "Aunt Etta, I'm leaving, but I'll be back later."

"Oh." She blinked. "The door will be open."

He went back to The Beer Joint, but he didn't go in. He watched and waited, wanting to make sure Lucky was okay. When the patrons started coming out, he parked in a ditch. The cowboys left along with the others. Still, he didn't move until he saw Lucky and Bubba Joe come through the door. He followed from a distance until she turned down the Littlefield lane.

On his way from Houston, he'd thought about what Cadde had said. If he didn't care about Lucky, Kid needed to get out of her life. If he did…that was the stumbling block. He wasn't sure what he felt. He only knew she was into something dangerous and he had to keep her safe. He hadn't been there for her years ago, but he would be there for her now.

He planned to win her over with kindness, but once he saw the black Dodge outside The Joint he knew that wasn't going to work. No way was he walking away and leaving her to face those yahoos. And to top off the evening, Luther had walked in. Nothing had gone his way. With a lot of kissing unbelievably ugly butts, he'd finagled himself out of a touchy situation.

All while Lucky was glaring at him.

He'd picked up on something, though. Lucky was interested in the two-bit cowboys for some reason. On the nights he'd been watching her, Bubba Joe always left with her. That meant she had to have asked Bubba to leave the night the cowboys waited for her. She'd wanted to talk to them. Why? That boggled his mind.

And then there was cattle rustling. Somehow he felt it was all tied together. But what did Lucky have to do with stealing cattle in the middle of the night? It didn't make sense.

He turned off his lights and drove into the Littlefield lane. He stopped the truck halfway to the house. Parking on the road wasn't a good idea. Due to the rustling, the sheriff, the constable and the ranger were checking all roads he was sure, and he didn't want Lucky to know he was here.

Opening the console, he pulled out a baseball. On it was written *Hardin* with a Magic Marker. He'd bought it in Houston earlier. He slipped out of the truck quickly, trying to minimize the brightness of the interior light. The night was warm and peaceful as he strolled toward the cemetery. A cow bellowed in the distance, crickets chirped, leaves rustled—all normal country sounds.

The house was in darkness as he made his way to

the chain-link fence. Once inside, he knelt by his son's grave.

"Hey, buddy, it's your dad." The moment he said the words he had to gulp a breath. He was a father and with that came responsibility. It didn't matter that the baby had died. It mattered that he had been conceived—in love. It mattered that Kid had to shoulder the responsibility of his death, as the thirty-nine-year-old man he was.

A coyote howled close by and the eerie call settled in him. He sank back on his boots. "I was going to put this baseball in the basket your mom has on your grave. It has *Hardin* on it. That's who you are." He twisted the ball in his hand. "But I can't do it now because it would upset her and that's a humbling thought for a man my age. Most of my life I've been carefree, fun-loving, the life of the party. I never knew about you and that's the most humbling experience of all. I'm not sure what kind of father I would have been at eighteen, but I would have loved you." He took a breath. "I love you now and when your mom says it's okay, I'll put the baseball in the basket. Bye, son."

As he walked away he thought this was a hell of a way to grow up. But if he'd learned anything from the past few days he knew Kid Hardin had finally achieved adulthood—the hard way.

WHEN HE WOKE UP, HIS AUNT and uncle were gone for the day. He made coffee and then showered and dressed.

As he was pouring his second cup, Aunt Etta rushed through the door.

"I brought your breakfast." She placed a plate of scrambled eggs, bacon and two biscuits on the table. "It's hot, so eat."

"You don't have to wait on me," he told her. "I've been on my own for a long time and managed to survive."

"God only knows what you've been eating."

He shrugged. "Mostly doughnuts, sweet rolls and sometimes nothing. Just coffee. That's the good thing about being an adult. I get to do what I want."

"Now that's a mouthful."

"I guess I should be eating healthy, huh?"

"Yes, and always a good breakfast. That gets you started for the day. Now I have to run. Sky is helping Coop today and I'm watching the kids."

His aunt was in her seventies and worked all the time. "Do you ever think about retiring?"

"Retiring?" Her eyes opened wide. "When they put me in a coffin."

He leaned against the cabinet, drinking his coffee. "Wouldn't you like to go somewhere? Take a vacation? I'll pay for everything."

"Ru and I were born and raised here. This is our life and my heart is full since Cadde and Chance moved home. I wouldn't be happy anywhere else even for a week."

"But I want to do something for you."

She shoved her hands into the pockets of her apron.

"Then find some peace within yourself. That's what you can do for me."

He grimaced. "It would be easier to send you to the Grand Canyon or somewhere."

She shook her head, those patient eyes looking all the way into his soul. She knew him better than anyone and he could tell her anything.

"I...I..." He told her what he tried to do last night. "I couldn't, though. Something held me back."

"Conscience?"

"Maybe."

"Talk to Lucky and get all of this bad stuff out of your system so you can see the future—with or without Lucky. Don't just charm your way into her heart. Let it happen naturally."

He pulled out a chair and sat at the table. "I'm working on it."

"See you tonight."

"Oh, Aunt Etta." He stopped her at the door. "I'll be in and out so don't wait up for me." He just needed a place to sleep and that made him think about the beds. "How about if I buy a new bedroom set for our old room?"

"There's one in the attic that Dane and the cowboys took out. I rather like the room the way it is. It reminds Ru and me of when you boys were here fighting over the bathroom, who gets the first pancake and what TV show to watch."

"Okay. Nothing new." That old mattress was about to kill him, though. Aunt Etta liked it so he wasn't changing a thing. He could sleep at his brother's, but that was honeymoon central and he didn't want to invade their privacy.

After breakfast, he thought he'd try and talk to Lucky. As he passed the general store he saw her truck and turned around. He wanted to set a time for when they could talk. Showing up uninvited was like the old Kid. There were rules of conduct and they were meant for him, too.

As he slid from his truck, Mrs. Farley and Mrs. Axelwood came out the door.

"Good morning, ladies." He tipped his hat.

"Cisco, how nice to see you." Mrs. Farley shook his hand, as did the other woman. "And it's so wonderful to have your brothers back in High Cotton."

"Yeah, they're married and settled. Me, I'm still a bachelor."

"You just haven't met the right woman."

"I have a niece..." Mrs. Axelwood spoke up.

He held up his hands. "Thanks, but no setups." And to steer the conversation in another direction, he added, "It was great seeing ol' Luther the other night."

"Where did you see Luther?"

"At The Beer Joint."

Mrs. Farley bristled. "I beg your pardon. My son does not frequent that place."

"Now, I know it was Luther."

"You're mistaken." At that moment Lucky walked out of the store. "It's the devil's workshop—" Mrs. Farley glanced at Lucky "—and the people who work there are the devil's helpers."

"Well, then, Luther must be on first name basis with the evil-doer himself because he was there."

"Let's go, Gladys," she snapped and they hurried to a tan Buick.

"Tell Luther I said hi," he called after them, running to catch Lucky before she drove off.

Her window was down so he was able to talk without yelling. "Could we talk, please?"

"No." She started the motor.

"Come on, Lucky. A few minutes, that's all I'm asking."

Her blue eyes stared straight at him. "I do not need your protection so stop butting into my life. I can handle those old bats any day of the week. I'm used to it."

"You shouldn't have to be."

She sighed and he wanted to run his hand over the back of her neck to comfort her. He curled his hands into fists to keep from doing so.

"I'm going home and I'll give you fifteen minutes to say what's on your mind. Not one minute more."

"Thank you."

"And please stop saying 'come on, Lucky.' It just annoys me now."

"Okay." It used to make her smile, a poignant reminder of the past.

She backed out and drove away.

He had a short amount of time to cram a lifetime of

forgive-my-sins into. But as he thought about it he decided to do the exact opposite of what she was expecting.

LUCKY HURRIED THROUGH the front door, threw her purse on the sofa and carried a carton of milk to the refrigerator.

Her father was sitting in front of the TV. When *The Price Is Right* was on, an elephant could walk through the house and he wouldn't notice.

"Dad, Kid's coming over."

He didn't answer. She put glasses and cups into the dishwasher and waited for a commercial. When it came on, she shouted to him again. "Dad, Kid's coming over."

"What the hell for?"

She'd made a connection. "He wants to talk."

"So? People in hell want ice water. You don't see me shoveling it out."

"Dad..."

There was a knock at the door and she went to let Kid in. He smiled that cocky grin and her stomach fluttered just like it used to. But now she was immune to his charm. Almost.

"Hey, Bud," he said, removing his hat. She noticed he had some papers in his hand.

"You got a Magic Marker in your pocket?"

"No."

"Good. You're not writing on any of my walls." Her dad tried to look around Kid to the TV. "Move. You're blocking my view."

"Oh." Kid immediately took two steps sideways.

"We can talk in the kitchen," she said, and he followed her to the table, hooking his hat on a chair.

Ollie sniffed it.

"No," she scolded and Ollie trotted back to his spot.

Kid eased into a chair. "How is Bud getting *The Price Is Right* on a Sunday?"

"I taped a lot of the shows when he was in the hospital and when there's nothing else on, he watches them."

"Oh. Aunt Etta watches it, too."

"Are you going to waste your fifteen minutes talking about a TV show?"

"No." He pushed the papers toward her. "I'd like to talk about leasing your land to Shilah Oil."

That shocked her. She'd thought he'd gotten the message the first time. And she had braced herself for a battle over the headstone. She had to completely readjust her thinking. Was that what he'd intended? To befuddle her?

She shoved the document back to him. "The answer is still no."

"Read it," he insisted. "Check the signing bonus, the royalty rate. It's top dollar and no one is going to beat it."

"I'm not interested."

He stood with a long sigh. "Don't do this to get back at me. This could be very good for you."

She lifted an eyebrow. "And get me out of The Beer Joint?"

"Well, yeah."

She got to her feet and then wished she hadn't. He was a little too close for her comfort zone. A musky sandalwood scent reached her and she bit her lip to keep her emotion on a leash.

"I do not need your help. I'm doing fine on my own. I only have one problem—your unwelcomed intrusion into my life."

"Okay, things got out of hand with the cowboys, but there's something going on..."

"Nothing's going on that concerns you, and what were you doing buying them drinks last night?"

"You're into something dangerous and it involves those cowboys. I'm going to keep kissing their ugly butts until I find out what it is. I didn't count on ol' Luther coming in when he did so I had to keep up the farce. If I'm good at anything, it's talking my way out of sticky situations."

"Yeah, I know that better than anyone, but I just don't understand how you feel this is any of your business."

"I wasn't there for you years ago, but I will be here for you now."

She sighed. "Why is that so important to you? Your intrusion into my life is only making me angry."

He shrugged. "Sorry. I wasn't able to do anything for our son, but I will keep his mother safe."

Her nerves stretched taut at his mind-boggling attitude. She thought quickly and knew of a way to get him out of her affairs. If she didn't, he was going to jeopardize the whole case. "I'll sign these papers if you'll promise to go back to Houston and get out of my life."

He rubbed his jaw and she wanted to reach out and touch his roughened cheek. She had to restrain herself from doing so. "Nah, that's a no go. I have family here and High Cotton is my home."

"But you don't have to see me. You don't have to come to my house."

His eyes narrowed. "My son is buried here and I plan to visit his grave a lot, with your permission, of course."

She closed her eyes and wanted to pull out her hair. She was getting nowhere with him. "Please leave."

"You've said that so many times I'm beginning to believe you don't like me anymore."

She gritted her teeth. "Goodbye, Kid, and take the lease with you."

"No." He waved a hand toward the papers. "Read it. Talk about it with Bud. My number is on the attached card. You can call me at any time."

Don't hold your breath, she wanted to say, but decided not to let him get to her. She followed him to the front door and was surprised her dad didn't add a few scathing words, but he was too interested in the TV.

As they went out the door, Ollie eased out, too. On the porch, Kid said, "I'm not trying to butt into your life. I'm just worried you're in some sort of danger."

"Kid, you have no right to worry about me. I haven't seen you in years."

"That's my fault."

"Please." She held up a hand to stop him. "We can't keep stepping back into the past. It's too painful. I really loved you, but the sad truth is you didn't love me enough."

"Lucky…"

An old blue Ford inched up the lane, interrupting him.

"You've got company."

"It's Mrs. Grisley." She hoped the woman was coming to see her dad and not to complain about Bubba Joe working too hard. She was about to mother the poor man to death.

"Bubba Joe's mom? I haven't seen her since I left for the university."

"You haven't missed a thing." She forced herself not to smile.

A tall big-boned woman got out of the car with a huge purse on her arm.

"What the hell is that on her head?" Kid asked. "It looks like a dead raccoon."

"It's a wig. Don't mention it." Again, she had to suppress a grin.

"Lucky, I want to talk to you." Wilma stomped up the steps. "Thelma Lou is messing with Bubba Joe's head. You need to fire her."

"Messing?" Lucky had no idea what the woman was talking about.

"She's always asking him over to fix stuff and he takes her home after she works at The Joint. She has a husband somewhere and four wild kids. My boy doesn't need to get mixed up with that."

"Wilma, I have no control over Bubba Joe or Thelma Lou."

"Ah, you're no help. Where's Bud? He'll make you see reason."

"In the house." Lucky stepped away from the door.

Wilma finally noticed Kid. "Who are you?"

He held out his hand. "Kid Hardin, ma'am."

"My, my." Wilma shook his hand. "You were always getting my boy into trouble."

"Now, ma'am—" he smiled that silly grin "—that's a slight exaggeration. Kids were always picking on Bubba and I tried to help him. Yeah, it ended in a fight, but we didn't take any crap, either."

Wilma pointed a finger at him. "Leave my boy alone. He's all I got." She yanked open the door and stomped inside.

"Poor Bubba," Kid muttered, and then looked at her. The mirth she'd been holding inside could no longer be stifled. Laughter bubbled from her throat and she held a hand over her mouth.

Their eyes met and at the gleam in his the amusement turned serious. She ran a hand through her short hair, searching for words that had to be said.

At that moment Ollie leaped for Kid's hat and took off for the barn.

"Come back here!" she shouted, and jumped off the porch to catch the dog. She could hear Kid's boots pounding behind her. When she entered the barn, Ollie lay in a pile of loose hay, chewing on the Stetson. "Give me that hat." Ollie darted around the hay and she followed on the right. Kid headed the dog off on the left. They both jumped for him at the same time. Bumping into each other, they fell backward into the hay. Ollie dashed away.

Kid rolled on top of her, looking into her eyes. His brown hair was tousled over his forehead, his eyes dark and warm. The handsome face in her dreams was right there—a breath away.

Move, Lucky. Move.

But she couldn't make her body obey.

He stroked her hair. "Lucky."

The moment he said her name she was lost.

His head bent and she met his kiss with a fire she remembered well. It had been so long. Their lips and tongues renewed a familiar hunger that enclosed her in a world where only he existed. Her arms wrapped around his neck, pulling him closer and closer. He moaned, pushing her into the hay. Twenty years came full circle as she embraced the passion of two teenagers who were now adults. The emotions were still there. Driving. Forceful. He yanked her blouse from her jeans and she ripped open his shirt, her hands caressing the firm muscles of his back.

She'd forgotten how good he felt. How good he tasted.

His lips trailed to her cheek, her jaw, and she arched her neck from the sheer pleasure. Hot kisses blazed a path to her breasts and all conscious thought left her. Maybe they were always going to be eighteen, like he'd said.

"Lucky," he groaned against a breast and then took her lips once more.

When the world started to spin away, he suddenly broke the kiss and rolled away, taking deep breaths. It took her a moment to gather her pride and then she pulled her blouse over her aching breasts.

He stood, brushing hay from his clothes.

She sat up, wishing she could crawl away and hide. He'd exposed all her vulnerabilities and she wanted to say something to regain a measure of control, but even she knew it was too late for that.

His darkened eyes held hers. "I'm sorry."

"It's…it's okay."

He buttoned his shirt with quick, sure movements. "Back then…I did love you…enough. I just wasn't man enough to accept it."

CHAPTER NINE

KID TURNED OUT OF THE Littlefield lane and had to stop. He switched the air-conditioning to full blast, letting it cool his heated emotions. All these years he'd been looking for Lucky in every woman he'd met. He knew it the moment his lips touched hers and he also knew if he went any further she would never forgive him. He'd used up all of his get-out-of-jail-forgive-me cards.

Resting his head on the steering wheel he took another deep breath. It was uncanny how he remembered the curves of her body, the smoothness of her skin, the smell of her hair. The last thing he wanted to do was stop kissing Lucky. The old Kid wouldn't have thought twice about it. The new Kid, the one who had a son buried on the hill, knew he couldn't do that to Lucky—have sex like two hot-blooded teenagers. She'd hate herself and then she'd hate him all over again. It was the right decision. He wished his body understood that.

He pulled onto the road, planning to go to Aunt Etta's and change into shorts and a T-shirt. Then he'd try to outrun his frustrations. Before he reached the High Five ranch, he noticed a lot of trucks at Chance's. Something had happened. His gut twisted in a familiar sickening way—the same as it had the night his parents had died.

Jumping out of his truck, he saw Chance and his stomach eased somewhat. He was okay. What about the rest of the family?

Walker, Judd, Cooper Yates and a man Kid didn't know stood by Chance talking.

"What's going on?" he asked.

"Someone stole my damn cows," Chance replied. "When I left this morning, I didn't notice them so later I called Shay to check when she got home to see if they had come up to the barn. They hadn't. She got on her horse to look for them and found the cut fence."

"This is getting serious," Judd said. "And I want something done. Now!" He directed his words to the stranger.

"This is Travis Coffman, a special ranger with Texas Southwest Cattle Raisers Association." Chance made the introductions. "This is my brother Kid Hardin."

They shook hands but the ranger's attention was on Judd. "We're doing everything we can. All law enforcement agencies have been notified. Brands have been run through our Fort Worth database. We keep a constant check on auctions barns to see if the cattle have been sold. I'm running down every lead. Nothing pans out. These are some crafty criminals and they're getting bolder."

Kid stared at the man. He looked familiar and then it clicked. The night Lucky had told him about the baby it had hit him like a ton of bricks and he'd sat in the gravel at The Beer Joint for a while. Travis had stopped to ask if he was okay. He didn't remember much after that but Travis's face was clear in his mind.

What had he been doing there at that time?

"Rest assured these criminals will be caught. We have undercover people on the job and someone is going to slip up."

Undercover?

Before Kid could mull it over, Walker's cell beeped. He glanced at a message. "I've got a domestic violence call. I have to go. Why don't we meet at The Beer Joint tonight to discuss this further? A lot of ranchers go in there and they need to be aware and on guard."

"Sounds good." Judd nodded. "I'll be there about seven."

"I'll be there, too," Cooper added. "Then I'm going to sleep with my cows because I can't afford to take a hit of losing any."

"Get the cameras up as soon as you can," Travis urged, and the men walked to their trucks.

"I can't believe this." Chance swiped a hand across his brow. "This is High Cotton. What the hell is the world coming to?"

Kid wondered that, too. The country town was a safe place to live and raise a family. He thought about Jessie's door always being open.

"Is Cadde worried about Jessie?"

"Why?" Chance looked confused.

"She never locks her door."

"They don't hit houses. These are cattle rustlers."

"Still…I can check on her if Cadde wants me to. I'm around."

Chance stared at him.

"What?"

"You're around. That doesn't sound like you. Isn't there a party going on somewhere? Isn't there a woman or two waiting for you in Houston?"

The words hit Kid like a blow, but he knew Chance spoke the truth. Over the years he'd lost himself in parties and with women. But the biggest part of him, the part that mattered, he'd left right here in High Cotton… with Lucky. She had his heart. He knew that beyond a shadow of a doubt.

"I've been a real bastard, haven't I?"

"Nah. You're just Kid."

He thought about that for a minute. In his twenties that explanation was acceptable. Facing forty, it wasn't. "I told you I've grown up. I'm responsible. Levelheaded. And if you laugh I'm going to…hug you."

Chance laughed anyway. "I don't think you can pull that off."

Kid shot him the finger with a grin.

Just to ease his mind he drove to Cadde's. Someone had broken in on Jessie when they'd lived out of Houston and he didn't want her to be afraid. He'd play with Jacob—that always made him feel better.

He lay on the floor while Jacob crawled all over him. Jessie was busy going through baby clothes to see what she could use for the new arrival.

His cell beeped and he saw he had a message. It was

from Cadde. Two words: "stay there." He hung around so long he knew Jessie was getting suspicious. Fortunately, Cadde came home early and she didn't have to kick him out. He knew his brother would explain and arrange for Rosa to be there during the day until the no-good thieves were caught.

While he had supper with his aunt and uncle, they looked at him suspiciously, too. He was never around this long. They might have to get used to it.

Cattle rustling was the topic of conversation. Uncle Ru and Cooper were going to take turns watching the cattle. His uncle was too old to take night duty and Kid thought he'd help out. He'd love to come face-to-face with the low-down bastards who were wreaking havoc on his hometown.

LUCKY SPENT A LOT OF THE DAY on the phone with Travis. He gave her the heads-up about the meeting at The Joint tonight. She was still reeling from the rustlers hitting another place so soon. Chance was a nice person and liked by everyone. She didn't understand it.

"I think we might be after the wrong people," Travis said. "The cowboys should have let something slip by now."

"They apologized for scaring me, but they haven't said anything about being arrested. They've been very cordial."

"We're missing something, Lucky."

"I feel that, too. Someone knows this area very well and it's like they're choosing certain places."

"I'll check the auction barns again tomorrow. Other than that we wait for them to make a mistake."

"Notifying everyone is a good idea."

"Yeah. I'll see you tonight."

She ended the call and stared toward the cemetery.

Kid.

She could barely keep cattle rustling on her mind for thinking about him. How could she give in so easily? One look, one touch and she was right back where she'd started—giving in—to Kid. She got up and went to the only place that gave her comfort—her son's grave.

Kneeling, she said, "I'm sorry, baby. I swore I'd never forgive your father for what he did to us, but today I felt like that young girl whose whole life was worthwhile because he was in it. I know that's crazy and I have to admit to you I don't think I'm ever going to get over him. That first love is so hard to forget, but I will be stronger for both of us."

She hurried down the hill and found her dad on the porch.

"Girl, you visit that grave too much. You have to let go."

She sank onto the stoop. "He's my son. I will always visit him."

"Mmm. Why did you let that old bat into the house?"

"Wilma? She wanted to talk to you."

"She yammers on and on about Bubba Joe. Someone needs to hit her with a stun gun."

"I'm not on her side, but Bubba is getting himself into a sticky situation. Thelma's husband's been gone for about a year. He sends money every now and then but Thelma's barely getting by with food stamps. I guess she's lonely. Bubba is, too."

"Now, Thelma, she's got an edge that'll cut through a T-bone steak. Bubba doesn't need another domineering woman in his life."

She stood. "I'm staying out of it."

"That's my motto, too, so don't let that old bat in the house anymore."

"You talk to her on the phone. I don't see a difference."

"I can hang up a phone but in person Wilma doesn't have an off switch."

She kissed his cheek. "I think you protest too much."

"Humph."

"I'm going to work. Need anything?"

"Nah. I saw the lease papers on the table."

"Yeah. That's what Kid wanted to talk about."

"You sound disappointed."

Was she? She had so many regrets concerning Kid that he had a special storage place in her brain. But she was almost certain that getting him out of her life was paramount for her sanity.

"I read the lease. It's a good deal."

She bit her lip. "I don't plan on looking at it."

Her dad twisted his neck to look at her. "Now, that's just crazy."

"I offered to sign it if he'd go back to Houston and leave me alone."

"And he refused?"

"Yes."

"That's just guilt talking. He'll soon tire of this cat and mouse game and hit the road like he always does. There's money on the table, girl, and when that happens you never walk away. Besides, it will enable you to quit your other job and concentrate on a life for a change."

She opened the door, knowing it was useless to talk to him. Her dad gave new meaning to the word *grouchy.*

Inside she stared at the lease on the table. She'd gotten past her pigheadedness in not signing or talking about the lease the first time Kid had approached her. It was the main reason he was in High Cotton. If she'd used her head and not reacted out of years of resentment, Kid would no longer be a problem. Now he was a huge one jeopardizing everything she'd worked for in the past few months. But like her father had said, he would soon tire. She was counting on it.

LUCKY WENT TO WORK EARLY because she knew there would be a big crowd tonight. She'd called Thelma Lou to help out. By seven the place was packed with angry ranchers wanting answers. Judd, Walker and Cooper came in with their wives, Cait, Maddie and Sky. Chance and Shay squeezed in at their table, as did Travis.

Wilma sat on the end bar stool, sucking on a Coors, oblivious to what was going on around her. Her beady little eyes were pinned on Thelma Lou, but Lucky didn't have time to deal with that situation. More people were coming in and since there was no seating left they leaned against the wall.

"Damn, Lucky, we're gonna run out of beer," Bubba Joe said.

"The cooler in the back is full," she replied above the chatter.

"I'll transfer some," Thelma Lou offered, but stopped by Bubba first. "Tell your mom to go home. She's gettin' on my nerves."

"She doesn't listen to me. Just let her be."

"Bitch," Thelma Lou muttered under her breath as she headed for the storeroom.

Lucky and Bubba kept serving beer. Suddenly, Travis got to his feet and everyone quieted down. He introduced himself and went into his speech about security, safety and how knowledge is the best weapon against thieves. He went on to say to report any suspicious behavior or strangers around their property and then handed out his card.

Questions followed and sometimes things got heated when Travis didn't have any answers.

"You mentioned undercover agents. Are there any in High Cotton?"

Kid. Lucky almost dropped the beers she was carrying. How did he get in here without her seeing him? Why was he asking questions? He didn't own a cow.

"Mr. Hardin, I can't divulge that kind of information. But rest assured we have a lot of hardworking people on the case."

Lucky noticed Kid had wedged a chair between Cait and Sky. Naturally he'd want to sit with the women.

"Where can we buy the infrared digital cameras?" Tyler Jakes asked.

"Nell at Walker's is getting a shipment in tomorrow and most sporting goods stores have them."

There were a few more questions and then men began to leave. Now there was some breathing room. Travis made his way to the door and was careful not to look her way. Most of the patrons called it a night except the Belle sisters, their husbands and two of the Hardin boys and Chance's wife.

As Lucky made her way to the bar, Wilma asked, "What was that man talking about?" Sometimes Wilma didn't hear too well. If it didn't concern Bubba, she tuned it out.

"Cattle rustling," she told her.

"What? Where?"

"In High Cotton and surrounding towns."

"Nah. Can't be." She shook her head and Lucky was afraid the atrocious wig would fall off. "Bubba's not going to get hurt, is he?"

Lucky wiped the bar. "No. He doesn't own any cows."

"My boy's a fragile soul." Wilma took a swig from the bottle. "No one understands that. He needs his momma."

Wilma was hard enough to deal with when she was sober, but drunk put it into another realm of insanity.

"Hey, everybody, it's time for some fun." Kid headed for the jukebox.

"Nobody's in the mood," Chance told him.

But Kid wasn't listening. "Bubba, how do you make this thing work?"

"Just hit it," Bubba shouted. "The records haven't been changed in years and it only has old country songs."

"No problem." Kid whacked the side with a hand and "Born to Boogie" by Hank Williams Jr. came on. "Hot damn, Caitlyn, that's our song."

"My wife doesn't feel like dancing," Judd said in a stern voice.

"Excuse me." Cait got to her feet with a whole lot of attitude directed at her husband.

Kid whirled her onto the small place in front of the jukebox.

"I knew that was the wrong thing to say, but it just slipped out." Judd took a swallow of his beer and watched his wife and Kid. Their fast steps matched as they danced, laughing. Kid twirled Cait round and round until she landed in Judd's lap.

Kid then pulled Maddie to her feet. "Don't you dare lick me," she warned to no avail.

He licked her cheek anyway. "Ah, Maddie, you're as sweet as a lollipop. I just had to." She remembered Kid doing that when they were young. Most girls would have slapped him, but Maddie was so good-natured she took Kid's antics in stride.

"You're going to hell, Kid Hardin," she said as they fast-stepped to the music.

"Ah, Maddie, as long as my body goes to heaven."

The crowd guffawed that.

The song came to an end and Kid kicked the jukebox again. Maddie escaped to her husband. The sounds of "Boot Scootin' Boogie" by Brooks and Dunn filled the room. Kid jerked Sky to her feet and they linked arms over each other's shoulders and kicked and scooted to the beat. When Sky reached Cooper she let go and pulled her shocked husband onto the floor. Kid then grabbed Shay and Chance immediately cut in. As the music ended, Kid was left standing alone.

The group got to their feet. Judd slapped Kid on the back. "You were right. We needed some fun tonight." He lowered his voice. "I'm just hoping I don't have to sleep on the sofa."

Cait wrapped an arm around her husband's waist. "Don't push it."

As they made their way to the door, the jukebox came on again without anyone hitting it. Suddenly "A Fire I Can't Put Out" by George Strait held everyone spellbound. Lucky stopped wiping the bar that was spotless. *Oh, no. Their song.* She raised her head and her eyes locked with Kid's. His eyes were dark, his expression serious, no laughter in sight. Her stomach knotted and her hands were clammy. *No. No.* She forcefully tried to push the memories away, willing herself to go into the storeroom and lock the door. But all she could do was stare into the eyes of the man who had broken her heart.

"A fire I can't put out."

He walked over and held out his hand.

No, no, no!

"Come on, Lucky." He smiled and without a sane

thought she placed her hand in his. He held her close and they slowly moved to the lovely music. Her body, her traitor, welded into his and everything she wanted to forget was there, raw and new. Powerful. Just like in the barn.

His roughened cheek rested against her forehead and she breathed in the heady scent of him. Unable to stop herself, her fingers stroked the taut muscles of his shoulder. His hand caressed her back. She sighed, and knew beyond a doubt that she was losing her mind.

But he would always be the fire she couldn't put out.

The melody stopped but they kept moving for a second longer. Clapping broke them apart. The group at the door slowly filed out. Her cheeks burned in embarrassment. Just as she was going to say something, Wilma threw the remains of her beer at Thelma Lou.

"Stay away from my son, bitch," Wilma screeched.

Lucky stepped between the two women. "Everybody calm down."

"Momma, what are you doing?" Bubba was outraged.

"Let's go, boy." Wilma slid from the stool and staggered. "You need to get away from this trash."

"I'm gonna punch her senseless." Thelma made a move toward the older woman and Lucky held her back.

"Let it go."

Bubba helped his mother to the door. "I'll take her home and come back to help clean up."

"I'll do it," Kid said. "Take care of your mom."

Lucky didn't say anything because she knew it was useless. She couldn't keep protesting and then falling into his arms like a besotted teenager. The three of them worked for thirty minutes throwing away cans and bottles, wiping down all the tables and sweeping the floor. She took the money and receipts and shoved them into her bag.

While Thelma Lou was getting her purse, Kid reached for Lucky's hand across the bar and stroked her palm. Her whole body tingled in awareness.

"Kid." She had to put a stop to this.

"Don't say anything."

She nibbled on her lip, trying to think of something to break the spell she was under. "Your hat's at the house. Ollie chewed up the rim. Tell me what it cost and I'll pay you for it."

"Nah. No need."

She took a breath and wanted to pull her hand away, but it felt so comfortable in his. "About...what happened in the barn..."

His dark eyes caught hers. "If you're going to tell me it didn't mean anything, you'd be lying."

"Kid." She sighed. "We can't keep going down memory lane."

His thumb gently rubbed against her palm and warm, tantalizing feelings flooded her. "I know you don't trust me," he murmured, "but the sentiment of the song we danced to is still valid. You'll always be my first love and there's nothing on this earth that will ever douse that." He kissed her palm and walked out the door.

A tear slipped from her eye as she recognized the truth of his words.

CHAPTER TEN

FOR THE NEXT WEEK, KID didn't go inside The Beer Joint or attempt to see Lucky. He was busy helping Cooper and Uncle Ru keep a watch on High Five's herd. He took the early morning two to six shift. Staying awake at night was no problem for him. It was his thing and that wasn't something to brag about.

But he made it his business of being at The Joint at twelve to make sure Lucky made it home safely. She never saw him. He thought it best if they had some breathing room. Holding and kissing Lucky had awakened all the old feelings of first love. He didn't want to hurt her this time and he had to prove to himself that he had the stick-to-itness of forever in him.

He had a lot of time to think—alone in the dark with his conscience and a few hundred head of cattle for company. He hadn't been on a horse in years, not since he'd cowboyed for Dane, but he got the hang of it quickly. As long as Rusty, his horse, didn't do any trick moves, Kid was fine. A couple of Cooper's Australian Blue Heelers, Boots and Booger, followed him as he kept a close eye on the fences bordering roads. A couple of times the dogs shot out after an armadillo rooting in the grass, but they were never away for long. Soon they were back on duty.

The moon was full and the night had an eerie calm as the ranch land was cloaked in iridescent shadows of darkness—and the unknown. A rifle was in his saddle scabbard and he felt like Clint Eastwood riding the range.

He stopped to listen. Sounds carried a long way out here, but he only heard an occasional cow bellow, a coyote howling, crickets serenading and unusual noises of the harmless nocturnal creatures—no trucks or clanging trailers.

As always, his thoughts turned to Lucky. For her, he had to look deep at his own character, his flaws. He liked the nightlife, the ladies. He couldn't deny that. But lately he enjoyed spending time with his aunt and uncle, visiting his brothers and their families. The last time he had a date, hell, he couldn't remember. Probably right before Jacob was born. Nah, it couldn't be that long. Once his nephew had come into the world, though, a whole new realm of excitement opened up for him.

He could spend an hour watching the expressions change on Jacob's face. And all the while his own son lay cold in a grave—a son he'd abandoned. He took a deep breath. He was never going to get over that. Another black mark on his soul.

The thing about the past—a person could never go back or relive it. It was done. Over. Now he had to find some peace with Lucky without seducing her.

Ironically, he'd never forgotten Lucky's smile, her

laugh, her sweet disposition. He'd searched for it in every woman he'd ever dated, in every woman he'd been with. None were right for him because he'd left the perfect woman behind. He remembered telling Chance when he and Shay were having problems that if what Chance felt for Shay was the twenty-four-carat-slip-on-the-left-hand kind then he'd better think twice before throwing it away. Yet, Kid had done that very thing.

He was still blown away by their song coming on when it had the other night. In their teens Bud would sometimes allow them to do their homework in a booth before the bar opened. The songs on the jukebox were old then and Lucky knew how to make them play without putting a quarter in. They'd drink a Coke with peanuts in it and try to focus on their work, but when that song came on, and Bud wasn't looking, they'd scoot closer. And he wasn't the only one doing the scooting.

A fire he couldn't put out. Kid realized for the first time that he never had extinguished the flames she'd ignited in him. He'd tried. God help him, he'd tried.

His head started to hurt and he saw the sun creeping up over the trees, washing away the darkness with a soft yellow glow.

Kneeing his horse, he galloped toward the barn, the dogs following. He met Uncle Ru saddling up.

"Your aunt is waiting for you at the big house," Ru said, raising his boot to a stirrup. "We appreciate your help. When you get ready to go back to Houston just say the word." His uncle shot out of the barn.

Why did everyone think he was leaving? Maybe because he hadn't been home in years. And when he was, leaving was always on his mind. Like Chance had said, being around wasn't his thing. There were too many sad memories in High Cotton. The good ones were all linked to Lucky and suddenly he didn't want to leave—ever.

As he unsaddled his horse, Coop walked in. "Hey, Kid, see anything?"

"Nah, everything was quiet. I think the word has gotten out and the rustlers are lying low."

"Yeah. I've gotten the cameras up and feel a little more secure. We don't need to do night duty anymore."

Kid slapped the rump of his horse and he trotted into the corral for feed. "To be honest, and please don't tell Uncle Ru, but he's not up for extra duty."

"Yeah, try telling him that." Coop squatted to pet the dogs. "Breakfast is waiting for you and thanks for all your help. Just let me know what I owe you."

Kid leaned against a barn post. "Now, Coop, I've given up fighting as of about a week or so ago, but if you offer me money again we're going to come to blows. Dane Belle was there for the Hardin boys and I'm gonna be here to make sure High Five doesn't suffer a loss. Besides, I've got time on my hands as I try to figure out my messed-up life."

Coop stood. "Sky told me about Lucky. I'm sorry, man, but you two seemed pretty tight the other night."

"Just an illusion, my friend." Kid headed for the house and food. He couldn't talk about Lucky. Those emotions were so complicated he had a difficult time explaining them to himself.

He had breakfast with Sky, the kids and Miss Dorie. Aunt Etta rushed around waiting on them. Sky tried to get her to sit down but that was like trying to move a mountain with your bare hands. Aunt Etta loved to feel needed. Kid wasn't going to try and change her. He loved her just the way she was.

Afterward, he crashed and slept until two, got up, showered and dressed. He spent the afternoon visiting with Jacob and Cody. Then he put on his shorts and sneakers and ran through High Cotton. He stopped several times to talk to friends he hadn't seen in years. Home was where everyone knew his name. He had never understood Chance's need to stay in this small country town. He did now.

LUCKY BRUSHED HER SHORT blond hair into the stylish cut—the one Kid didn't like. All week she'd waited for him to show up at the house or The Joint, but he'd done neither. She'd heard through the daily gossip that he was helping Coop to guard his cows. That threw her. That wasn't like Kid. There was no fun, no party in such tedious labor.

She'd hoped he'd returned to Houston to his job. That way her heart would be safe, unscathed by Kid's untimely interruption of her life.

Her cell buzzed and she grabbed it from the dresser. "Hi, Travis, any news?"

"Just a couple of calls about suspicious behavior. A

pickup was parked in a lane and someone called it in. Turned out to be a rancher's daughter necking with her boyfriend."

Lucky felt a familiar ache in her stomach. How many times had she and Kid done that? Too many to remember. Seemed young girls were still gullible and naive, or maybe just in love. And, like Lucky, they had no idea what love really was beyond the sex.

"The other call—" Travis was saying "—was called in by Thelma Lou Harris. Seems an elderly woman was parked outside her driveway for hours."

"Wilma Grisley?" The old lady just never gave up.

"You know her?"

"She's Bubba Joe's mother."

"Oh. I notified Walker and this is the third time he's gotten a call about this. Ms. Harris wanted to press charges, but Walker talked her out of it if Mrs. Grisley stays away from her trailer. It took some doing, but Walker got the older woman to promise to visit her sister for a few days. If he gets another call, he's going to arrest her."

"I can't believe he got her to agree. She's so afraid Thelma Lou is going to take Bubba away from her. This is good, though. Everyone will have time to cool off."

"These are not the kind of calls I was hoping for," Travis mused.

"No news about the rustlers."

"Not a peep. It's so quiet it's scary, but they have to move the stolen cattle and goods soon. I'm just worried they're a step ahead of us and they've moved the operation out of this county."

"Mmm. The cowboys haven't been in for the past two nights. Have you gotten any more information on them?"

"As I told you when I suspected them, they're cousins. Melvin and Earl are brothers, both divorced and living with their mother in Cameron. Clyde's married, but he seems to spend very little time at home."

"Do they go back to Cameron at night?" she asked.

"They head out for U.S. 290, but I'm not sure where they actually go."

"They said they work cattle for people and Mr. Wallace was in here the other night talking to them. They'd worked for him so that part of their story is true."

"They worked for Mr. Barton, too. Everything seems legit."

"We're missing something, Travis."

"Yeah. I just can't put my finger on it." He paused. "Has Hardin been back?"

Her hand froze on her cell. "No. Why?"

"That was spooky when he asked about undercover agents."

She'd thought of little else since, except their heart-stopping dance. Kid couldn't have figured it out she kept telling herself, but she had moments when she thought Kid was smarter than she was giving him credit for. That's why she'd expected him to show up all week. But he kept surprising her. First, he wanted her to sign a lease. Next, he demanded his name on their son's headstone. Then he was back urging her to sign his papers. And to top that off he came into the bar for the cattle rustlers meeting asking pointed questions. Now he'd stopped all contact, which was a good thing, and she tried hard not to feel any differently.

"Don't worry about Kid. He bores easily and will go back to Houston soon."

"Lucky—"

"I'll call if anything happens tonight." She cut him off because she heard that caring tone in his voice. That gave her a big clue as to where her heart was and always would be.

Damn Kid!

In the living room she kissed her father's cheek. "I'm going to work."

"That old bat called," he said in his grumpiest voice.

"Wilma?"

"Yeah."

"What did she want?"

"She wants me to go down to The Joint and make sure Bubba doesn't go home with Thelma."

"What was your answer?"

"I told her I'm not moving from my chair and that her wig must be on too tight 'cause her damn brain is shrinking."

"You didn't say that?" She didn't know why she was surprised. Her father said what was in his head uncaring of anyone's feelings. Must be a right that came with old age.

"Sure did. She needs to get her nose out of Bubba

Joe's life." He waved a hand at the air. "Ah, what do I know? If I'd been stricter with you, maybe Hardin wouldn't have crushed your heart like an empty beer can."

"Dad..."

"I let y'all study at the bar and at the house and I knew you were stealing beer for him. I should have stopped all of that, but you were happy and that's all I ever wanted for you."

"It wouldn't have changed anything. I would have found a way to be with Kid."

Her dad shook his head. "Never dreamed the boy wouldn't come back for you."

She hadn't, either.

"If he had showed up after the baby died, he would have been roadkill."

"Dad, you told me not too long ago that I needed to let go and you were right. We both need to let the past go and live in the present."

He stared straight at her. "But you're not doing that, girl. You're different since he's been here. It's like he's lit your pilot light and you're full of warmth and glowing."

She touched her cheek. "I am not."

"Remember when he'd drive up and you'd run through the house shouting 'He's here. He's here'? You're doing that now except you're shouting it in your head and then you have to go up on the hill to remember the pain."

Oh, my God! She was. She buried her face in her hands. "I don't know how to forget him," she muttered.

"Sign the damn lease and get him out of our lives." Her father reached for her trembling hand. "Baby girl, don't let him hurt you again."

She sank down by his chair and he stroked her hair and she soaked up his comfort and support. For a moment. Then she came to her senses. How pathetic could she get? Slapping away tears, she got to her feet.

"I'm going to work."

"Girl…"

"It's okay, Dad. I'm stronger, a lot more mature and I can handle whatever happens."

"If you say so."

Ollie rubbed against her leg and she petted him. "I'm still mad at you."

"Why are you mad at Ollie?"

"He chewed up Kid's hat." And put me in a compromising position. She didn't think she'd mention that to her father.

"I trained him right."

"I'll see you later." She headed for the door.

"If that old hag comes in tonight, just shoot her."

Lucky told him about Walker's intervention and Wilma leaving town.

"Humph. I don't believe that for a minute. You better be careful she doesn't come in there and shoot Thelma Lou."

Oh, good heavens, just what she needed.

As SHE DROVE TO THE BEER JOINT, she noticed a neighboring rancher, Mr. Hopper, parked on the side of the road. He and a little boy were searching for something in the bar ditch. He was one of the church members, but was always friendly to her so she stopped to see if they needed help.

"Is anything wrong, Mr. Hopper?"

"Oh, Lucinda." The older man turned toward her. "My grandson stuck his head out of the window and his hat blew off. We were trying to find it."

"Grandpa, I got it." The little boy who looked about eight came running with the battered hat jammed on his head.

"You sure did." Mr. Hopper patted the boy's shoulder. "This is Lucinda Littlefield and this is my great-grandson, John."

John raised a hand. "Hi."

"Hi," she responded.

"They're having a teacher workday at John's school so my grandson brought him to spend the day with me and my wife. He's been upset since someone stole his four-wheeler and the saddle I was going to give him."

"It was mine," John said. "Why did they have to take it?"

She bent down to his level. "Sometimes it just happens, but the authorities are doing everything they can to get your items back."

"They are?" His eyes opened wide. "Are they going to get Grandpa's cows back, too?"

Oh, goodness, what had she gotten herself into? But

John looked so sad she couldn't resist giving him some hope. "We'll have to wait and see. It's going to take some time to catch the thieves."

"Good." He bobbed his head. "I hope they put them in jail for a long time." He held out his little hand. "Nice to meet you, Miss Lucinda."

She shook it with a smile. "Nice to meet you, too."

As the boy ran to the truck, Mr. Hopper said, "I've been telling him that for days, but he never seemed to hear me. Thank you, Luc—I believe everyone calls you Lucky, right?"

"Yes."

"Then that's what I'll call you, too. Thank you, Lucky."

They shook hands and the moment was surreal but it gave her an insight into her own motivation for continuing in a job her father hated. She could help people and it made her feel good about herself, her life. It kept her going on days when she felt as though she couldn't spend one more minute in that bar.

"I hope I didn't lift his spirits for nothing," she had to say.

"You gave him faith, Lucky, and we all need that from time to time."

"Yes." She needed it every day—a faith and a belief that she could make a difference.

She waved as they drove away and stood staring down the long expanse of blacktop. Kid used to give her that faith in herself, but she didn't need him for that anymore. She could make it on her own.

As the September sun bore down on her she realized her feelings for Kid were changing. She didn't analyze that beyond the fact it wasn't a bad thing.

WHEN SHE GOT TO THE BAR, she had a talk with Bubba Joe.

"Don't worry, Lucky, she's gone to Aunt Mable's."

Like her father, she didn't quite believe that. "I'm not one to give advice, but if you want a life you're going to have to tell your mother what you will and will not tolerate."

"She's my momma and worries about me."

She sighed in frustration. "Bubba, when we were in first grade, your mother brought you a hot lunch every day and practically spoon-fed you. That was maybe understandable when you were six but at fourteen and sixteen that was a little over-the-top, especially since she sat and ate lunch with you. I don't want to sound cruel, but that's why kids laughed at you. Sometime before you reach forty you need to say the word *stop* to your mother and mean it."

His big chest heaved. Oh, no. Was he going to cry?

"Bubba…" She felt bad.

"You're right, Lucky, I have to do something."

She exhaled. "Yes. If you're serious about Thelma Lou…"

The woman in question came through the door. "Did I hear my name?"

"We were talking about Momma," Bubba replied.

"Don't mention her." Thelma threw her purse into the

back room. Where Bubba was tall and round, Thelma was short and plump. Her brown hair was always in a ponytail, and as Lucky's father had pointed out, she had a sharp tongue.

"Okay," she said to them. "I'm not getting involved in y'all's business, but Thelma, if you're serious about Bubba, get a divorce and keep the relationship out in the open because I'm not having Wilma coming in here, sitting at the end of the bar, stone drunk with murder in her eye."

"If I could find that sorry bastard of a husband, I would," Thelma snapped.

Lucky walked off and started to fill bowls with pretzels. Why had she said anything? It was none of her business.

Luther and Frank were the first ones to come in. "Hey, Lucky." Luther slid onto a bar stool. "Party not started yet?"

"What do you want, Luther?"

His eyes slid over her in a way that left no doubt as to what he was thinking. For once she didn't let it slide. She was tired of taking crap from sleazy men.

"I keep a gun below the bar and if you don't back off, I'm going to put a hole right in the center of your forehead."

His ruddy skin paled.

"He's just joshing, Lucky," Frank spoke up.

"I'm not, and if you don't treat me with the respect I deserve, then you can get your ass out of here permanently."

Both men just stared at her.

"Now, once again, what would you like?"

"Coors Light."

"Bottle or can?"

"Can."

She placed the order and ticket in front of them.

Luther popped the top. "You're getting hard like Bud."

"I'm not taking any more crap, and you only get one warning."

"Yes, ma'am." Luther raised his can. "Frank and I will be gone for a couple of days. You're gonna miss us."

"Don't count on it."

As she walked away she marveled at the difference her standing up for herself had made. Luther backpedaled immediately and his tone of voice changed, too. It wasn't degrading. She'd even detected a little of that respect she was demanding.

It was a Wednesday night so the place wasn't too lively. She stilled when the cowboys came in. They were excited, laughing and joking.

"Hey, Lucky," Clyde called, "how about a beer?"

She grabbed some bottles and moved to the bar in front of them.

"We're sorry if we scared you that night we were drunk."

"It's okay. Just don't do it again."

"We're headed back to Cameron," Melvin said. "Not much work around here."

They were leaving. This was big. That meant if they were involved in the rustling, they were likely going to move the cattle to get rid of them.

"Good luck, boys." She tried to appear as calm as possible. "If you're in this area again, the bar is always open."

She hurried to the back room to text Travis. No response. Where was he? He usually responded immediately. Then she remembered. He had a meeting with another ranger and two market inspectors in Georgetown, but he always checked his phone. She waited, but she knew she didn't have much time. If they were going to find out anything, the cowboys had to be followed.

When no message came through, she went to the bar and sneaked her gun to the storeroom. She motioned for Bubba Joe.

"What's up?"

"I have to leave. Please close up for me."

"Sure."

Being Bubba, he didn't ask any questions.

Stuffing her gun into the back of her waistband, she hurried out of the bar through the side door, holding her phone in her hand. She scanned the parking lot and saw the black Dodge nosed up next to her pickup.

She waited a second, willing the phone to beep. It didn't. What did she do? She called Walker and got a message. He was in Giddings and wouldn't be back until later. If it was an emergency, the voice mail said to call 9-1-1. Damn! She'd try the sheriff but she knew he was in the meeting with Travis and she didn't know who to trust at the sheriff's department. What should she do now? If she did nothing, the cowboys would leave and everything they'd possibly stolen would be moved out of the county and sold, including little John's saddle. And they'd get away with the biggest robbery in this area.

Her options were a little murky, but she knew one thing—she had to do something. Her stomach felt queasy at the thoughts in her head. She had her phone. She had a gun. She could do this. Without another thought she walked to her truck and dropped down, making her way to the Dodge. Part of the vehicle was in the dark, away from the spotlight. Grabbing one of the sides, she swung into the bed and crouched low against the cab, hoping with everything in her that she wasn't detected.

CHAPTER ELEVEN

KID PLAYED A GAME ON HIS PHONE to keep from being bored, all the while keeping an eye on The Beer Joint. He'd gotten here early because he was tired of his family giving him odd stares. He knew they thought he was staying in High Cotton out of guilt, but they were wrong. He was searching for something inside him that would make him feel good about himself—something of substance. There had to be more to him than Kid the kidder. Or Kid the ladies' man.

Shoving his phone into its case, he saw a movement on the left side of the building. *Lucky.* Was she going home early? To his astonishment she swung into the back of the Dodge.

What the hell?

He jumped out of his truck, leaped across a ditch and sprinted to the vehicle and dived inside the bed. He heard a muffled scream.

"It's Kid."

"What the hell are you doing here?" she snapped.

"What the hell are *you* doing?"

"This doesn't concern you. Get out." Her voice grew angrier by the second.

The bed of the truck smelled like diesel and cow crap—not pleasant. He shifted closer to her.

"Get out," she repeated.

He didn't heed the warning. "I've been thinking and I keep telling myself it can't be true. But you're an undercover source for Travis what's-his-name, aren't you? This is the dangerous stuff you're into."

He could feel her breathing rapidly. "All right, you've figured it out. Now get lost."

"You're not facing these guys alone."

"I just need to know where they're going. That's all and then I'll get out."

But it was too late. The cowboys were coming to their truck. The gravel crunched beneath their boots as they drew closer. Kid pulled her flat against the bottom of the bed.

"Too bad we can't take Lucky with us." That was Melvin.

Lucky stiffened.

"The boss said to leave her alone so that's what we're doing." Clyde chuckled. "Doesn't mean we can't come back later and have some fun." The doors slammed shut and the motor roared to life.

"Check the time on your watch," she whispered.

He glanced at the lighted dial. "Yeah, it's always good to know the time when you're going to die."

The truck backed out and moved onto the highway.

"We're turning left," she whispered.

"That's my guess."

The lights from the bar faded away and the truck

bumped over uneven ground as it traveled through the night. The rough road jostled them against each other.

"Stop touching my breasts," Lucky said under her breath.

"I'm trying to hold on."

"Hold on to something else."

The truck stopped and they burrowed further against the bottom of the bed.

"Check the time," she said again.

"Nine-minute thirty-second drive, if that's what you wanted to know."

"Shh."

"Don't know why I have to open the damn gate," Melvin grumbled as he got out.

The vehicle pulled through and stopped again. Suddenly they heard Melvin peeing and Kid hoped he wasn't close to the truck, but it sure sounded like it. Don't look. Don't look, he chanted in his head.

He breathed a sigh of relief against Lucky's cheek and she felt damn good beneath him—not exactly an appropriate thought at the moment. Their lives were in danger.

The truck bounced on rougher terrain.

"Where are they going?" Lucky whispered, almost as if she'd accepted him being there.

"Not downtown High Cotton, for sure."

Bushes and trees scraped against the truck and it finally stopped. The cowboys got out. Doors slammed. "Let's get to work," Clyde ordered. "It's all scheduled. The boss wants this done tonight."

They heard movement and then silence. "Stay down," he told Lucky, and peeped around the cab. An old mobile home sat among the bushes, which he could see because a small light was burning outside. Otherwise there was nothing but woods. Where were they? And where had the cowboys gone?

"What do you see?" Lucky asked.

"Dense woods and a rundown mobile home. Let's get out before they return." He jumped to the ground, as did she. Grabbing her hand, they ran into the woods and sat in the thicket. Darkness surrounded them.

"I have to contact Travis," she said, "but I'm afraid they'll see the light."

"Hold it close to your chest. The woods are so thick I don't think they'll notice. I just wish I knew where they were."

She leaned against a tree and pulled out her phone. He scooted closer to help shield the light.

"I got a text from Travis. He's on his way and he says for me to wait for him."

"You've blown that one," he remarked.

"Don't start." She looked around. "I have to text him back."

"From the tone of your voice I'm guessing chasing criminals is not part of your job description."

She fiddled with her phone. "No. I just gather information."

"Then let's get the hell out of here."

"No. The stealing has been going on for months and

it's time the thieves were caught. Chance's cows were stolen. Don't you want to know who did it?"

"Those two-bit cowboys who just walked into the woods."

"We don't know that for sure. We have to follow them."

"Oh, God. I had a few gray hairs before I came back to High Cotton, but now I can feel them sprouting by the minute and every one has *Lucky* written on it."

"Poor Kid."

"Do you know how dangerous this is?"

"I have my gun."

"I know. I felt it poking in places it shouldn't have."

He heard a snicker.

"Are you laughing?"

"No."

"Yeah, right." He reached for his cell. "I'll text Chance. Travis should hear about this in person, and the sheriff and Walker need to be notified. Let's try to figure out where we are."

"We turned left which is east and drove nine minutes and thirty seconds. This has to be near the old Wilkins' property, heavily wooded and the son never tends to it. He tried to sell it, but no one wanted to spend the money to clear the land."

"So you think the Wilkins guy is involved?" he asked.

"I don't know."

"Be on the lookout while I try to text." He wasn't quite sure how to word the message. So he poked in letters fast: L and I r following 3 cowboys involvd in catt rust. Think old Wilkins place. Contact T. Will txt later.

He got back one word: What?

Do it. He punched in the letters and turned off his phone.

"Make sure your cell is off," he said.

"Already done it." She got to her feet. "Let's see if we can find them."

Kid stood and stopped. "Listen." The bellow of cattle broke through the silence of the night.

"Cows. They're agitated so they must be moving them. Let's go."

They walked to the trail the truck was parked on and followed it. Since they could barely see, they stayed close together. The track gave way to a clearing and Kid pulled Lucky into the bushes. Squatting, they surveyed the scene in front of them. A barbed wire fenced pen held about thirty head of cattle. He saw Chance's black ones right away and Judd's white Brahmas stuck out like old lady Grisley's wig.

"There are all the cows they've stolen," Lucky whispered.

"Yep. Just wondering what they're going to do with them."

"I don't see a cattle trailer but it could be hidden in the dark."

The beams from the cowboys' flashlights were the only way they could see anything. Earl walked toward a tin shed on the left and opened the door. Lucky gasped and quickly covered her mouth against his shoulder. He kind of lost his train of thought when she did that.

"Just look at all that stuff." Her voice was barely a thread of sound. "There's Mr. Hopper's beautiful saddle."

Inside the shack were four-wheelers, two Polaris Rangers that he could see from the flashlight, saddles, tack and other items they'd stolen from ranches across the area. A putt-putt sound grabbed their attention and a green tractor with headlights and a flatbed trailer attached slowly moved from around the shed and then backed up to it. Melvin jumped from the seat and the cowboys began to load the items. Motor sounds mingled with the bellows. The cows grew more agitated as they jostled against each other looking for a way out.

Once the loot was loaded, Melvin backed the trailer next to the pen of cows.

"I don't understand what they're doing," Lucky murmured.

"Me neither. How do they plan to move that stuff?"

As soon as the words left his mouth, the sound of a train echoed through the night. Clyde was talking on something that looked like a walkie-talkie. He waved his flashlight as the train came into view, and slowed until it came to a complete stop. Two cattle carriers were in front of Clyde.

"Son of a bitch! They're carrying everything out of here by train. This is a professional criminal operation."

"Yeah."

In a stupor they watched. Melvin pushed opened the big door of the car. Clyde and Earl adjusted ramps, which were laying on the ground, to the opening and threw up cow panels for the sides. Clyde opened the barbed wire gate and with whips and yelling they herded half the cattle up the ramp into the car. A couple of cows fell and as soon as the whip stung their hide they staggered inside. Melvin shoved the door closed.

Clyde was on the walkie-talkie, flashing a light. The train inched forward and they started the process over again. When the cattle were safely in the carrier, the train moved and the loot was loaded into a boxcar. Earl drove the tractor back to the shed and ran to join Clyde and Melvin as they jumped aboard. The train revved up and slowly began to roll.

Lucky jumped to her feet. "I'm going with the train."

"What!" Before he knew her intentions she was running toward it. He was a step behind her. "Lucky," he screamed, uncaring if anyone heard him. His breath came in gasps as he tried to stop her. To his horror, she reached a boxcar and swung inside. Without having to think about it, he dived right after her, but misjudged his strength and slid across the floor of the car and almost went out the other side. Half of his body was hanging out. The train picked up speed and all he could see was Texas rail flashing before his eyes. His heart jackknifed into his throat.

This was not the way he wanted to die.

Lucky.

It took a moment for Lucky to catch her breath and then she almost fainted when Kid flew past her and hung out of the car. Oh, my God! She grabbed his boots and pulled. He did a half turn with his body and flipped back inside, knocking her down.

"Lucky?"

She took a couple of deep breaths. "I'm okay." She rose to a sitting position and scooted against the wall of the car. He joined her, both of them breathing heavily.

After a moment, Kid asked, "What is this stuff scattered in the car?"

"From what I can see it looks like a busted bale of cotton. I guess someone was too lazy to dispose of it."

"Mmm. Comfy." He jammed a wad behind his back. "You know, Lucky, there are a lot of other fun ways to get the adrenaline going instead of risking your life."

"You didn't have to follow me." But she was glad he did. She was scared out of her mind. Yet, here she was hopping a train chasing criminals.

She could feel him looking at her in the dark. "My brothers ask me this all the time. Now I'm asking you." He paused. "Are you insane?"

Leaning back her head, she replied, "Probably, but if someone doesn't follow them they'll get away with stealing all that stuff. Little John Hopper wants his great-grandfather's saddle and I'm getting it back for him."

"Lucky, this is dangerous. The saddle is a material thing. It can be replaced."

"Some things can't be replaced," she said as old

memories surfaced. "When I was eight, rustlers wiped out my dad's small herd right before Christmas. He always sold calves to buy gifts for me. Grandma told me I wouldn't be getting the pink bike I wanted. She said Santa ran out of them. But Christmas morning there was my pink bicycle. I was happy." The clap-clap of the rails seemed to intensify. "My mother left me her beautiful sapphire ring my father had bought for her when they were dating. It was small but I loved it and would stare at it in her jewelry box and play with it. It was mine and Dad said I could wear it when I was older. Soon after Christmas I noticed it was gone. I heard my grandma and Dad talking. He'd sold it to buy me the bicycle and other gifts. That's when I knew there wasn't a Santa Claus and mean people took things that didn't belong to them."

"Lucky." He scooted closer to her, his thigh touching hers, and her stomach fluttered in stupid excitement. More excitement than she needed tonight.

She took a breath. "I don't plan to confront the criminals. I just want an idea of where they're taking this stuff and then I'll get off and let the authorities handle it."

"Okay. I'm with you all the way."

For a while there was silence as they watched the night fly by. The hum of the rolling wheels against the rail was the only sound.

She was curious about something. "How did you just happen to be outside The Joint tonight?"

"I'm there every night."

"What?" She tried to see his face in the dark.

"I get there about closing to make sure those cowboys don't hurt you and I follow you to see you get home safely."

"That's stalking." She was trying to dredge up some anger, but it wasn't working. She couldn't help but feel touched that he was concerned about her.

"Really? I kind of looked at it as worried out of my freakin' mind about what you're into, and I was right. We're on a damn train headed into God-knows-what."

That obliterated every retort in her head, but one. "You can get off at any time."

"Not likely." She felt him move restlessly. "And since I'm fessing up. I visit the baby's grave, too."

That threw her. "When?"

"Usually right before I go to The Joint to make sure you're okay. I just sit there for a while praying for his forgiveness."

They both needed to get a grip or the past was going to cripple them. "You can visit the baby's grave any time you want."

"That wasn't on the table the last time we talked. I believe you threatened to have me arrested."

"That was about the headstone."

"Yeah. My name's not on it."

She heard the sadness in his voice and she weakened. "We'll talk about it when we get back. Okay?"

"Works for me."

Something else occurred to her. "Why were you there so early tonight?"

"Ah, my aunt and uncle were giving me suspicious looks. They can't figure out what I'm still doing in High Cotton. I just needed some breathing room."

"Why are you still here? Don't you have a job in Houston?"

"Cadde keeps asking me the same question, but I'm not going anywhere until I know you're safe."

"Kid..."

"I know you don't understand that, but it's the only way I can make up for the bad stuff I've done. It's the only way I can live with myself."

She didn't know what to say to that. He had to deal with his own demons in his own way and she had to let him. It was the only way they could get through the horrendous mistakes they'd made.

He reached for his cell. "I better call Chance and let him know where we are. Any idea where that might be?"

"The rail runs north and south through High Cotton. My guess is we're going south."

"Well, I have three messages from Chance and one from Cadde. Let's see what the bros have to say. Chance's messages are all the same 'Where are you?' Cadde's is 'What the hell are you doing?'"

She pulled out her phone. "I have three from Travis and they're all the same 'Call me.'"

He clicked a digit. "Let's see how they feel about us hopping a train."

The wisecracking Kid was back. The serious Kid

didn't surface too often like it had a moment ago. But their son was a solemn subject for both of them.

"Kid, are y'all okay?" Chance came right to the point. Kid had the cell on speakerphone so she could hear. There was some static but the voice was recognizable.

"I'm not sure." She could feel those dark eyes pinning her.

"I'll put you on speakerphone. Travis, Walker and the sheriff are here."

"Oh, dandy."

"What happened?" Travis wanted to know.

Kid told them the story glossing over Lucky's part. "We thought we'd follow this party to its destination. The cows and goods are going somewhere."

"Let me talk to Lucky," Travis demanded.

"I'm here," she said.

"Get off that train. It's too dangerous."

Before she could say anything, Kid jumped back in. "Now, Trav, this train is going pretty fast and I'm not in a mood to risk my life or Lucky's."

She gave him a glare. She knew he couldn't see her face clearly, but she hoped he felt it. "Travis, I'll be careful and get off before anyone sees us."

"Kid, you've been involved in some harebrained schemes but this is—"

"Hey, Cadde, I know I'm topping stupid this time, but listen up. I don't want to use up all my battery. By our calculations we're guessing the cows were kept on the old Wilkins place. This train is probably headed south out of High Cotton. There has to be someone you can contact at Union Pacific to find out the stops and its destination. And the engineer of the train is also involved. He stopped that train in the middle of nowhere so they could load the cattle."

"And they mentioned a boss who's in charge," she added.

"I'm on it," Travis said.

"Girl, where's my girl?" She tensed. She was planning to call her father as soon as they finished talking. What was he doing there?

"Lucky." Chance's voice came back on. "I had Uncle Ru pick up Bud. I knew you wouldn't want him to worry."

"Thank you, Chance. I appreciate that."

"If you get any nicer, Chance, we might have to put you up for sainthood or something," Kid wisecracked.

"Girl, are you okay?"

"Dad, I'm fine. Please don't worry."

"You're on a train chasing criminals with that no-good Hardin boy and you don't want me to worry?"

"Well, I guess they're not putting *me* up for sainthood."

"Shh," she hissed at Kid.

"Dad, please." Her composure shook at the pain she was causing him. What was she doing? Kid was right. This was insane. She needed to get off this train and deal with her messed up life instead of risking it.

"Tell Aunt Etta I'm fine," Kid shouted as they lost

connection. He clicked off and nothing was said for some time.

As the train rolled, her emotions settled down. She would see this through to the end. It was her job and she wasn't stopping now.

"Could we talk?" Kid asked.

The last thing she needed was to dredge up the past. "I'd rather not."

He stretched out his long legs. "I'd like to try and explain."

Maybe it was time for them to expose those raw feelings so they could finally heal. She scooted to face him. "I'm listening."

"When I left, I was down all the way to Lubbock. I missed you. I was going to call the minute I got to my dorm just to hear your voice, but the phone wasn't hooked up. I went down the hall looking for a pay phone and found a party instead. I was glad to make new friends and we partied to the early morning. When I woke up, about a day late, I had a gigantic hangover. You were the first thing I thought about, but I figured I'd wait until I could form a sentence before calling. Then there was another party and a week had gone by. I knew you were going to be mad so I kept putting it off."

"Were there girls at these parties?" she had to ask, even though she knew the answer.

"Yeah, lots of them."

She swallowed and wondered why she was going to ask the next question but she couldn't seem to stop herself. "Did you sleep with any of them?"

The answer was a long time coming. "Not at first, but…"

"You don't have to say anything else." Her stomach cramped and she didn't want to hear the rest.

"I called her Lucky," came quietly through the darkness.

"What?"

"The first time it happened I called the girl Lucky. I knew then I'd screwed up big-time. I wanted to call and come home, but I couldn't face you so I tried to forget you in every way I could."

She licked her lips. "Did it work?"

"Not entirely. Someone would laugh or bite their lip and I'd think of you. Sometimes I'd see blond hair and you'd pop into my head. I avoided coming home because of you even when Dane and Aunt Etta begged me. I thought the best thing was for me to stay away."

While she was searching for words to say, he continued, "Then there was the sadness. In High Cotton everyone knew about my parents' deaths and the grown-ups never seemed to know what to say to me. They just looked at me with that 'you poor kid' look. In Lubbock no one knew about my parents and there were just happy, fun times. I know that doesn't sound very nice, but I enjoyed that freedom."

"And I would have tied you down."

"I suppose. Aunt Etta said we got too serious too quick and I think she's right."

Lucky had to dig deep for the truth, but it was there and she had to say it. "We thought we were in love but we weren't. We were just two kids who needed each other at that particular time in life."

"Yeah. I'm sorry I hurt you. I'm sorry I wasn't there when you needed me."

"I was, too, and I was angry for a long time. I'm not anymore." Since they were being honest, there was something else she had to ask. "Did you ever fall in love?" She used to dread that someone would say, "Did you hear Kid Hardin got engaged?" or "Kid Hardin got married." She didn't think about it too much anymore, but she was still curious.

"Not even close." He shifted against the wall. "I'm afraid I'm just like my old man and I'll never be able to love any woman completely."

She was startled for a moment. She had no idea he knew about his father. "He was not very discreet about his affairs."

"You knew about Blanche Dumont?"

"Who? I just knew he brought women into The Joint not a mile from your house."

"You saw him with other women?"

By his tone of voice she knew that he never had. "Yes. Sometimes if my grandma had a doctor's appointment or something, the bus would drop me off at The Beer Joint and I'd do my homework in back until Grandma came. When Dad wasn't looking, I'd peep around the door and I saw your dad several times with other women sitting in a booth on the same side being very friendly."

"You never told me."

"Why would I? You adored your father."

"Yeah, he was quite a man. *Not.* The night they had the wreck he told my mom he was leaving her for another woman, who turned out to be Blanche Dumont. My mother started hitting him and he lost control of the car. Chance heard all of it."

"Isn't that Jack Calhoun's ex?"

"Yes, and Shay's mother."

"What? Is…?"

"No. She's not Jack's daughter. It was a sordid mess, but luckily Shay is nothing like her mother. I pray every day I'm not like dear ol' Dad, either. God, I can't believe he met women in High Cotton."

"I'm sorry, Kid." She wanted to touch him, hold him, but refrained from doing so. She couldn't get caught in that emotional wringer again.

"How about you? Did you fall in love with someone else?"

"No." She watched the night whiz by. "I have a hard time trusting anyone."

"But this ranger guy is interested, right?"

"Travis? I gather information for him. That's it."

He reached out and tucked her hair behind her ear. "Lucky…" Her name was a sultry breath against her skin. All her restraints broke free and her hand touched his roughened jaw.

He caught her hand and pulled her forward. Before her lips could taste his, the fast train clanged to a slower pace.

"We're stopping," she breathed.

"Show time." Kid moved toward the opening as they prepared to finish the job they'd started.

But a part of her wanted to finish something else.

CHAPTER TWELVE

THEY STOOD AT THE OPENING, feeling the warm wind against their faces and staring into the night's darkness.

"I don't see anything," Lucky said.

"Me neither," Kid replied, "but we're slowing down for something. Wait a minute, there are lights. A crossing, I think."

"We must be going through a town."

"Yeah. Look for some sort of landmark or sign so we can figure out where we are."

Suddenly a man flung himself into the boxcar and Lucky and Kid jumped back. It took him a minute to stagger to his feet, and at that moment he became aware he wasn't alone in the car.

"Who are ya?" he growled. A foul odor emanated from him.

"Nobody," Kid spoke up. "We're getting off soon."

"No, ya ain't. You're after my stash, ain't ya?"

"I have no interest in your stash, whatever that is."

"Ya lying. Ya been following me for a year."

"I'm just riding the rails like you, man, and I don't want any problems."

"Ya not gettin' my stash. I got a gun."

For a brief moment a passing light reflected off the

pistol pointed at them. Kid pushed her behind him. "Whoa, mister. You can keep your stash. Just put the gun away."

Lucky reached for the gun tucked into her waistband just as the guy charged them, knocking her against the wall. Her head spun as she watched Kid wrestle with the hobo, trying to gain control of the gun.

The odor became pungent as they tumbled around the car. Marijuana. That was his stash. Her head was fuzzy and she forced herself to focus on the two men. The hobo was trying to swing the barrel toward Kid. *No, don't.* She tried to stand, but couldn't.

Abruptly a gunshot ripped through the night and Kid and the hobo fell backward out of the car.

"Kid!" she screamed, crawling on her hands and knees to the opening. "Kid!" She was about to fling herself out when she realized the train was picking up speed, moving again. It would be suicidal to jump now.

Pushing up against the wall, she took several deep breaths and the dizziness eased. Was Kid shot? Was he dead? She had to get help. Pulling out her cell, she tried Kid's number, glad she remembered it from the card he'd left at her house. If he answered, he was okay. It rang and rang and then went to voice mail. An errant tear slipped from her eye. She swallowed hard and poked in Chance's number.

He answered before the ring even stopped. "Lucky." Then there was nothing but static.

She waited and tried again. This time she got a stronger connection. "Some…something bad has happened."

There was a slight pause. "What? Wait. Let me put it on speakerphone so everyone can hear."

"I'd rather my dad didn't."

"He's in the kitchen. Nettie fixed him something to eat."

"Okay, then."

"What happened?"

"A hobo jumped into our boxcar and he was nutty, rambling on about us not stealing his stash. Kid tried to reason with him, but he pulled out a gun and charged us. I hit my head and was a little dazed. Kid wrestled with him and then there was a gunshot and they fell out of the car. I'm so afraid Kid was hit and he's lying out there bleeding to death."

Static intervened and then there was complete silence on the other end.

She poked the number in again, afraid she was going to use all her power. Cadde's strong voice came through. "What does the terrain look like?"

"I can't see much. It's dark, but I've noticed flat land with mesquites and we just went through some sort of crossing or small town."

"We could follow the track with the chopper, but we don't know exactly where Kid is and it's dangerous at night. Kid's very resilient, but if he doesn't check in in the next fifteen minutes we'll have to do something."

Chance joined the conversation. "Travis and the sheriff are working with the railroad, but it's difficult getting information at this time of the night. Hang in there and get off that train as soon as you can."

"Is my dad okay?"

"Nettie's keeping him entertained." The connection went dead again. Damn!

She settled back, her head aching. *Nettie was keeping her dad entertained.* That was odd. Nettie was a very colorful, eccentric lady and her father was as down-to-earth as he could be. But she was glad he had someone to talk to.

She tried Kid again. Still no answer. *Kid, please answer.* Please. As the train moved through the night, she prayed he was all right.

KID HIT THE GROUND WITH A THUD that jarred every bone in his body. He rolled to his feet like a stuntman and sprinted for the train.

"Bastard," the hobo screeched, firing after Kid with wide shots.

Kid didn't have time to think about the crazy man. The caboose came into sight and he had to run in cowboy boots to catch it. For a moment he thought his overworked lungs would explode. He made a dive for the tail end and leaped aboard. Then he half lay and half sat sucking in precious air.

He looked up and saw a ladder going to the top. He had to get to Lucky and that was the only way. He swung to his feet, wincing, and climbed up. He'd seen this done in movies so it should be a piece of cake. Finding Lucky's boxcar would be the toughest part. He'd heard the crack of her head against the wall and he hoped she was okay.

The insanity of what he was doing flashed through his mind as he reached the top of the car, but that didn't stop him. The trick now was to run across the top until he could pinpoint the right boxcar. He gingerly stood and the force of the wind almost sent him flying into outer space.

Damn it!

He took a deep breath. All he had to do was get his balance and it would work. The second time he was ready for the wind and ran the length of the car before he fell to his knees. Without thinking it to death, he jumped to the next car and the next trying his best not to be tossed aside like a piece of garbage. He was getting the hang of it. Hell, he could be a stuntman.

When the scent of the cattle reached him, he knew he'd gone too far. He'd passed the car Lucky was in. He had to go back several boxcars. This time the wind gave him a push and it was at his back so he had to adjust his balance. He squatted at one car and shouted "Lucky," but there wasn't an answer. He jumped to the next one and tried again.

"Kid!" she screamed, and he swung in and landed flat on his back.

"Kid, Kid, Kid!" She stroked his face, his chest. "Are you okay?"

"You keep doing that and I'll be A-okay."

She hit his shoulder. "Stop it. I thought that hobo shot you. We've all been worried. I have to call Chance."

She grabbed her phone, poked in a number and put

it on speakerphone. "Chance, Kid is okay. He made it back to the train."

"Yeah," Kid piped in, "I'm thinking of joining the summer Olympics. I didn't know I could run so fast."

A loud sigh echoed. "Were you shot?"

"Would I be talking to you if I was? That old fool couldn't hit the side of a barn. The authorities need to check into that guy—he reeks of marijuana and he's dangerous."

Static intervened again. "Wait a minute," Kid shouted through the noise.

"Kid, when you get back here I'm going to kill you." Cadde's voice came on and then there was a pause. "Just stay safe and stop pulling stunts. My blood pressure can't take it."

"Will do, big brother. Have they found out where this train is going?"

"Not yet. Travis and the sheriff are working on it."

"It's not like we have a lot of time here. This train will stop before it reaches its destination and those cattle and stolen goods will be gone so fast that Travis will never catch the real boss behind all this."

"As soon as it's daylight we'll take the chopper and follow the track," Chance said, but before they could say anything else the phone went dead.

Lucky laid her cell on the floor. "Why didn't you answer when I called you?"

"I lost my phone somewhere. That damn hobo is probably calling his weed dealer on it."

"Are you sure you're okay?"

"Hell, no. I'm bruised from head to toe. I'm tired and smell faintly of marijuana, but I'm back with you so I'm okay."

"How did you manage to get back?"

"Fortunately, the fall didn't knock me out. I rolled to my feet and dashed to the train while that crazy hobo was firing at me."

"Oh, no," she gasped.

"As I said he couldn't hit a thing. I saw the caboose coming and I ran like hell to catch it. But I was a long way from you. I climbed to the top and ran across the cars until I reached you."

"Are you insane?"

"Actually, the vote is in on that. Yes."

"I think you're high from smelling that guy's weed."

"Could be." Suddenly he had to touch her. After this horrendous night he just needed her. He ran a hand through her hair to the back of her head and felt the knot. "Are you all right?" he whispered.

She wrapped her arms around him, her face in his neck. "My head's a little sore," she breathed against his skin. He pulled her closer and just held her, stroking her hair. Her soft yielding body and the scent of strawberries flooded him with memories of two teenagers whose hormones were out of control. They were adults now, but those feelings were there. Stronger. Powerful.

"Sometimes…"

"What?" He smoothed back her hair, just loving the feel of her.

"Nothing."

"Come on, Lucky."

"Sometimes…I just want you."

His hand stilled. "Lucky…"

She kissed his neck, his cheek and he eagerly met her lips, renewing a fever they knew well. The kiss deepened and she moaned as they discovered all those little things they remembered about each other.

Leaning back, she unbuttoned his shirt, her hands splaying across his chest. Any sane thoughts he had were slowly leaving. "Lucky," he groaned.

"Shh." She slipped the shirt from his shoulders and kissed him all the way down to his jeans. He caught his breath and they quickly helped each other remove cumbersome clothes. He pulled her into his arms and turned until they lay in the cotton on the floor of the car, the heat from the rails warming his back.

"A comfy bed left just for us." Tucking her into his side, he caressed and kissed her soft breasts. "They're fuller," he murmured.

"Since the pregnancy."

He buried his face between them. "I'm sorry I wasn't there." Unexpectedly a tear slipped from his eye.

She kissed it away. "I know."

Gathering her nude body against him, he found solace in the softness of her pressing into his hard planes. Their lips and hands renewed a vow of long ago; they would always love each other. He kissed her deeply, their tongues mingling and tasting as they discovered new delights—stronger than ever before. His hands touched every inch of her and her hands were equally at work on him.

Butterfly touches and bold strokes drove him wild. He caressed the triangle between her legs and she sighed blissfully. When she rubbed against his hardness, he could stand it no longer and thrust into her, gently, securely, and the rolling of the train enhanced the rhythm of their bodies. She cried his name as she reached that pinnacle of unabashed pleasure, her nails digging into his back.

When his release came, he felt as if he were sailing off the train into clear blue skies, buffeted only by Lucky's arms. It took a long time for him to come down. It was as perfect as he remembered. He cradled her in his arms and wondered again why he had left behind everything he'd ever cared about.

Maybe he was crazy.

WHEN LUCKY WOKE UP, SHE was lying on top of Kid, feeling rejuvenated in a way she hadn't in years. His body had matured with hardened muscles and strength, but he was still a gentle, explosive lover. She wasn't going to analyze what had happened. It would be futile to feel outraged. She'd wanted it as much as Kid. Maybe more. Now she had to decide what she could live with or live without.

She smoothed the hair away from his forehead. The brothers had the same dark hair and eyes, but Kid was strikingly different in looks. As his mother used to say, "Too handsome for his own good," and he was. With sculpted features, brown hair that curled into his collar, a smile that could move the weakest of hearts, he was a charmer, the life of a party.

She, on the other hand, was quiet and reserved, yet somehow they'd formed a connection. That was the past, though. She now had to concentrate on the future and what the night had meant. She'd never had a man risk his life for her as Kid had last night. But then no one had hurt her as bad as he had, either. How did she balance it with true emotions, true feelings?

But in her heart she knew it all came down to one thing—would she ever be able to trust him again?

Looking outside, she saw the night fading away to an early morning glow. They had to get dressed. She shook Kid. "Wake up."

"Oh, crap."

Lucky found her panties and bra and slipped into them.

Kid sat up, his dark eyes on her. "You know, I'm just going to get hard watching you do that."

The train started to slow.

"Oh, hell, so much for being aroused." He stood, wincing.

She zipped her jeans. "Are you hurt?"

"My body is a little bruised from my stuntman work." A teasing glint brightened his eyes. "But you can kiss it better."

"I already have," she said, slipping on her sneakers.

"And it was much appreciated." He hopped around trying to get his boots on.

She picked up her cell and gun and went to peep around the opening. From the dim morning light she could see clearly. "There's nothing but mesquite and dry barren land."

"Could we talk?" His breath fanned the top of her hair and she felt a weakness in her lower abdomen.

"Not now. Something is fixing to happen."

"About last night," he said as if she hadn't spoken.

She turned to face him. "It happened. I'm okay. I'm not angry anymore."

"You're very nonchalant about it."

"I'm more focused on what's going to happen now and…"

Suddenly voices erupted outside. "Where's your gun?"

She held it up in her right hand and he took it from her. "Hey."

"I'll be doing the shooting," he informed her. "Now let's get off this ride."

The train came to a slow stop. Voices drew closer and they pulled back into the car. When the voices faded, Kid took another sneak peep.

"There's a barbed wire pen, trucks, cattle trailers and a box truck. They're getting ready to move the stolen property."

"Do you see anyone?"

"Clyde and the boys. Text Chance so they'll know what's going down."

She looked at her phone. "There's a text from him. The train is headed for Brownsville and the chopper is on the way. They're following the track. Hopefully they're not far away."

"So we're somewhere outside Brownsville?"

"Yep. Do we get off now?"

"See if there's anyone on the other side?"

Lucky edged her way over, her nerves tense. She took a quick look. "It's all clear."

"Men are getting out of trucks. What the hell?"

She hurried back. "What?"

"Listen."

"How many head?" a man asked.

"Thirty-two prime beef. One bull."

Lucky froze. "That voice. It couldn't be."

"Sounds familiar," Kid whispered in her ear.

"It can't be."

"Look but be careful. Could there be two of this person?"

She did, but still couldn't believe her eyes. "This is crazy."

"There's a boxcar full of stolen property. Make me an offer," the familiar voice said.

She and Kid listened closely as the man inspected the items. Money exchanged hands. "You got a good deal," the voice said.

"Get your boys to unload the cattle and my guys will haul them out of here with the goods. We have to do it fast. We don't want to draw any attention and this train needs to get moving."

"Hey, Clyde, you heard the man."

"The deal's done?" Clyde asked.

"You bet. We made a pretty penny. Now I can buy that house in Austin on a lake for my boy and get him away from that trashy Thelma Lou. It feels good sticking it to the people of High Cotton. Judd Calhoun wouldn't hire my son so the next hamburger he eats will be his own prize Brahmas."

"You're a cruel bitch, Wilma."

"But a rich one. Lie low for a while. We'll start up again in about six weeks. I'll be in touch." Wilma walked away and turned back. "I'm not happy with the Hardin grab. You did that without my permission."

Kid stiffened beside her.

"Hardin messed with us so we messed with his brother to get even. Those Hardin boys are close and that was as good as hitting the Kid himself."

"Bastards," Kid hissed.

"But he was good to my boy so lay off the personal stuff."

"Yes, ma'am. We're headed down to Mexico. See ya when we get back."

Lucky watched Wilma as she strolled away to a pickup Lucky didn't recognize. A Mexican man walked beside her. The woman even looked different. The atrocious wig was gone and her gray hair was cropped short. She just couldn't believe what she was seeing and hearing. Wilma was the leader of the cattle rustling ring that had been operating for months. Unbelievable. Of course, no one even suspected her. Lucky certainly hadn't. Wilma was just a crazy old woman obsessed with her son.

"Do you think Bubba Joe's involved in this?" Kid asked.

Lucky shook her head. "No, but I'm not sure about anything."

"Come on. It's time for us to leave before this train starts moving."

He took her hand and they crept to the other side. After looking both ways, they jumped to the ground. "Let's head for the mesquites," Kid said, and they started to run.

"Hey!" Melvin shouted. "We got company."

They ran for their lives, and as bullets whizzed past them Kid dragged her into a gully. Dust blanketed them. "Okay, we got one gun, one clip. We have to make it last until the chopper gets here."

"You're a dead man, Hardin!" Melvin thundered.

"He's getting closer." Lucky watched as the man charged toward them with a large gun. It looked like an AK-47.

Kid quickly rose and fired at Melvin's feet.

Melvin flinched and backed up. "Son of a bitch! He's got a gun."

"Lucky." Kid sank down by her, breathing heavily. "I'm not really into cops and robbers. I'm an oil well driller. I'm comfortable in that role."

"I'm sorry I got you involved in this."

"Come on, Lucky." He touched her cheek. "I'd die for you, don't you know that?"

She kissed his hand, feeling that closeness they'd always shared. "I hope it doesn't come to that."

"Yeah, where in the hell is Chance and the chopper?"

The sound of gunfire echoed kicking up dirt above their heads. "Prepare to die, Hardin."

Kid rose and fired again, and then he pulled her to his side. "Please say you forgive me. I need to hear that now and I need you to mean it."

In her heart she knew she already had. She rubbed her face against him. "I forgive you."

"What the hell is going on?"

Wilma.

"Lucky and Kid Hardin followed us. We have them cornered in the gully."

"Now that's a shame. Lucky's always been nice to my boy, but she used him like everyone else."

"What do you want us to do?"

"Kill 'em."

CHAPTER THIRTEEN

A SECOND ROUND OF RAPID gunfire blasted over their heads. Kid pulled Lucky lower. "Text Chance. Tell him we need help."

Lucky wiggled to get her cell out of her pocket. "I'm low on power. I hope it goes through."

"Give it up, Hardin!" Melvin yelled. "You're outnumbered."

"You come anywhere near this gully and I'll plant a bullet right in the middle of your chest. Come on, Melvin. You want to be the first to die?"

Kid had no idea if he could kill someone, but he'd pull the trigger before he'd let them touch Lucky. Sinking back against dried grass and good ol' country dirt, he took a deep breath and looked into her beautiful blue eyes.

"You know I'm getting used to that short hair."

She smiled that special smile and it made everything right in his world, except for those guys trying to kill them.

"Concentrate, mister. We have to find a way out of here."

He cocked an eyebrow. "Any ideas?"

Lucky looked both ways down the barren gully.

"Let's crawl farther along so they don't surprise us. They'll think we're here in this spot, but we won't be. It'll give us an edge."

"I love the way you think. You go first and keep your head to the ground."

She inched away and he followed on his stomach, staying as low as possible. He tasted dirt and spit it out. The sun was now out and the heat was going to be a factor in this desolate landscape.

Where was that damn helicopter?

The train still hadn't moved and the rustlers had to be anxious to get it going. Bellows of frightened cows pierced the silence. Suddenly, another barrage of bullets sounded at the place they'd been hiding, taking out the top of a mesquite bush.

"Good thing we moved," he said, scooting up next to her. Dirt was in her hair, on her face and clothes and she never looked more beautiful. Her eyes glinted with excitement—and fear. Yep, they both were afraid, but they now had each other. Ever since his parents had died, he'd felt alone. Even though he'd had his brothers and his aunt and uncle, that deep-seated emptiness was always there. He'd tried filling that gaping hole inside him with other women, but no one filled it like Lucky.

Kid brushed dirt from her cheek. "We'll make it out of here."

"Hey, Hardin," Melvin called. "Just come on out. It's getting hot and I'm not a very patient man."

"Keep quiet. Let them keep guessing our location," Lucky whispered.

Just then Earl came up from the back of them and jumped into the gully. He didn't look right or left, only at the shattered mesquite bush. "They're gone," he yelled to Melvin.

"What?"

Earl turned and saw them, his eyes big. Kid stood quickly, pointing the gun at Earl's chest. Caught off guard, Earl's gun was down by his thigh.

"You raise the gun or shout and I'm going to put a bullet through your heart." Kid was surprised at how steady his arm was, and maybe Earl was, too. He didn't move a muscle.

"Earl, what's happening?" Melvin yelled.

"Put your gun on the ground slowly," Kid said in a voice he hardly recognized. Or maybe he did. It sounded like Cadde's. "One false move and you're dead." How many times had he said that as a kid playing cowboys and Indians with his brothers? But this was real—as real as it could get.

Earl eyed him for a moment and then laid the weapon on the ground.

"Kick it toward me."

Earl slammed his boot against the gun and it spun toward Kid in a cloud of dust. But he didn't flinch or take his eyes off Earl as the man was probably hoping.

"Earl?" Melvin's voice drew closer.

Lucky picked up the gun, wiping the dirt from it.

"Tell Melvin—"

"Hardin, the party's over," Melvin said above Kid's left ear.

"Ah, Melvin, I really hate it when a party ends." Kid kept his weapon on Earl. "And this one's not. I still have Earl in my sights."

"And I have an AK-47 pointed at your head. Drop the gun."

Kid went over his options and none of them were in his favor. Someone was going to die. He'd seen this standoff in movies a hundred times, but he couldn't remember one damn ending. That might have something to do with the AK-47 pointed at him.

Before he knew her intent, Lucky swung around and fired at Melvin who staggered backward. A sea of bullets sprayed toward the sky. Earl ran off and the sound of a chopper was like a breath of fresh air.

Reaching for her, he pulled Lucky into his arms. They held on tight. She trembled against him, or at least he thought it was her. He could be trembling, too.

"I didn't kill him, did I?" she cried into his chest.

"Shh." He stroked her hair. "Let's take a look." They peered over the rise of the gully. Clyde, Wilma, the Mexican and Earl were running to cross the train to get to their trucks. Melvin limped behind them.

"Looks like you got him in the leg. He's on his feet."

"Thank God."

The helicopter came in low and Clyde raised his AK-47 and fired off a round. The chopper turned and lifted higher. The sounds of sirens echoed in the distance and Cameron County sheriff's cars burst onto the scene. Officers got out, guns drawn, and it was over.

The aircraft landed. Cadde, Chance, Walker and Travis jumped out.

"Kid, where are you?" Chance called.

Lucky sagged and he caught her before she hit the ground. He pushed her hair from her hot forehead. "You okay?"

"I just need a minute. I was so scared."

She was pale, jittery, and he wrapped his arms around her. What an awful night, but they had gotten through it together. A part of the night had been out-of-this-world good, though.

"I'm okay, now." She stepped back and straightened her shoulders.

"Kid, where in the hell are you?"

"We better go or Cadde's going to have a heart attack." He took her hand and they climbed out of the gully.

Cadde and Chance charged at him and caught him in a fierce bear hug. He couldn't breathe. "Hey, hey, I didn't die."

They let go and Chance hugged Lucky. "Are you okay?"

"Yeah."

Chance frowned toward the group the deputies had surrounded. "Isn't that Bubba Joe Grisley's mom?"

"Yes," Kid replied. "She's the boss—leader of the cattle rustlers. Seems she devised a plan to get back at everyone who had ever been mean to her son. She was planning on getting him out of High Cotton and away from Thelma Lou."

"You're kidding."

Wilma broke loose from the group, but two deputies grabbed her. She fought back, swinging her purse, her fists. "I have to go to my son," she screeched, flailing her arms. "He can't live without his momma. Bubba Joe, Momma's coming."

The cops managed to restrain her and put her in a squad car. She bumped her head against the window, screaming. Two officers drove away with her still screaming. The others were arrested and escorted to waiting cars.

Travis ran over and went straight to Lucky. He hugged her and she hugged him back. Cradling her head, he said, "I was so worried."

Kid stiffened. *Stop touching Lucky.*

She finally let go. "I'm okay, and you were right. We were missing something. Wilma was in the bar a lot of nights and I never listened to her and she probably dropped a hundred hints." She brushed back her hair. "Do you know if Bubba is involved in this?"

"No. Walker's going to pay him a visit when we get back." Travis turned to him and held out his hand. "Thank you for helping Lucky."

"You don't have to thank me for that." He stared at the man's outstretched hand and had no intention of shaking it. Why, he wasn't sure. Or maybe being an ass was more his style. Or maybe he was so jealous he couldn't think.

Chance poked him in the back. Cadde cleared his throat in a way Kid knew well—the lecture-type voice on good manners. Because he'd graduated to adulthood, he took the man's hand. No one could say he wasn't a gentleman.

"Travis, do you know who the Mexican is? Or the buyer?" Lucky asked.

"Wilma's brother-in-law, her sister's husband, Manuel Ortiz. He steals cows every now and then to make ends meet. According to Manuel, Mrs. Grisley got him caught up in it big-time. She was set on revenge for the wrongs she'd thought had been done to her son. She knew the people in the area so she was aware of their schedules and when to hit. It has worked for several months." Travis took a breath. "The buyer is Raymond Hatch, a friend of Manuel's and a big-time crook selling stolen cattle to a slaughterhouse and fencing the goods. There'll be more arrests as soon as we know who's working with Hatch."

"I've never done anything to Bubba Joe," Chance said, his face creased into a big frown.

"That was because of me," Kid had to admit. "I got into a fight with Wilma's goons and they did it to get back at me."

"I wasn't aware you had a share in my cows."

Kid slapped his brother on the back. "I think it's more of a blood thing. You hurt me. You hurt my brothers."

Chance's frown slid into a grin. "Are we related?"

Kid made a face. "Funny. I'll pay for the feed and transportation to haul them home."

"I do believe I know you."

"How did Wilma get the engineer involved?" Lucky asked, and the brothers became serious once again.

"We don't know yet, but I'm sure he'll start talking once he's in jail." Travis glanced toward the train. "We have to unload the cattle. They need water and feed until we can arrange for the owners to pick them up. We'll photo and number them to have a record for the trial."

"I'll call Judd and see what he wants to do." Chance reached for his cell.

Kid looked at Lucky and she avoided looking at him. That was not a good sign.

Chance put his phone back on his belt. "Judd is arranging for a cattle carrier to bring all the animals to High Cotton. They can stay on the Southern Cross until the owners are located."

"That's nice of Judd," Travis said. "I'll be busy here for a while, but Chance would you mind taking Lucky home? I'm sure Bud is worried about her."

"Will do. Is Walker going back with us?"

"I'll check."

As they walked to the aircraft, a news crew drove up, jumped out and started filming. Kid tried to shield Lucky as they climbed inside. She didn't say a word.

Walker hurried to join them, sitting across from him and Lucky. The helicopter was designed for use in the oilfields. Two leather chairs were on the left against the interior wall and one was on the right, leaving room for a stretcher in case a worker was injured. It also had room for materials or supplies that were needed fast on a site.

They buckled up as Chance took the pilot seat and Cadde sat beside him. The whirly bird revved up and soon they were in the air.

Lucky sat very still and quiet and Kid knew her protective walls were going back up. Didn't she remember the wonderful night they'd shared? And didn't she know he would never hurt her again? But he could almost feel her forcing herself to remember the pain he'd caused her. That might be one obstacle they wouldn't be able to overcome. He was going to be in there trying, though.

"That was a very brave thing you did," Walker said, looking at Lucky. "Do you feel like talking about it?"

He felt her tense. "Sure."

"What made you follow them?"

Lucky looked down at her dirty hands. "They said they were leaving High Cotton and since Travis suspected them of being involved in the cattle rustling I knew they were getting ready to move the stolen animals and goods. I called Travis immediately but he didn't answer. If the cowboys left without being followed, it would be another unsolved crime. When Travis didn't call, I hopped into the back of their truck."

Walker blew out a breath and winced. "That was dangerous."

"It was dark and I had a gun. I figured I'd sneak out as soon as I knew where they were going."

"How did Kid get involved?"

"By sticking his nose in where it didn't belong."

"Hey, that's not nice." Kid stretched out his legs, feeling aches all over his body, especially in his heart. A giant step forward and a thousand little ones backward. Oh, yeah. Damn it!

"I saw her jump into the back of their pickup," he said. "Being of sound mind and body I knew that was dangerous so I joined her and she was madder than hell."

"The cowboys came to the truck before I could get Kid out." Lucky took up the story. "They drove about ten minutes from The Beer Joint to a rural area."

"We followed up your tip about the Wilkins place and you were right. I called David Wilkins last night. He said he's leased the land to Wilma for about two years now. I sent a deputy out there before dawn. I heard from him a little while ago and he found the barbed wire pen and building. The main fence had been taken down so they had easy access to the train."

"Kid and I sat in a thicket and watched the show unfold. They were running around with flashlights and we had no idea what they were going to do. We heard the train and figured they'd hide."

"But they didn't?" Walker asked.

"No. They flashed a light and the train slowed and stopped when the cattle carriers were right there. They loaded everything quickly and hopped aboard. I knew this was how they were getting the animals out of the area undetected."

"Why did you jump on that train?"

Lucky twisted her hands. "That's hard to explain."

"I'm just trying to understand why you'd risk your life."

"I'm wondering that now, too." She brushed dirt from her jeans. "I saw Mr. Hopper's great-grandson earlier and he was upset that his four-wheeler and the silver inlaid saddle Mr. Hopper was going to give him was stolen. I told him the authorities were doing everything they could to find his things and he believed me. I saw the saddle as they loaded it onto the train and I knew it would be gone just like all the other stuff that had been stolen from the people of High Cotton." She folded her hands in her lap. "Suddenly, I couldn't let that happen. We'd worked on this case for months and I just wasn't going to let them get away with it."

"And Kid followed you?"

"Yes. He was like gum on my shoe I couldn't get rid of without a lot of muscle power." She took a breath. "I was glad he was there in the end."

Oh, now we're talking!

"Kid." Cadde spoke above the whirl of the chopper turned in his seat to look at his brother. "After the incident with the hobo and you caught the caboose, how did you get back to Lucky?"

Before he could answer, Lucky spoke up, "He ran across the top of the train."

"What!" Cadde shook his head. "Are you crazy?"

"Yep. Certifiable."

"I don't know how you did that," Walker said.

"It was scary. The first time I stood up the wind almost took me as if I weighed no more than a beer can. It's all about balance and once I got the hang of it I was off like a stuntman. Jumping from one car to the next was a problem in the dark, but I wasn't letting Lucky face those goons alone."

Complete silence followed his words. No one moved or said a word. He was hoping Lucky would look at him, but she didn't.

Walker leaned forward, his eyes on Lucky. "I still can't believe you risked your life to catch these thieves."

Lucky just shrugged.

"A lot of people in this town will be grateful."

Again, Lucky looked down at her hands as if she was uncomfortable with the conversation.

"May I ask a favor?" she asked.

"Sure."

"Can I go with you when you talk to Bubba Joe?"

Walker looked at her long and hard. "Yeah. I think you've earned that right, but you'll have to fill out a report about the shooting at the sheriff's office. Even though it was self-defense it has to be documented."

"Okay."

"We're fixing to land," Chance called.

Lucky scooted forward. "Could you give me a few minutes to see my dad and get cleaned up?"

"Call me when you're ready."

The craft landed smoothly on the pad they had built between Chance's and Cadde's houses. Chance helped Lucky out before Kid could. He didn't object because they were all glad to be home safely.

"I'm going to check on Jessie and my son and I'll be ready to leave for Houston in an hour." Cadde strolled toward his house. "We have to get back to work." Now that all the excitement was over Cadde was back to his usual workaholic self.

The four of them walked toward Chance's house. Bud and Nettie came out the back door. Bud shuffled as fast as he could toward Lucky. She took off running. Bud dropped his cane and caught her, his hand trembling against her hair. "Baby girl, I've been so worried."

She drew away and Kid noticed she wiped away a tear. 'I'm fine, Dad."

Bud looked her up and down. "You don't look fine. You're a mess."

Lucky brushed at her dusty clothes. "I just need a good bath."

"Did y'all catch those thieves?"

"Yes. The authorities are tying up the loose ends."

"Who were they? Anybody we know?"

Nettie picked up Bud's cane and handed it to him. He leaned on it heavily.

Kid could see Lucky was grateful for the distraction as she seemed to gauge her next words.

"Girl, was it anyone we know?" Bud asked again.

"Yes. Wilma."

Bud's eyes narrowed. "Wilma who?"

"Bubba Joe's mom."

Bud laughed. "Wilma couldn't rustle up a leaf on a windy day."

"It was her, Dad. She didn't have the wig and she was shouting orders like crazy—a totally different person. She had us all fooled."

"Why would she do something like that? Her only interest is Bubba Joe."

"That's it exactly. She targeted people she thought had been mean to Bubba. She wanted revenge and money to get Bubba Joe out of High Cotton and away from Thelma Lou."

Bud shook his head. "If that don't beat all. I knew that woman was loony."

Lucky put an arm around her father's shoulder. "Let's go home." She stopped suddenly. "Oh, my truck is at The Joint."

"I'll take you to get it," Walker offered.

"My truck is there so can I hitch a ride, too?" Kid asked.

"No problem."

Nettie patted Bud's shoulder. "It was nice to meet you."

Bud smiled and Kid couldn't even remember that phenomenon happening before. "Thanks for the coffee, food and company."

They climbed into Walker's truck. He tried to help Bud, but Lucky was there blocking his way. It didn't take long to reach The Beer Joint.

Before Walker could drive away, Kid said, "I'll get cleaned up and meet you at Bubba Joe's. If he's not involved, he's going to take this hard. If he is, you'll need some help with him."

"There's no need," Lucky snapped, stopping on the way to her truck. "I can handle Bubba. He's not a violent man."

Their eyes met and locked. "I'm Bubba's friend and I'm going to be there."

"Suit yourself. You're going to do what you want anyway."

And just like that the walls were slammed up and sealed tight—just as if the night had never happened. She didn't trust him and he couldn't really blame her. As he watched her drive away he knew what he'd probably known for years. He still loved her.

But how did he prove that to her?

CHAPTER FOURTEEN

LUCKY TOOK A SHOWER, washed her hair and changed clothes. All the while she forced herself not to think about Kid. She was good at that. She'd done it for years.

She'd thought her father would want to talk, but he was on the phone with Nettie. He'd just left the woman. What did they have to talk about?

Realizing she was grumpy for no reason, she went out onto the porch to relax and to take a deep breath. She wanted her father to have a friend. Lord knew Wilma wasn't that person. There were signs the woman was unstable, but everyone in this town called it nutty, out-of-control smothering. But it turned out to be so much more.

A light breeze touched her skin. A strong hint of fall was in the air. This wasn't her favorite time of the year because it brought back so many memories of when she was pregnant and alone in Austin. The baby was due in January. When the doctor had first told her that, she'd been shocked, unable to believe it. How could she go so long and not know she was pregnant?

At the time the only thing she could focus on was Kid's leaving. They hadn't been apart since they'd gotten serious and she didn't know how she was going to live without him. Since they always used protection, pregnancy never crossed her mind. And she was used to skipping her period. Her cycles were never regular.

Oh! She clenched her hands into fists. Why was she thinking about this? It was over. Done—twenty years done.

But it wasn't over. She closed her eyes. Last night she'd acted like that young girl, carelessly, recklessly. And she'd added stupid to the list. They hadn't used protection. The young Lucky had been smarter than that.

But when Kid went flying out of the boxcar, she had visions of him lying out there bleeding to death. All she could think about was him and how she'd gotten him involved in a dangerous situation. Because of her he might be dead. At that moment she'd known that she didn't want Kid out of her life, no matter how many times she'd told herself otherwise.

When he swung back in the car, she was so happy she'd just wanted to touch him, hold him and never let him go. And she had been uncaring of the consequences. But now in daylight reality she was waffling with all the feelings she'd said she would never have for Kid again. Evidently, she'd been lying to herself.

She glanced toward the hill and all of yesteryear's pain centered in her heart. Vividly. How could she ever trust him?

She'd trusted him last night and this morning. She wasn't sure what she would have done if he hadn't been there. It was nice not to be alone in a moment of crisis—to have someone to lean on. Even when Melvin had the gun pointed at Kid's head, he was still cracking jokes, but Lucky knew he was dead serious. To prevent Kid from being shot, she did the only thing she could and fired at Melvin. She'd been trained to protect herself but nothing prepared her for the startling reality that she might have killed someone. It left her weak and trembling.

Kid understood. That startled her even more.

On the ride home she'd come to the conclusion that she didn't want to risk her life or anyone else's again. She had to stop worrying her father and face life head-on instead of living dangerously on the edge, searching for validation from a group of people who cared nothing for her. How psychotic was that?

Travis was right, she should be a wife and a mother. But no one had ever come close to filling the emptiness inside her that Kid had left. Now he was back and she was falling into the same old trap of loving him. Maybe that's what she'd been waiting for all these years.

She drew another long breath. Out of self-defense she'd snapped at him earlier. Eventually they would have to talk and she wanted to be well armed with her pride intact when that happened.

Her father came out the door without his cane and sat in a rocker. "Hey, girl, I thought you had to meet Walker."

"I do." She got to her feet. "I just needed a moment."

"Mmm. Confronting Bubba Joe will be difficult."

"I'm just hoping he's not involved." That would crush

her if he was. They were good friends and she couldn't even remotely see him interested in cattle rustling.

"Nah." Her dad shook his head. "Wilma made him weak, dependent, and she would never let him get mixed up in anything like that because she'd be afraid he'd get hurt."

She leaned down and kissed his cheek. "I'm sorry I worried you."

"Ah." He waved a hand to dismiss it. "You know, Nettie reads palms and she said I didn't have anything to worry about, that you would come home safe. She was a soothing comfort."

"Mmm." She eyed her father who wasn't his usual grouchy self. "You like Nettie?"

"Yeah. She's a nice lady. A bit different, but I like different."

"Really?"

"Yep. She said there's a thing at the Senior Center on Wednesdays for men and women. They bring food, play cards, dominoes, some of the women knit. It's just a fun get-together. I think I'll go next Wednesday."

What? Her father never went anywhere. Nettie had certainly cast a spell over him.

She kissed his cheek again. "I'm sure you'll enjoy it. And to make you feel even better you'll be even happier to know that I'm quitting my job with Travis."

He turned his head to look at her clearly. "You mean that?"

"Yes. Travis will probably fire me anyway because I crossed the line. But that doesn't matter. I needed that job to make me feel better about myself. Not anymore. I don't care what people say or think about me. If they don't like me, it's their loss. I'm not putting you through any more hell because I need to prove something to myself. I think I'm a pretty nice person the way I am."

"Damn straight. And I want you to think about closing The Joint or selling it."

"Dad."

"I mean it, Lucky. I never liked you running that place. It's time to think about you—your life. Go to nursing school like you planned. Check in Brenham or College Station. I'm sure they have a program."

"I'm thirty-eight years old."

"So? You're never too old to achieve your dreams. You're never too old to be happy."

Lucky cocked her head. "This doesn't have anything to do with Nettie, does it?"

"We're not talking about Nettie." His voice became testy for the first time. "And what was that Hardin boy doing with you?"

Oh, yeah. The grouchiness was back.

"Kid saved my life last night and I was glad he was there." She told him about the hobo and Kid's daredevil stunt to get back to her.

"Oh, girl." He sighed heavily. "Don't get tangled up with him again. He'll break your heart just like before."

Unable to stop herself, she looked toward the hill. "I don't think I've ever become untangled. There's a permanent link that binds us."

"Oh, crap, girl. Don't do this to yourself."

"I'm not, Dad. I don't know what I want and Kid doesn't, either. It's like running through a fire and hoping you don't get burned."

He squinted at her. "How many times do you have to get burned before you learn not to run through a fire?"

She placed her hands on her hips. "My, aren't you a bundle of wisdom." He made to speak and she held up a hand. "No more advice. This time I'm making choices that are right for me and now I have to go."

Ollie was stretched out in front of the door. As he moved away, she said, "I'm still mad at you."

The dog whined.

"Stop picking on Ollie."

She squatted and hugged him. She couldn't really blame Ollie for her weakness in letting her guard down with Kid that day in the barn. It was the first crack in the armor she'd thought she'd perfected against the world—against Kid.

But it was strange. Ollie had never done anything like that before. Maybe he'd sensed the tension between the humans and acted on instinct to ease a difficult situation. And she was dawdling. She went inside and grabbed her phone off the charger and headed for the door.

Her dad was on the phone again with Nettie.

This could get interesting.

ON HER WAY TO BUBBA'S she called Thelma Lou to test the waters. She told her everything that had happened and added if she cared anything about the man she should be at Bubba's in thirty minutes.

The Grisley house wasn't far from The Beer Joint. The small white frame two-bedroom sat on five acres. Wilma paid someone to mow it because she didn't want Bubba Joe getting too hot.

She often wondered why Wilma let him work in the bar. She was so protective of him and then it hit her. It was a way for Wilma to get information. Poor Bubba Joe. Wilma probably grilled him every night. He was going to have to grow up fast. That was going on the assumption that he had nothing to do with the rustling.

She pulled into the driveway behind Walker. Kid whizzed in behind her. She tried not to look at him, but failed. His hair was still damp from a shower, curling into a blue polo shirt, which showed off his broad chest and strong arms. His jeans clung to his long legs. All that was sexy as hell, but it was the five o'clock shadow that made her weak in the knees. Or maybe it was remembering the feel of it as it had brushed across every inch of her sensitive body.

He looked at her, his eyes dark, and then he spoke to Walker. "How do you want to handle this?"

"I just got a call from the sheriff," Walker said. "Wilma totally lost it in the jail, beating her head against the bars and shouting for Bubba Joe. They restrained her and took her to a hospital for a mental evaluation so let's play this by ear. I'll start the conversation." Walker strolled toward the steps.

Kid lightly touched her arm and her skin tingled. "Are you okay?"

"Yes," she replied, following Walker.

"You seem upset…with me." He persisted.

"I'm not. I'm just upset by everything that has happened."

"Everything?"

"We'll talk later," she said, going up the steps. They were close to Walker so Kid didn't say anything else.

Walker knocked on the door. Bubba Joe greeted them in jeans and a white T-shirt, strands of hair sticking up at the back of his balding head. He'd obviously been asleep. He always slept during the day because he was up most of the night.

"Sorry to disturb you," Walker said.

"I was just snoozing in my chair before I go to work." He glanced at Lucky. "Did you come for the money from last night? I put it in the bag like I do when I close. It's in my room I—"

"Bubba, that's not why we're here," she said. "Can we come in, please?"

"Okay." He opened the door wider and it was very cool in the house, probably cooler than Wilma would allow him to have it. The place was neat and clean but it had an old musty scent. Walker and Kid sat on the threadbare sofa while Bubba took his seat and she pulled a straight chair close to him.

"Something has happened, right?" Bubba's friendly expression changed to one of fear.

"Yes," Walker said.

"Momma went to see Aunt Mable and something's happened to her."

"Yes," Walker said again. "But not like you think." Then he told him the whole story.

"Nah." Bubba shook his head and looked at Kid. "This is a joke, right? Like you used to pull in school?"

"No, Bubba." Kid scooted forward. "I wouldn't do that to you. This is serious and Walker needs to know if you were involved."

"Me?" Bubba was shocked. "I don't even like cows. Momma wanted me to work on the Southern Cross but Judd wouldn't hire me for that reason. Momma got mad and said she'd get even."

"She did, Bubba," Lucky told him. "She got even with a lot of people."

His bottom lip trembled and Lucky knew he was going to cry.

Kid got up and knelt by his chair. "Come on, Bubba, you're gonna have to grow up now."

"But Momma takes care of me. I give her my check and she won't let me touch the money. She gives me twenty dollars a week. Momma says I don't know how to manage money."

"I'll help you with all that now, but you better not be lying to us or Walker will find out."

"I'm not, Kid, I wouldn't lie to you. You're my friend." Lucky feared Bubba was always going to be in third grade, but it was very clear Bubba looked up to Kid—his hero.

"You bet." Kid smiled and she had a moment of revelation. She didn't think for one minute that Kid would take the time to fool with Bubba, but he was and it made him look so different in her eyes. Grown-up. Mature.

"Where's Momma, Kid?"

Kid took a moment and she knew he was measuring his next words. "When she was arrested, they took her to jail, but apparently she had a mental breakdown. She's being evaluated in a Brownsville hospital."

"Oh." Bubba choked up again, running his hands down the thighs of his jeans. "I'd like to see her, but Momma won't let me drive anywhere but High Cotton."

"I'll take you in the chopper."

"You will?" Bubba's eyes grew big. "I've never been on one. I might be scared."

"I'll be right there," Kid promised him.

"Okay." Bubba made a decision for the first time in his life.

"But do you understand your mother is not coming home?"

Bubba wiped at his eyes. "I do."

Walker stood. "Bubba, you'll probably have to sign some papers since you're the next of kin. All those involved will be transported to the Giddings jail since the crimes were committed in this county. After your mother is evaluated, we'll know more about where she will be located—jail or a hospital."

"I don't know what to do."

"Don't worry," Kid told him. "I'll be there to help you."

Bubba pushed out of his chair. "I'll go change my clothes."

Kid got to his feet. "We have time. I'll have to call Chance first to see when the chopper is available."

"Oh." Bubba looked disappointed.

"But it doesn't hurt to be ready."

Charming Kid was out in full force, but that's who Bubba needed right now, someone strong and self-confident to boost his low self-esteem. And Kid was good at that. As a teenager he'd given her confidence in herself—in life, only to shatter it. He wouldn't do that to Bubba, though. Why she was so sure of that she couldn't explain.

"Bubba, do you know of anyone who works for the railroad?" Walker asked.

"Yeah, Aunt Mable's son-in-law drives a train. When we visit, he's always talking about it."

"What's his name?"

"Philipe Mendes. Why?"

Kid patted him on the shoulder. "I'll explain later."

Suddenly the squeal of a car that needed new brakes sounded. Thelma Lou. She burst through the door without even knocking. She looked around at the group. "So the old bitch finally cracked."

Lucky leaned over and whispered. "Cool the attitude."

"That's mean, Thelma." Bubba's face knotted in pain.

Thelma flung out an arm. "Did y'all tell him what she's been doing?"

"Yes," Kid answered. "But we didn't cut him with a razor blade while we did."

Thelma got the message quickly. She went over to Bubba and put her arm around him. "I didn't mean to hurt your feelings."

"I don't want you mad at me." Bubba sniffed.

Good heavens, Bubba. Get a backbone. Then something hit Lucky like a smelly fish in the face. Was she this pathetic when she was a teenager, leaning on Kid to boost her spirits? Maybe he was glad to finally get away from her neediness. Oh, no!

Bubba went to change. Walker left and since Kid didn't have a cell he was on Bubba's landline to Chance.

Lucky was in frozen disbelief.

Hanging up, Kid said, "It will be a couple of hours before Chance can get here."

"I wish I could go, but I have four kids."

"Don't worry. I can handle Bubba," Kid assured her.

"You know, I like Bubba, but he has to grow up. I don't need another child." Thelma headed for the door. "See ya tonight, Lucky."

Kid walked over to her. "What's wrong? You're very pale."

"I…I just got a glimpse into how I was as a teenager. Needy. Needing you to lift my spirits. Needing your presence to face people. Just needing you to live. How pathetic I must have been. No wonder you never came back." She took a couple of deep breaths to calm her racing heart.

"Lucky…"

"Don't say anything." She stepped back toward the door. "I wouldn't believe you anyway."

"Lucky, don't do this," he begged.

But she wasn't listening. She ran out the door. She ran for her very life.

CHAPTER FIFTEEN

KID WAS HEADED FOR THE DOOR to go after her when Bubba Joe came out of his room.

"Kid, I'm ready to go see Momma." He had on baggy jeans, a T-shirt and sneakers, not much different from before.

He was torn between going after Lucky and helping an old friend. "Where does Thelma Lou live?"

Bubba pointed east.

"I have some things to do first so I'll drop you off there and pick you up later."

"Okay."

In less than ten minutes he was on his way to Lucky's. A cloud of dust followed him as he sped down the lane. She was sitting on the stoop, staring off into space. He got out and sat beside her. Neither spoke for a few minutes.

He wanted to put his arms around her and hold her, smell the scent of strawberries, touch her smooth skin and taste her sweet lips. For so long he wasn't sure how he felt about her, but now he knew he loved her. He also knew she wasn't ready to hear that. Even though he wasn't a patient man he would bide his time.

"Why aren't you helping Bubba?"

He watched the stubborn line of her jaw. "I can't until we talk."

"Kid." She glanced down at her clasped hands. "I saw myself clearly in Bubba today. As a teenager I was shy and had a hard time talking to people, even my classmates, but as long as you were there boosting my spirits I could. I never had the strength to stand up for myself. I needed you for that."

"I needed you, too. My parents died and people were distant, not knowing what to say to me. When I was with you, I was myself, strong again. I needed you just as much as you needed me. I missed you all the way to Lubbock and in the days that followed."

"But you never called or came back."

He swallowed. "No."

She brushed a hand through her short hair. "We were teenagers, Kid. We didn't know what real love was. We played grown-up games, but we were still kids without a clue. I was angry for so many years and I blamed you. I don't anymore. If I hadn't kept waiting for you to make decisions for me, our son would be alive today. If I had stood up for myself and come home, my life would have been so different." She clasped her hands again and he couldn't help but remember them touching his body and making him feel empowered like he hadn't in years.

"I have to stop looking back," she continued. "I have to make decisions now that are good for me. I'm going to stop chasing criminals because it makes me feel good about myself. I'm going to rent The Joint or sell it and then I'm going to do something for me—something I want, and build a life I deserve. My dad suggested nursing school and I might just do that. Never again will I be needy."

He took a deep breath. "What about us?"

She turned to look at him, her eyes as bright and sincere as he'd ever seen them. "We were two teenagers who needed each other, but now we're adults with very different lives. And the sad truth is if you had really loved me, you would have come back. You wouldn't have noticed those other girls. I don't think you even realized that until you got to Lubbock. There was a whole other world out there, without the pain, and you embraced it totally."

He couldn't deny her words but he had to ask, "What about last night?"

She studied her hands. "We got a lot of frustration out of our systems."

"It was more than that," he said stubbornly.

"We just got caught up in the moment. That's all it was."

"Not to me."

"Kid." She sighed. "The honest truth is you like women. Even though you don't want to hear it, you're a lot like your father in that regard. I can't live my life wondering where you are and who you're with."

His cool slipped a little. "Have you heard of the word *trust?*"

"Yes. I trusted you twenty years ago."

That pretty much spoiled every retort in his head.

"It's over, Kid. We have to admit that and we both

need to move on." Her voice was calm, practical and he hated that.

He got to his feet, his eyes holding hers. "It's not over for me, Lucky. It will never be."

He strolled to his truck, trying not to look back at everything he wanted, but would now never have.

Life sucked sometimes.

LUCKY CRIED HERSELF TO SLEEP, but it was cathartic, cleansing. She'd meant every word she'd said to Kid. It just wasn't easy saying them and watching the pain on his face. She'd asked herself so many times how did she go forward without looking back? Making peace with the past and letting go. It was simple. The only way to accomplish that was by being strong enough to stand on her own, uncaring of what people said about her. She gave them power when she walked away from their snide remarks, when she didn't confront them, when she allowed them to treat her like a second-class citizen. But not anymore.

When morning arrived, she felt better, but somewhere in her mind she knew Kid would always own a piece of her heart. That first love wasn't going to be easy to forget. She wasn't sure she had to forget. She just had to overcome it.

As she went into the kitchen, she noticed her dad on the phone again with Nettie. They must have a lot to talk about. She smiled at her father's new interest. Maybe he'd get out of the house more.

Coffee was made so she poured a cup, spotting the

lease papers on the counter. She sat down to read them. Now that she was starting a new life she would need the money. She'd sign it and drop it by Cadde's or Chance's.

Her father shuffled into the kitchen without his cane. Refilling his cup, he said, "I'm going over to Nettie's. She used to be a masseuse and she's going to massage the tight muscles in my leg to relax it."

"Really." She lifted an eyebrow. "And what will this massage include?"

He shrugged. "I don't know, but I'm going to find out."

With a smile he shuffled to the door.

"Dad, you forgot your cane."

"Don't need it."

Her dad was like a kid again. Maybe there was hope for her, too. She touched the lease papers for a moment, saw Kid's handsome face and immediately let it go.

A knock at the door had her on her feet. It couldn't be her father. She'd heard his truck leave. Travis stood on the doorstep.

He removed his hat. "May I come in?"

"Sure." She opened the door wider. "Have a seat. Would you like a cup of coffee?"

"Thanks."

Travis had a wad of newspapers under his arm. Was he planning on reading the paper here? She placed a cup of coffee on the end table and sat in her dad's chair. Ollie curled up beside her.

"How did things go?"

He took a swallow of coffee. "We worked into the

night and even arrested Philipe Mendes, thanks to Walker's tip. Since the crimes were committed here, they're being transported back."

"Walker mentioned that."

"I went by to check on Mrs. Grisley and she's had a complete mental breakdown. She's just lying there muttering 'Bubba Joe' over and over. I was there when Kid arrived with her son. Bubba cried like a baby asking her what he was supposed to do now. Kid took him outside and told him to straighten up. It wasn't a time to be a sissy. He had to be a man. Bubba cut it off—" Travis snapped his fingers "—just like that. Kid's good with him and Bubba listens."

"Kid's very good with people." She knew that better than anyone.

Travis sipped his coffee and then placed it on the table. "Lucky, what you did was dangerous...and heroic."

"And I'm fired," she teased.

He reached for a newspaper and handed it to her. It was a Brownsville paper and her face leaped out at her. Kid was beside her helping her into the chopper. Hometown Heroine, the caption read, and went on to tell everything that had happened.

"How did they get this?"

Travis shifted uneasily. "It's my fault. A guy was there who I thought was with the sheriff's department. He kept asking questions and I finally asked the sheriff about him. He was a reporter, but the damage had been done. I'm sorry, Lucky."

She shrugged. "It doesn't matter. At least it didn't run in a paper around here."

He frowned.

"What?"

"The story was picked up by The Associated Press and it's running in a lot of papers across the country—human interest type story."

"Oh, no." That was the last thing she wanted, but at least there would be less or no fuss in High Cotton. "I guess my cover's blown."

"Yeah, but it doesn't say anything about you being my undercover source. It just tells about a young bar owner who heard bits of information and took it upon herself to stop a cattle rustling ring."

She fingered the paper. "I've decided to quit anyway. When I start risking my life, I have to question a lot of things."

"This has a lot to do with Kid?"

"Yes. I just never got over him." She ran her hand along the arm of her father's chair. "But now I'm ready to start a new life. I'm going to rent or sell The Beer Joint and then I'm going back to school."

An eyebrow rose. "Are you sure about Kid? He seemed pretty protective the other day."

Her hand clenched into a fist. "There's a lot of history between Kid and me, but it's time for both of us to move on."

"You deserve the best, Lucky." There was that note in his voice again, but her emotions were too raw to start anything with Travis and she sensed the man knew that.

She smiled. "Thank you. I enjoyed working with you." She paused, needing to think about something else. "How's Melvin's leg?"

"You grazed his thigh. They took him to a hospital, gave him an antibiotic shot and stitched it up. It wasn't bad enough to keep him out of jail."

That was a relief. She didn't want to harm anyone, including Melvin.

Travis reached for something on the sofa. "I brought you a gun. Yours is being tagged and entered into evidence." He laid it on the coffee table. "Melvin and Earl's mother has been calling wanting to go their bail. There's an attempted murder charge against them so I don't think they'll be getting out any time soon. In case they're stupider than I think, I want you to have a gun."

That gave her a jolt, but she wasn't going to be paranoid about it. She couldn't live her life that way.

"Please keep it. I'll be fine," she assured him.

"Lucky..."

"When you offered me the job, I was so excited to be doing something worthwhile. It boosted my spirits and made me feel good about helping people. At that time in my life I needed that. But now..."

"You can handle anything life throws at you," he finished for her.

"Yes." She smiled. "But I'll miss you."

"Same here. The job was exciting when you were around."

They'd gotten personal without her realizing it, but they were good friends and they always would be.

Travis cleared his throat. "Do you think you can go to the sheriff's office in the morning and speak with an investigator about the shooting? It's standard procedure."

"Yes. Walker mentioned that, too."

"Good. We want to have an airtight case against these guys."

"Do you know how Wilma got involved with them?"

"At The Beer Joint."

"My place?"

"Yes. They stopped in there late one night about a year ago when she was in her crazy-old-lady-wig mode. She heard them whispering about an ATV they needed to get rid of. She told them if they wanted to make some big money to call her and they did. Up until then they'd been just petty thieves stealing when they needed money."

Lucky leaned forward. "What did Mr. Hopper ever do to Bubba Joe? He's a nice Christian man and I just can't see him being rude."

"Clyde, Melvin and Earl are doing a lot of talking. Seems Mr. Hopper was putting gas into his truck at the convenience store. Bubba Joe had stopped for a Coke, candy bar and chips. When he backed out, he clipped the tail end of Mr. Hopper's truck. The gas nozzle came out and splattered Mr. Hopper with gas. Startled, he called Bubba an idiot. He then apologized but it was too late. Wilma heard what had happened, and two weeks later Mr. Hopper's cows were gone along with his great-grandson's ATV and the silver inlaid saddle he'd won in his rodeo days. There are a dozen or more stories like that."

"This has hit Bubba hard."

"How did he even start working for you?" Travis asked.

"Bubba and I were in school together and sometimes he'd stop in to say hi. One night I was really busy and he jumped in to help. I stopped him because he wasn't licensed to serve beer. He wanted to know how to get a license and I told him. The next thing I knew he had one. He did that all on his own and he's been working at The Joint since. I thought Wilma would put a stop to it, but she didn't."

"How will he cope now that everything is out in the open?"

"He has a cousin here who will help him. Bubba loves her kids because he's a big kid himself. And Kid will help him."

"Are you sure? Kid's part of a big company in Houston. I wouldn't think he has a lot of available time."

"He'll be there for Bubba."

"Are you saying he's trustworthy?"

What? This was confusing. She didn't trust Kid. How could she say that Bubba could? "Yes, in a lot of ways," she replied. But not in the ways that counted.

She thought about her answer long after Travis had left. Her emotions were slipping and sliding like a bar of soap on a tiled floor. One thing was very clear. She was afraid of being hurt again. She'd gotten through all the pain and she couldn't live through another betrayal.

Like she'd told Kid, they were young and the agony of what had followed was that much more vivid.

She'd told herself she was ready to move on, but here she was stepping back into the past with the same old heartache. She had to make some hard decisions in the next few days and she would make them with her eyes wide-open. Maybe by then her emotions would be stable. Maybe by then she would be focused on the future instead of the past. Maybe.

Getting ready for work, she stalled. She really didn't want to serve beer to drunken men anymore. Before she had a reason, a cause. Now it just seemed like paving a road to hell, as Mrs. Farley would say. She laughed at the thought, the sound easing her mind. If she could laugh, there was hope for her.

She heard the door open and went to greet her father, who was rubbing Ollie.

"You've been gone all day," she said.

"Yeah. Nettie likes *The Price Is Right,* too, so we watched it together and then she fixed lunch. She takes care of Chance and Shay's baby while they work. He's a cute little booger. When Cody went to sleep, she gave me a massage."

"And did you have to take your clothes off for this?"

"Uh..." He looked at her with startled eyes. "Well, yes." He limped into the kitchen, not shuffled, to avoid eye contact.

She laughed. "Do we need to have the sex talk?"

"No," he shouted. "I gave it to you and it didn't work."

"I'm going to The Joint. I'll see you later."

She smiled all the way to her truck.

THE NEXT MORNING WHEN SHE got up, her dad wasn't there. She found a note on the table: "Gone to Nettie's." She hoped he wasn't wearing out his welcome. They might have to talk about this.

After coffee, she dressed and drove to Giddings and spoke with the investigator, giving him the details of what had happened. It was quick and easy and the man said they'd have a ruling on the shooting in a few days, but added there was nothing to worry about. He congratulated her on a job well-done. That was a welcome relief.

They were out of milk and orange juice so she stopped at Walker's General Store. As she was getting the items out of the cooler, Mrs. Farley and Mrs. Axelwood came in. Usually she would tense and immediately leave the store. She did neither.

Mrs. Axelwood tried to grab for some brown construction paper from a top shelf, but she was too short. Without thinking about it, Lucky walked over, reached for the paper, while juggling the milk and orange juice in one arm, and handed it to the startled woman.

"Ah...thank you," the woman said.

"Can I help with anything else?"

"I...I was wanting the orange paper, too. We're making turkeys in our Bible study class for Thanksgiving."

"My grandmother used to take me to church. Making those was fun."

"I remember Mrs. Littlefield." Mrs. Farley joined the conversation. "She was a nice lady."

"Yes. I still miss her." The milk and orange juice were cold against her breast, but she would stand there forever staring these two ladies in the eyes, just to prove she would never shy away from their remarks again. After a moment, common sense prevailed. "Have a nice day."

Easy breezy. Nothing to it. People could only hurt her when she let them. She placed her items on the checkout counter with a confident smile.

"Lucky, the whole community is grateful to you," Nell, Walker's aunt, said, dropping some licorice sticks into the bag because she knew her father liked them.

Before she could respond, Maddie came in and immediately hugged her. "You're my heroine. I could never do something so dangerous unless my kids were in harm's way."

"Thank you," she replied, feeling out of breath.

Caitlyn came up behind her. "I'm going to personally do something nice for you," she told Lucky. "I've had to listen to Judd complain for over a week and believe me it wasn't appealing. Thanks to you he's got his cows back and he's happy. I'm happy. I'll take you out to lunch or something. I'll let you know."

Cait waved and made her way to the door. Lucky slowly followed.

As she walked to her pickup in a daze, a truck and trailer drove up.

"Lucky," the man shouted, getting out.

She turned to see Mr. Hopper and he held out his hand. She juggled the bag and her purse to shake it.

"Thank you," he said. "I'm so grateful. I got my cows. See." He pointed to the trailer. "My saddle, too. And the ATV. My great-grandson is so happy. I'm giving the saddle to him over the weekend before it's stolen again. I just can't believe a young girl would put her life in so much danger for her neighbors."

She leaned over and whispered, "Don't tell anyone, but I'm not that young."

He laughed and Mrs. Farley and Mrs. Axelwood came out.

"Hello, Ben," Mrs. Farley said. "We haven't seen you at church lately."

"I've moved my membership to the church on First Street."

"Why?"

"I'm a Christian and I don't like associating with hypocrites."

Mrs. Farley bristled. "What do you mean?"

"You tote the Bible in one hand while your son has a beer in both of his."

"My son does not drink."

"Frances, who are you trying to fool? Luther has run into my fence three times drunk as a skunk. The next time I'm calling Walker." He turned his back on them and spoke to her. "We'd love to have you join us in services one Sunday, Lucky."

"Thank you, Mr. Hopper." A smile seemed to be plastered across her face. "I just might do that."

"You can consider our church, too," Mrs. Farley said in her huffy natural way.

This is where she got even and told the old windbag what she thought of her. But to her surprise she couldn't be that cruel to anyone. "Thank you, Mrs. Farley. I appreciate the offer." She didn't think she needed to say any more than that.

Mr. Hopper patted her shoulder. "That's class, Lucky. You took the high road." He strolled toward his vehicle and turned back. "I don't drink, but I might stop in and have a soft drink with you one day."

"That would be nice." She got into her truck and froze. Kid was standing at the door listening to the whole thing. Their eyes met for a brief moment and then he went inside. He looked hurt and her heart ached. Was it always going to be like this when they met?

Driving home, she thought about the incidents and how she'd handled them. Instinctively most people were nice and if she hadn't shied away from them, her life would have been much different. She didn't need to hop a train and risk her life to get their approval. If she had made an effort, Mr. Hopper would have treated her as cordially last week as he had today. And if she had spoken to Mrs. Farley and Mrs. Axelwood, they would have responded like they had today. They had a picture of the type of woman she was and she'd never made the effort to show them otherwise. That was a revelation in itself.

Since she hated going into The Joint, she decided she would close it. After Bubba Joe's life settled down, he might want to take over the business. At least Kid would be happy she wasn't serving beer to men.

And sometime in the near future she might have to ask herself why that mattered.

CHAPTER SIXTEEN

KID WATCHED THE SCENE with pride. Lucky handled the naysayers of High Cotton with grace and dignity, not sinking to their level. She didn't need him to protect her. Would she ever need him again?

How he wished she could understand there was a difference between need and needy. They'd needed each other. Needy was Bubba Joe being dependant on his momma, and that was a whole different ball game. He couldn't understand how Wilma could emotionally cripple her son. She never let him have a life or make a decision without her supervision. The only thing Bubba had done on his own was get a job at The Beer Joint. He was proud of that, but if Lucky closed the place Bubba would be left without an anchor.

Kid was in the process of going over Bubba's finances with Bubba's cousin, Nancy. The sheriff wanted a full record of Wilma's banking. Fortunately, Bubba had his own account where Wilma deposited his check every week. Kid turned the information in to the sheriff and he was in the process of seizing Wilma's accounts. Bubba's was left alone and Nancy was helping him to manage his own money.

Kid talked to Nancy about Bubba renting The Beer

Joint and she thought it was a good idea. It would keep him busy. Nancy offered to continue managing the financial records, but Bubba took offense to the idea. He said Lucky taught him how to handle money and how to pay the beer delivery people. He was now taking care of his own money and he would talk to Lucky about renting the place.

It was nice to see Bubba growing into manhood so quickly. He was on a high experiencing life for the first time. Everyone in this town thought Bubba was slow, but Bubba was proving them wrong. He'd just been kept back for so many years and was now having his first taste of freedom. Bubba was still seeing Thelma Lou, but he refused to let her take control, either.

The judge had signed an order for Wilma to be moved to a state mental facility in Austin. Bubba hadn't asked to go see his momma again, but Kid knew he'd get a call one day soon and he'd take Bubba to Austin to visit. With the way Bubba was staking his independence, though, he might go on his own.

Everything had settled down in High Cotton and everyone was feeling secure again, except Kid. He was never more restless in his life.

He hadn't stopped for anything at the general store. He saw Lucky's truck and Mrs. Farley's Buick and thought Lucky might need him. But she hadn't. Maybe he needed to be needed…by her. Now, there was a thought.

Since he hadn't seen Cody in a couple of days, he

drove to Chance's. Knocking on the back door, he heard Nettie shout, "Come in."

He stopped short in the kitchen. Bud sat at the kitchen table with Nettie, drinking coffee.

Bud frowned. "What are you doing here?"

Nettie placed a hand on Bud's arm. "Franklin, Kid is Chance's brother and he's always welcome here."

"Ah, he hurt my girl."

Nettie rubbed Bud's arm. "I've done things in my past I'm not proud of—haven't you?"

"If I told you, you'd never see me again."

They shared a secret laugh and Kid stared at them. What was going on? "Is Cody awake?" he asked, rather puzzled.

"He just woke up," Nettie said, and pointed to a baby monitor on the counter. Kid heard the soft coos. "He wakes up happy and I'm letting him watch the horse mobile his father bought for him. I'll get him up in a few minutes."

"Do you mind if I do?"

"No. Go ahead."

"You don't know nothin' about babies," Bud told him.

"Franklin," Nettie scolded.

"Sorry."

Kid left the room, but glanced back. They had their heads close together, whispering. Could they be? Nah, they were too old. But did one ever get that old? Lord, he hoped not.

Cody lay in his crib kicking his legs and flailing his arms as he watched the horse mobile go round and round. "Hey, big boy," he said, and Cody kicked that much faster, turning his head to find the voice.

"Want to get out of the crib?" Kid gently lifted him into his arms. "Uh-oh, someone's wet. But that's okay. Uncle Kid will change you." He laid the baby on the changing table and unsnapped the blue all-in-one outfit. Removing the wet diaper he wadded it up and put it in a plastic bag like he'd seen Chance do and dropped it into the trash can. Quickly wiping Cody's butt with a baby wipe, he reached for a fresh diaper and put it on him, snapping the onesie, all before the baby could pee on him as Kid had seen him do to Chance.

"Hey, that wasn't so bad." He scooped Cody into his arms and cradled him against his chest. Looking down into that sweet face reminded him of his own son. "You know, I had a son once. He'd be about twenty now and we'd probably be arguing about cars, the speed limit, school and girls, but he would know that I loved him."

He looked up and saw Bud standing in the doorway with a look of disbelief on his face. Suddenly, Bud turned and limped away.

Kid drew a deep breath. No matter what Bud thought of him he knew in his heart he would have loved his and Lucky's child.

LUCKY LOOKED INTO NURSING programs, but couldn't get into a fall class because everything was full. She'd start in the spring. Even though she would be with students half her age, she was still excited. Starting over at thirty-eight wasn't so bad after all.

Bubba Joe came by and talked about renting The Beer Joint. She knew he could do it because he took care of the place when she wasn't there. Thelma Lou was going to help him but Bubba was the one paying the rent. She was just glad the people of High Cotton hadn't blamed him for his mother's mental illness.

She sat down and read the lease papers Kid had left and signed them. The deal was a good one and she was being stubborn in not signing them in the first place. Her father had just come in from Nettie's and he was flipping through the TV channels.

"I'm taking the lease papers over to Cadde's," she said. "I'll be right back."

"Why aren't you taking them to Kid? He's still around, you know."

"Cadde's the CEO of Shilah Oil so I'll just take them to him."

"Are you afraid to face Kid?"

She placed her hands on her hips. "I thought you didn't like Kid and didn't want me anywhere near him."

"People change, girl."

"Where is this coming from?"

Her father turned off the TV. "I saw Kid the other day. He dropped by to see Cody. Nettie said he comes all the time to play with the baby and with Jacob, too. I could hear him talking to the baby on the baby monitor so I went down the hall to see what he was up to. He was cradling Cody and telling him about his son and how old he would have been and how much he would have loved him."

Her throat closed up and she couldn't speak.

"He's grown up, girl."

"Dad, please. I don't want to talk about him." She headed for the door and realized how immature she was acting. Maybe some traits were inherited. She turned back. "Okay, here's the truth. I'm always going to love Kid, but I can't trust him and I don't know if I can live like that."

"Did you trust him on that train ride?"

She swallowed. "Yes."

"Sometimes you have to go on faith. You're not going to get a guarantee for happiness in this life by avoiding what you want most. You have to fight for it."

"Got it." She winked.

"Don't be smart. I want you to be happy."

She looked down at the papers in her hand. "I want that, too."

"Then take those papers to Kid."

She shut the door before he could say anything else. She fully intended to go to Cadde's, but she turned at the High Five entrance. Her dad was right. She had to return the signed lease to Kid.

His truck was at the little house so that's where she drove. She knocked on the door.

"Come in," Kid shouted, but she wasn't just walking in.

She knocked again.

"It's not locked. Why can't you just come in?" Suddenly the door was yanked opened.

"Lucky." He stood there in jeans and a T-shirt, no

shoes. His hair was tousled and he looked as though he'd been resting. The sleepy eyes and five o'clock shadow made her heart race in excitement. She'd seen that look many times. They kept staring at each other and finally he moved aside. "Come in."

"No, thank you. I just came by to give you these papers." She held them out. "I signed them."

His eyes narrowed. "Are you sure?"

"Yes. I've rented The Beer Joint to Bubba and I'm starting nursing school in the spring. The money will help tide us over."

"Sounds as if you have your life sorted out."

"Yes."

"Without me in it."

She drew a long breath. "Kid."

"Okay. I get it." He took the papers. "I owe you some money but I don't have the draft book here."

"Don't worry about it. I tr..."

His eyes held hers. "You trust me?"

"Kid."

He covered the space between them and cupped her face with his hands. Looking deep into her eyes, he kissed her softly, gently. She moaned and wanted to melt into him and to forget that he'd ever hurt her. She rested her head on his chest and breathed in his masculine heady scent.

"All I'm asking is for you to take a chance on us."

Her emotions wobbled and she stepped back to gain a measure of control. *She trusted him.* Could it be that easy? "I'll think about it, but I'm not promising anything. Just give me some time." She walked to her truck and her knees felt weak. But for once she'd admitted the truth. She needed time.

THE DAYS PASSED QUICKLY and it was the middle of October before she knew it. And true to her word Cait arranged a day out. Judd was footing the bill. Lucky didn't hesitate or shy away from the offer, but she didn't expect all the Belle sisters to go along and Jessie and Shay, too. Well, why not? They were having a spa day in Austin with manicures, pedicures and massages. The six of them went in Cait's Escalade. Lucky never had any real close friends except for a girl in Austin who lived next door. When she'd moved away, Lucky missed her.

These ladies were different. They knew each other and joked a lot. The sisters playfully argued. Cait missed a turn so Sky insisted on driving and she did not know the meaning of the word *slow*. She whipped in and out of traffic. Jessie closed her eyes, saying she was afraid she'd have the baby early if she didn't. But they made it safely to the pricey spa. It was a luxury that Lucky could have never afforded and she enjoyed every minute.

Afterward they had lunch and decided to shop. The kids department was their favorite place as the women bought things for their children. Lucky felt a moment of sadness but quickly brushed it away.

Jessie wanted to look for a dress to wear to the baby's christening. After the baby was born, due in late November, she wouldn't have the time or feel like doing it.

The scene that followed was hilarious and Lucky found herself giggling at times. Since Jessie was very pregnant she asked that someone her size try on the clothes.

Sky said Maddie's breasts were too small and Maddie pretended to be indignant. Jessie informed them that her breasts were not always that big. They all laughed. Then Sky decided Cait was out because her butt was too big. Cait came right back at her calling Sky a hippo. Maddie had to part them before the women said too much they didn't mean. They all agreed that Shay was too slim and they hated her because she'd lost her baby weight without even trying. That left Lucky as the designated model. She was self-conscious at first but got into it.

The clothes were to die for and when Lucky noticed a price tag she almost fell out of the high heels the store had provided. Dress after dress and Jessie still couldn't make up her mind. Finally Lucky put on an off-white ivory V-neck dress with a beaded jacket. The long skirt came to midcalf and the back was longer. It was lovely and Jessie bought it along with another simpler outfit.

On the way home Cait said they needed margaritas so they stopped, and then she declared they needed another. Since Jessie was pregnant she drank ginger ale and drove them safely home. By the time they reached High Cotton they were happy, singing, and Lucky felt a part of the group.

After Jessie dropped her off, she fell into a dead sleep wondering if she'd ever get the chance to wear beautiful clothes like Jessie.

ON SUNDAY AFTERNOON KID DROVE over to Cadde's to give him the lease papers. Jessie was resting and Jacob played at Cadde's feet.

Jacob stood up, holding on to the coffee table and then suddenly shot across the room to Kid. "He's walking." Kid lifted the baby into his lap.

"He's been doing that for a couple of days and he's so proud of himself," Cadde said.

Jacob pushed out of his lap and took off again.

"Is Jessie okay?" he asked. "She's not usually asleep this time of the day."

"She was out late last night."

Kid frowned. "What do you mean she was out? Weren't you with her?"

"No. The Belle sisters, Shay and Jessie took Lucky to Austin for a day out."

"What? And Lucky went?"

"Yes, and they had a great time."

"How come no one told me about this?"

Cadde shrugged. "I haven't seen much of you lately. Where have you been?"

"Aunt Etta's and helping Bubba Joe."

Cadde shook his head. "Only you would do that. I hope he appreciates it."

"He does."

"And might I remind you that you have a job. When are you coming back to work?"

Kid laid the lease on the coffee table. "Here's something that will make you happy."

Cadde reached for the document and flipped through it. "You've had this for two weeks."

"Yep." He stood. "I'll leave on that note of enthusiasm."

"Kid, this is important."

Hearing the sternness of his father's voice, Jacob stuck out his lip, tears welling in his eyes.

Cadde picked him up. "It's okay, son." Stroking Jacob's head, Cadde looked at him. "Why did you keep it so long?"

"I wanted to give her a chance to change her mind. I wanted it to be her choice."

"Now it is?"

"Yes, drill your oil well. Make lots of money."

"You'll make money, too. Have you forgotten that?"

"No, Cadde, I haven't forgotten, but it just doesn't mean that much to me anymore."

Cadde watched him. "Isn't it ironic that Kid Hardin can get any woman he wants, but he can't get the one he loves?"

"Screw you."

"Kid, get your head on straight and come back to work. Let things cool off for a while."

He pointed a finger at his brother. "I remember saying that to you about two years ago, but I let you work through all that misery. Ah, forget it. I'm going to converse with the coyotes. They make more sense."

"Kid…"

He walked out. The more he tried to get his head

straight, the more muddled it got. He pushed Cadde's words away. Lucky said she needed time and he clung to that.

THE HOLIDAYS ARRIVED. Lucky hated this time of the year. Her son had died on December twenty-third and she hadn't celebrated Christmas since. But she did prepare a big Thanksgiving and a Christmas dinner for her dad. As she was writing out a grocery list, her dad came in.

"Whatcha doing, girl?"

"Sorting out what I'll need for our Thanksgiving meal."

"Ah, girl, you don't have to do that." He got a Dr Pepper out of the refrigerator. "Nettie invited us for dinner."

"What? You never said anything."

"I guess I forgot."

"This is their family time and we shouldn't intrude."

"Nonsense. We're going."

"Dad…" The ringing of the phone cut her off. She reached for it. "Hi. Oh. Are you sure? Okay. What should I bring?" She frowned at her father as she talked.

Hanging up, she continued to frown. "You told Shay to call me?"

"No. They invited us."

She wrinkled her nose as an unfamiliar scent reached her. "What's that smell?"

"I don't smell anything."

She walked over to him. "Is that Old Spice?"

"Maybe."

She smiled and hugged him. "I'm glad you're happy, Dad."

For so long he'd been a recluse and it was uplifting to see him changing before her eyes, getting out and seeing people. He was putting on weight and the shotgun wasn't in the living room anymore. He must have put it in his room. She wasn't sure what to expect next.

He limped to his chair without his cane. He hadn't used it in weeks. "Oh, before I forget. After Thanksgiving dinner, we're going to High Five for dessert and coffee."

Protesting was out of the question so she didn't, but she sensed she was being manipulated by a crafty old man.

The day turned out better than Lucky had even expected. She felt right at home helping Shay and Nettie in the kitchen. Darcy was a delight and Lucky couldn't seem to take her hands off baby Cody. He was very affable and smiled a lot.

Later they drove to High Five. The Belle residence was packed with family, but she didn't feel out of place like she thought she would. As usual the Belle sisters poked fun at each other and kept them entertained. The kids played out on the veranda, except Jacob and Cody, who were too little. Her dad and Nettie sat on a swing watching them. After helping Etta and Maddie wash the last of the dishes, she went into the parlor for a breather.

The men were talking cow prices and oil prices. Jessie sat on the sofa, looking miserable.

"Are you okay?" Lucky asked.

Jessie grimaced. "I feel like a beached whale. I don't know if I'm going to make it one more week."

"Can I get you anything?"

"No, thanks."

Cadde sat by his wife and began to rub her back. That seemed to give her some relief.

Lucky found a chair and relaxed for a moment, but then Kid drew a chair close and joined her. He had Cody in his arms. They'd spoken when she'd first come in, but they hadn't had a moment together.

"Look at this baby," he said. "Don't you think our son would have looked like this?"

Lucky drew back. Why was he asking that? She wanted to smack him. Instead, she bit her lip and replied, "Probably."

Jacob noticed Kid holding Cody and he toddled over, trying to push the baby out of his lap.

"Hey, partner." Kid reached out with one arm and pulled Jacob onto his knee. "We can't be mean to Cousin Cody."

Lucky watched in amazement at how easily he handled his nephews. Her father was right. He was good with kids. This was a whole other side to Kid.

Suddenly, he said, "We should be married with our own kids."

She was so startled her throat closed up.

He looked at her. "Let's forget the past and fly to Vegas. We could be man and wife by morning."

"Are you drunk?"

"I don't think so."

"Your marriage proposal stinks." She got up and went down the hall to the bathroom. She'd often dreamed of Kid asking her to marry him. The dream was nothing like reality, which sucked, to say the least.

Inside the bathroom, she felt faint and dabbed her face with a damp washcloth. What was wrong? Kid was doing what he did best—kidding—and aggravating her.

Bile rose up in her throat and she sank down by the commode and lost her dinner. Had she eaten something bad? She washed out her mouth and blotted her face again. Then she sprayed the room with deodorizer. The scent made her nauseous again. What…? She thought for a moment and then it hit her. This feeling was familiar. She couldn't be.

No, no, no!

She couldn't be pregnant.

CHAPTER SEVENTEEN

THE NEXT MORNING LUCKY was sick again and she knew she was pregnant, but she had to be sure. She drove into Giddings to buy a pregnancy test. An hour later she sank to the floor in the bathroom and wrapped her arms around her waist. Her life had come full circle. Twenty years, maturity and age hadn't made a difference. She was still making the same mistakes.

Yet this was not a mistake. She placed her hand over her stomach. This was a second chance to be a mother. A second chance to correct all the choices she'd made. She was thirty-eight now, and that would be a factor in her pregnancy, but she would embrace it with all her heart.

She couldn't shake that feeling of déjà vu, though. At eighteen she was on the verge of starting nursing school, as she was now. Was she doomed to repeat the same mistakes? No, she would not hide in shame this time and she would do everything right with the pregnancy. And she would tell Kid. She wouldn't keep it from him. But she had some things to do first.

She made a doctor's appointment in Brenham and had the pregnancy confirmed. The baby was due in early June. She already knew that.

By the end of the week she was ready to tell Kid. He was back at work because Jessie had given birth to ten-pound four-ounce Cadde Thomas three days after Thanksgiving. Cadde took off to spend time with his wife and sons. Even though Kid was back at Shilah, he still came home to High Cotton every night. Her father brought home all kinds of tidbits about Kid—seemed he'd given up his bachelor pad in Houston. That surprised her but every day she was finding out new things about Kid and they were all good.

They'd started the oil well and it was located at the back of the Hardin property. A road had been built on the left side of Chance's house to get to it. A wooded area blocked the sight of the road so it wasn't intrusive. Late at night the hum of the rig could be heard across High Cotton. The Hardin boys were definitely back.

Kid was on the site most days, but she wasn't sure he was there today. She sat on the stoop, Ollie by her side, and tried to figure out a way to contact Kid. Her father was going to be late. He and Nettie were going to a school event of Darcy's. This was the perfect time.

Abruptly the sound of a helicopter whirled through the sky. She could see it as it hovered and slowly descended. Was it Kid? She waited a few minutes and poked in his number.

"Hey, Lucky," he answered.

That teasing masculine voice did a number on her senses. "Could…could you come over for a few minutes?"

"I'll be right there."

In less than ten minutes, she saw his truck coming up the lane. Ollie barked. "Shh," she said. "It's just Kid." That was a mouthful. The man who, after all these years, could turn her inside out, flip her world into a tailspin and have her smiling all the while, was here.

Her muscles tensed.

He got out of the truck and, despite the cool December breeze, walked toward her without his hat. He was probably afraid of Ollie stealing it again.

Kid's hair curled into his collar and her eyes were glued to his handsome face. Was she always going to feel giddy when she saw him?

He plopped down beside her. "What's up?"

She noticed he had a baseball in his hand. "What's with the baseball?"

"Oh." He twisted it. "I bought it right after you told me about the baby. I intended to put it in the basket on his grave. See." He held out the ball. "I wrote *Hardin* on the leather. That's who he is and I wanted him to know that."

With a Magic Marker no less. Her dad would laugh at that. Or maybe not. "But you decided against putting the ball in the basket?"

"Well, late one night I came here to do exactly that, but standing there in the dark I knew I was being immature. I told my son I wouldn't leave it there until his mother approved."

"Oh." He'd surprised her once again.

He looked at her and his dark warm eyes made her weak. "You're beautiful," he said, "and sexy as hell."

He touched her cheek with the back of his hand. "Your hair is getting longer. Are you letting it grow?"

She should get it cut, but she kept putting it off. It had nothing to do with him liking it longer...or maybe she was lying to herself. Again.

"I...I just haven't had time."

"Shay and Nettie cut hair. I could ask them if you want."

"You want me to get my hair cut?"

"Doesn't matter to me. I love it short, long, even bald. You're still my Lucky."

My Lucky.

"Do you mind if I put the ball in the basket?"

"Ah...no."

He stood and held out his hand. "Come with me."

Without a second thought she put her hand in his and they walked toward their son's grave. As they did, Lucky realized she hadn't been there for a while and she'd finally stopped grieving. That painful emptiness was gone.

Kid squatted at the small grave. He didn't even look at the headstone. "Hey, son, it's Dad. I brought the baseball, just like I promised, with your mom's approval." He placed it in the basket and froze as he finally saw the headstone. His hand shook as he touched the word *Hardin* engraved across the bottom.

He glanced at her. "You put my name on it."

Her pulse quickened at the joy in his eyes. "Like you said, he is a Hardin."

"Thank you." Kid got to his feet and gathered her

into his arms. "This is the best Christmas present I've ever gotten. Thank you, Lucky."

She'd done the right thing. She burrowed closer loving his tangy masculine scent and strong arms.

"I've asked myself a million times what kind of father I would have made at eighteen, but I know now I would have been a good father no matter what age."

This was it. She had to tell him now. She stepped back to get the words out. "You're going to get the chance to prove that."

"What?" His brow creased. "I can't. Our son is gone."

"I'm pregnant."

His eyes shot wide with disbelief. "What? We're having another baby?"

"Yes. It's due in early June."

"Oh, my God! This is great." He grabbed her and just held her for a moment. "Wait a minute. How long have you known?"

"A week. It's just like before. I was stressed about you being back and I wasn't paying attention to my cycle. I'm all set to go to nursing school and I'm pregnant again twenty years later. I must have a very hard head because I never learn."

"Okay, listen. You're going to nursing school. I'll help with the baby. But first we have to get married as soon as possible."

Have to? Something about the way he said the words didn't set right. "I don't have to do anything. My only concern is taking care of myself healthwise and making sure my baby is born safely." She turned and marched down the hill, fuming.

"Lucky." Her name carried on the cool breeze.

He caught her on the front porch. "Okay. That came out wrong, but marriage is the next step. I don't see it any other way."

"Then maybe you need glasses. I'm not marrying you because I'm pregnant." She pulled away, went inside, slammed the door and locked it.

"Lucky!" He beat on the door. "Don't do this."

She put her hands over her ears and went into her bedroom. When she finally heard the sound of his truck leaving, tears ran down her cheeks. Why couldn't he have said the right words? *I love you and can't live without you.* That would have healed all the old wounds. Not *have to.*

Maybe she was acting irrational. Her head spun, her heart ached and all she could hear was *have to.*

Not any time soon, Kid Hardin.

WHEN SHE HEARD OLLIE BARKING, she knew her dad was home. She sat on the sofa and tried to erase all signs that she'd been crying.

"Hey, girl." Her father paused as he looked at her. "Are you sick or something?"

It was a good time to tell him. "Or something." She made a face.

"What does that mean?"

She took a quick breath. "I'm pregnant."

"Uh..." Clearly that wasn't the answer he was expecting. He eased down by her. "Baby girl. Baby girl." She went into his arms and cried on his shoulder. "Shh, now." He stroked her hair.

She pulled herself together. "It seems like my past is repeating itself."

"Mmm…and with the same man. I knew I should have killed him."

"You're not killing anyone. It takes two people and I wanted it as much as he did."

He didn't say anything for a few seconds. "What do you plan to do?"

"Kid said we have to get married."

"Good." He nodded. "That's what you need to do."

She gritted her teeth. "I'm not marrying him because I'm pregnant."

"What?" His eyebrows knotted together. "Girl, you need to think about this."

She jumped to her feet. "Oh, you men are all alike."

"What did I do?"

She turned at the bedroom door. "The baby shouldn't be a reason to get married even if you and Kid think so. I'm thirty-eight years old and when I get married it will be about love and only love. And a little romance wouldn't hurt."

She slammed the door, fell across her bed and cried. Just because she wanted to.

KID WAS LATE FOR THE MEETING with Cadde and Chance and he didn't care. He was going to be a father again. He was ecstatic, so why was Lucky shutting him out now?

She'd put his name on the headstone. She'd forgiven him and said she'd think about giving him a second chance. But when he'd suggested marriage she'd said no. Why? They needed to be together to raise their child. Damn! He wasn't ever going to figure Lucky out and it wasn't for lack of trying.

He was going to be a father. Everything he'd ever wanted was right here in High Cotton. How did he make Lucky see that he was here to stay—for her *and* the baby?

Cadde's house was quiet as he walked through the back door. He went toward the study and he could hear Cadde and Chance talking.

He plopped into a chair.

"You're late," Cadde said.

"So? I'm sure Chance has brought you up to speed. Everything's going smoothly with the oil well. Hell, look out your back door. We'll reach the desired depth in a couple of days."

"Keep your voice down," Cadde whispered. "Everyone in the house is sleeping."

"Why? It's late in the afternoon."

"Because we're not getting any sleep. Jacob's not adjusting well to the baby. He's waking up in the middle of the night and climbing out of his crib. Mirry starts barking like crazy because she knows he's not supposed to do that. It wakes the baby and us. Then Jacob wants to get in our bed. And he doesn't want Jessie or me to hold the baby."

"He'll adjust," Chance said.

"I don't know." Cadde shook his head. "I don't think I ever adjusted to Kid."

"Funny."

"What's wrong with you? You haven't put your boots on my desk in months."

"I have other things on my mind instead of aggravating you."

"Like what?"

Kid leaned forward, his elbows on his knees. "I'm going to be a father."

Cadde pointed a finger at him. "I told you your past was going to catch up with you. Who is it?"

Kid got to his feet and lost whatever cool he possessed. "If that's what you think of me, I'm outta here for good."

Chance beat him to the door and stood in front of it. "Calm down. Cadde's sleep deprived. He doesn't know what he's saying."

"I'm sorry, Kid," Cadde apologized. "I didn't mean it to sound like that."

"Why can't either of you take me seriously?"

Chance patted his back. "Because you're always joking around and you're never serious."

"I am now. Lucky's pregnant and I told her we have to get married and she said no."

Chance frowned. "You didn't say it like that, did you?"

"What?" He had no idea what his brother was talking about.

"You didn't tell her that y'all *have to* get married."

The moment Chance said the words Kid knew he'd made a big mistake. He ran his hands over his face. "Oh, no."

"Of the three of us I thought you were the one with the romantic, sensitive side. When Shay was pregnant, she needed to know she was beautiful and wanted. Even after Cody was born, she went through all kinds of moods and it all had to do with me loving her. We made special times for us. That's what she needed."

"Oh, God, I have to go."

As he went out the door he heard Cadde say, "Think I'll go lie down with my wife."

Maybe one of these days the Hardin boys would get it right. Kid planned to do that real soon.

HE WANTED TO GO TO LUCKY'S but decided to wait. He had an idea.

Aunt Etta could not have been more excited about the baby. When Kid told her he needed her help she was happy to be of assistance. That night, sleep evaded him and he got up early to finish his plans. The morning light spurred him into action. He called Chance to tell him he wouldn't be back until after Christmas. Like the sensitive, understanding brother he was, he didn't ask questions. He just told Kid to be happy.

Kid had discovered Bud's new daily habit was to visit with Nettie, so that's where he went. He knocked and went in to see Bud and Nettie sitting at the table drinking coffee. Cody was in his high chair eating a cut-up banana, smearing it on his tray, face and clothes.

Kid kissed the top of his head. "Hey, buddy."

Cody smiled at him.

"Bud, could I talk to you a minute?"

"No. You made Lucky cry and I'm not happy with you."

Nettie gathered the baby out of his chair. "Franklin, you be nice. I'll get Cody cleaned up."

Kid sat across from Bud. "Did she cry long?"

"I don't know. She's mad at me, too."

"Why?"

"Because I told her you two needed to get married. It's been twenty damn years. It's time."

He could imagine Lucky's ire when she heard that.

"Has Lucky put up a tree yet?"

"Nah. She never puts up one."

"Why?"

Bud's eyes narrowed on him. "She didn't tell you?"

"What?"

"The baby died on December twenty-third and we buried him on Christmas Day. Ever since then we've never celebrated the holiday."

"Oh, my God!" He buried his face in his hands, feeling as if his chest had just caved in. All the pain she must suffer at this time of year was almost more than he could bear.

"You make it right, boy, do you hear me?"

He drew a breath so deep it hurt in a way he couldn't describe. "I will, Bud. I promise. And I'm sorry about the past. I'll never hurt her like that again."

"You better not. I still have my shotgun."

Kid spent the next few days putting his plan into motion. Only one problem remained. How did he get Lucky out of the house for a whole day?

LUCKY WAS HELPING BUBBA JOE with his books from The Joint. He had everything down pat, but he always wanted her to check it.

"I went to see Momma yesterday," he said. "I took her flowers for Christmas. She likes flowers."

"Did Kid take you?"

"No, I drove myself. Momma can't tell me where I can drive anymore."

She hugged him. "I'm so proud of you."

"Thelma's husband filed for divorce. He lives in Freeport with another woman."

"How did Thelma take that?"

"She was happy. Now the state will make him pay child support."

"Does this mean you and Thelma…?"

"Thelma and I are good together, but I'm taking it slow. She wants to manage my money but no one is doing that again."

She patted his arm. "Good for you."

"I can take care of myself, too. Luther said he wasn't paying his bill the other night."

"What did you do?"

"I told him that right after I kicked him out, I was calling his mother."

"And?"

"He paid up."

"Oh, Bubba. You're going to make it."

Bubba looked down at his big hands. "I couldn't have done it without Kid. He's my friend."

Kid had that effect on people. He made them feel special because he loved from the heart. Oh, God. Did she just think that?

AFTER BUBBA LEFT, CAIT CALLED. The girls were going Christmas shopping in Austin and they wanted her to go. She had nothing else to do so she said yes. They met at Walker's store and piled into Cait's Escalade. Jessie went, too. She said she needed a day out.

They laughed and talked like friends, real friends. The mall was decorated for Christmas and Christmas carols played on the intercom system. It was festive and exciting. She'd forgotten how infectious the holidays could be.

Again they spent a lot of time in the children's department and in a toy store. Sky and Maddie were looking for dolls for their daughters. Lucky stared at all the beautiful baby dolls and a feeling of warmth came over her. They looked so real she just wanted to hold one.

There in the middle of the aisle with people milling around them she blurted out, "I'm pregnant."

No one was surprised or startled.

"Y'all already knew, didn't you?"

"Yes," Cait replied. "High Cotton is a small town."

"But how did it get around so fast?"

"Well." Cait put an arm around her. "Etta was so excited she had to tell Gran and then Gran told Sky and, of course, as sisters we don't keep much from each other."

"We heard it from our husbands," Shay said.

"On that note, let's go have lunch." Sky linked her arm with Lucky's.

She wasn't upset they knew. She wanted the world to know and it felt good to talk about her pregnancy with friends. Over lunch she shared what happened at the birth of her first son. She'd never told anyone but her father and Kid. They all got up and hugged her and the pain from the past slowly ebbed away.

Cait resumed her seat. "You know we've been waiting for years for the right woman to get Kid off the bachelor merry-go-round."

"I think he's had her all along and just didn't know it. Men." Sky rolled her eyes.

"Has he popped the question?" Maddie asked.

"Sort of. He said we have to get married."

"He didn't actually say it that way, did he?" Shay was aghast.

Lucky played with her napkin. "Yes. That's why I'm here with you and not with him."

Cait laughed. "How could a ladies' man like Kid get that so wrong?"

"He's Kid," Jessie said, and they all laughed.

"When he gets around to getting it right, you don't have to shop for a wedding dress." A stricken look came over Maddie's face.

"What's wrong?"

Sky moved uncomfortably. "Okay. We have to fess

up. Remember when we went shopping and Jessie was looking for something to wear to the baby's christening?"

"Yes."

"That wasn't exactly true. We knew you and Kid were getting serious and we wanted, no matter how misguided, to do something nice for you. The dress is for you to wear to a party, reception or a wedding. That is if Kid ever gets it right."

"You bought it for me?"

"Sneaky, huh?"

Jessie reached for Lucky's hand. "The dress is at my house. You can use it or we can look for another one. Whatever you want."

"It's gorgeous. I just can't believe y'all bought it for me." A tear slipped from her eye and she dabbed at it with her napkin. No one had ever been this nice to her.

"Uh-oh. Emotional tears," Cait teased.

"Happy tears." She smiled through them.

They finished shopping and headed for home. The car was packed with toys, gifts and clothes. They couldn't get one more item in the back. Bags were on the floorboard and in their laps. And befitting of the season they sang Christmas carols all the way to High Cotton.

At Walker's store Lucky unloaded her bags and waved goodbye. They went home to their husbands and kids. She went home to her father, who may or may not be there.

Kid hadn't called or come by since she'd told him

about the baby. Even though she'd pushed him away, it seemed strange he hadn't come back. She expected pressure, anything but silence.

She placed her hand over her stomach. "If he doesn't come back this time, you and I will find him." Suddenly, deep in her heart she knew Kid would never hurt her again.

Now where in the hell was he?

She turned into the lane just as the sun was sinking in the west. As she drove closer to the house, she noticed it was decorated all over with Christmas lights. She could only stare at the hundreds of glowing bulbs. Her father couldn't have done this. He wasn't able to climb up to the roof. A beautiful red-and-green wreath hung on the door.

Who had done this? There wasn't a vehicle in sight. She got out and walked up the steps. With no idea what she was going to find inside, she paused and then reached for the doorknob.

Again, she could only stare. The lights were dimmed and a fire was burning in the fireplace. Red and white poinsettias were everywhere and garland was strung across the mantel. Candles flicked invitingly. What grabbed her attention was the big tree in the window. Beautifully wrapped Christmas gifts covered the floor and were piled up the wall. Along with the lights, red and white booties covered the tree. She stepped closer and saw, at the very top, a white angel, and a red glittery heart below it. Inside it was written: Lucky and Kid Forever.

A sob caught in her throat.

"What do you think?"

She whirled around to see Kid leaning against the kitchen doorjamb. In black slacks and a long-sleeve white shirt, he looked virile and handsome. His hair was cut short like Chance's and the five o'clock shadow was gone. She might miss that. Still the whole tantalizing package was Kid—a man any woman would want. Her heart skittered in awareness.

"You…you did all this?"

"Yes." He straightened and came toward her. "We're going to celebrate Christmas, Lucky, every year in a big way."

"Dad told you about the baby?"

He nodded. "I'm so sorry you had to go through that alone. I'll never get over it." He swallowed. "But from now on we're going to replace the bad stuff with good memories." Reaching in his pocket, he pulled out a small black velvet box and opened it. A beautiful oval sapphire nestled in diamonds sparkled at her. "Lucinda Lucky Littlefield, will you marry me? I love you. I've always loved you. I'm sorry it took me so long to realize that."

A tear slipped from her eye. This was romance like she never expected and for a moment she couldn't speak. The fire crackled and the vanilla scent from the candles wrapped her in a warm cocoon. She wanted to live in this moment forever.

Kid stroked her hair. He touched her face. "Come on, Lucky, this is where you say yes."

A sob clogged her throat and she had to take a deep

breath. "Yes! I love you. I tried to hate you, but I can't. I love you."

He reached for her left hand and slipped the ring onto her finger.

"It's beautiful," she breathed, twisting her wrist. "You remembered about the sapphire. I can't believe you did this. Oh, my, it's so gorgeous."

"I don't want you to be sad about your mother's ring. I don't want you to be sad ever again." He gathered her close and held her.

She curved into every hard angle of his body. Her arms went around his neck and he pulled her closer, kissing the sensitive spot below her ear, her cheek and finally capturing her lips in a drugging forever-like kiss. When they came up for air, she rested her head on his shoulder.

"Am I dreaming?" she whispered.

"No. This is real. This is forever."

She glanced at the tree and all the gifts. "Who are all these presents for?"

"You."

She looked into his warm brown eyes. "I haven't received that many gifts in my whole life."

He kissed her nose. "Get used to it."

"They can't all be for me."

"Well." His eyes twinkled. "Some are for the baby. I was going to buy one little outfit but then I saw a stroller, a car seat, a Pack 'N Play and a layette. I'm afraid I got carried away. The lady said we can bring it all back if you don't like it."

She stroked his chest. "If you picked it out, I'll love it." Her hand went to his clean-shaven cheek. "You've shaved and cut your hair."

"I'm going to be a husband and a father. I have to be respectable and it's going to throw ol' Cadde for a loop. He's always yelling at me to cut my hair and to get my boots off his desk. Some days I lived just to aggravate him, but not anymore. I've finally grown up."

She smiled. "I might have to start calling you Cisco." He would always be Kid the kidder, though, the jokester, the life of the party. That was okay as long as she was the light of his life.

Her eyes went to the beautiful tree. "Where did you get all those booties?"

"I asked Aunt Etta and the nice ladies of High Cotton for help and, boy, did they deliver. It has taken a whole village to get us together."

Her eyes narrowed. "You asked Cait to take me shopping?"

"I had to get you out of the house and Cait was happy to help." He kissed her lips. "Please don't be mad."

"I'm not." And she wasn't. With this much love and friendship, how could she be? The gorgeous dress was just waiting for her to step into it, to step into a new life with Cisco Hardin. The trust issue wasn't important anymore. The truth was she couldn't live without him and in her heart she knew he was home to stay.

"There's champagne chilling in the kitchen and I have chocolate-covered strawberries. Bud won't be back until twelve. What do you want to do?"

She slipped a button on his shirt through a hole. "I want to love you until I can't think straight."

He smiled his trademark cocky grin. "Works for me."

She moved against him, but he stepped back. "Wait, wait, I have to confess everything." Her heart stopped for a moment but he still had that grin on his face so she knew whatever he had to say wasn't bad. "Here's the plan. We're getting married and then spending Christmas with our families. Christmas Eve at Cadde's and Jessie's. Christmas dinner at Chance's and Shay's. That night we'll spend at High Five with the Belle sisters and the whole family. After that, we're flying to the Bahamas for the honeymoon of our dreams."

"You have it all planned."

He winked. "Subject to any changes you want to make."

"Let's see." She pretended to think, but she couldn't find anything wrong with his plans. For so many years it had been just her and her father. Now she was inheriting a big family and it felt right. She looked into his eyes. "The schedule seems full. When is our time alone?"

He kissed her nose. "Christmas morning. We may have to lock Bud in his room, though."

"We will not." She poked him in the ribs and they shared a long kiss.

"One more thing," he breathed against her lips. "I reserved the church that Cadde and Jessie got married in for the twenty-third."

No. Not that day.

He must have read the emotions on her face. "Lucky,

his birthday has to be a good memory and I have to believe he'd be happy his parents were married on the day he was born."

For a brief second the pain was there, but then it was gone.

He stroked her face. "Come on, Lucky."

EPILOGUE

May 5—The next year

THE HARDIN BOYS STOOD outside the old home place with their wives. Twenty-five years ago they'd left in an adrenaline rush to play in a state basketball championship. Their parents had died that night. They'd returned to sadness and heartache and they'd never stepped foot in the house again—until today.

They were all married, happy, with families. But they had to totally put the past behind them. The house was rotting away, an eyesore between Chance's and Cadde's homes.

Kid looked to the oil well pumping in the distance. It had come in good, just like Cadde had predicted. Their father would be so proud, but Kid couldn't dredge up much enthusiasm at the thought. His father was an adulterer. He had destroyed the family and Kid vowed every day that he'd never be like him. He cherished his marriage and would never do anything again to extinguish that light in Lucky's eyes.

At night he slept with his head on her stomach so he could feel their child kick. He read to it, too, all kinds of children's books he'd bought at a bookstore. When the baby was born he or she was going to know his voice. They decided not to find out the gender. They wanted to be surprised.

The past few months had been the happiest of his life. Lucky didn't want to move away from Bud so they built a house on the Littlefield property in record time. They just moved in and had a nursery ready. Four more weeks and they would be parents, the way they should have been twenty years ago.

The trial for the cattle rustlers was in March. Clyde, Earl and Melvin each received a thirty-year sentence for armed robbery and attempted murder. Manuel, Hatch and Philipe each got a twenty-year sentence. They wouldn't be out of prison any time soon. Wilma was in her own kind of prison.

His arm tightened around Lucky and she smiled. He kissed her and turned to his brothers staring at the house.

"Bros, let's go see what's inside." They followed him and the wives stayed behind. Cadde had the key, but the lock was rusty and it took a while to get the door open. They fought their way through cobwebs to the kitchen. An old Formica table sat in the middle of the room. The chairs were haphazardly strewn about as they'd left that day in excitement. Dust coated everything, even the mail on the counter.

Cadde drew a heavy breath. "The only thing I feel is the love Mom showered on us."

"Me, too," Chance said.

As they stood there they realized almost at the same

time that their mother had been the stabilizing force in their lives. She was always there for them, helping with their homework, class projects, baking cookies, being a room mother and all the while making a home for them.

"He was never here," Cadde said. "Mom built him up in our eyes, telling us what a great man he was and how much he loved us."

"He was home about ten days a month," Chance added.

"We doted on his every word because we craved his attention." Kid sneezed as the dust got to him. "At night he was down at The Beer Joint chatting up some woman." He'd told his brothers what Lucky had told him.

"I think we can safely say that none of us is like him. I'd never leave Jessie or the boys that long. I couldn't."

"Me neither," Chance said. "No one is taking me from my family."

"I thought I was most like him, but I'm not. Lucky is my life now."

They stood for a moment in silence.

Chance cleared his throat. "I want to make sure Henry Faust doesn't destroy the magnolia tree or Mom's rosebushes when he tears down the house. I'm going to put a brick border around them as a memory to her."

Kid spotted an old catcher's mitt on the floor and remembered the times their father had tirelessly pitched a ball to them. He picked up the mitt and placed it in the dust on the table. "In his own way I guess he loved us and I don't think we're going to have any peace until we forgive him."

Chance held out his hand, palm down. "Here today we forgive our father."

Cadde placed his hand on top of Chance's and Kid followed suit. They stood like that for a moment and then walked out. There was nothing in the house they wanted. Their future waited outside. As the door closed, they knew their past was truly behind them.

Lucky hugged him. "You okay?"

"Yep." He clapped his hands. "It's time to liven up this party." He started to sing. "We're living in High Cotton…"

"Ah…o-o-oh…"

He didn't think his singing was that bad. He turned to his wife who was making the noise. She was clutching her stomach.

"My…my water just broke."

All humor left him. "No. No! It's too early."

"Kid!" she screamed. Still clutching her stomach, she sank to the ground.

He grabbed her. "Take a deep breath. Calm down." He looked around but Chance had already left to get the helicopter. Jessie and Shay were gone, too.

"I'm having contractions just like before. Kid, please, we can't lose this baby."

His insides roiled with a sick feeling. "Hold on, honey. Chance is bringing the chopper. We're going to Houston to our doctor. Take deep breaths. Breathe like they told us. Hold on, Lucky."

The aircraft taxied to a stop beside them. Shay and Jessie came running with towels, sheets, pillows and blankets. Cadde swung open the door and Kid picked up his wife and carried her inside. Everyone climbed aboard.

"Let's go," Chance shouted, and the chopper lifted off.

Lucky screamed as another contraction hit her. Shay and Jessie spread blankets on the floor and he laid Lucky on them.

"Call the hospital," he shouted, and rattled off the number. "Make sure they contact our doctor."

"I'm on it," Cadde shouted back.

"We have to get her out of her clothes," Shay said. In a matter of seconds Kid had her clothes off. Jessie covered her with a sheet.

Lucky let out a tortured breath as another contraction ripped through her stomach.

"How far apart are the contractions?" Cadde asked, on the phone with the hospital.

"About every two minutes." Kid rubbed her back, trying to help her relax.

"He says the baby's coming. Be prepared. She can either sit or lay with her legs apart, her knees bent. Have something clean to catch the baby."

"What! Tell him it's too early. She's not due until June tenth."

"He said get ready."

"Damn it! Lucky can't have the baby here. We don't know anything about childbirth."

"Kid." She took several deep breaths. "We have to be strong. Ah…ah…o-oh."

Jessie and Shay propped her up with pillows, wiping her brow with bottled water and a washcloth. Kid positioned himself between her legs.

"Check and see if she's dilated," Cadde instructed.

"How in the hell am I supposed to know that?"

Shay made an annoying sound and scooted over to look beneath the sheet.

"Yes, a lot. This baby is coming now."

"Kid, no! It's just like before. No. Please!"

"Shh. Don't push. Try to relax." He wouldn't allow himself to think about the past.

Lucky screamed and the excruciating sound curdled his blood. He couldn't stand to see her in this much pain.

"I have to push. I have to push!"

Kid rubbed her lower stomach. "Relax, honey. Relax. Pant like we practiced."

She panted for several seconds and then screamed again. "It's coming," she gasped.

"Use something clean to catch the baby." Cadde relayed the message.

Jessie handed him a sheet, which he tucked under Lucky's buttocks.

"Can you see the head?"

Kid lifted the sheet farther away. "Yes. Oh, God, yes."

"Guide the baby's head out with your hands. Don't pull or push. The face should be down."

"Kid." His name was barely a sound as her strength waned. He had no idea how she was enduring this. How did women do this?

"It's okay, honey. I'm right here. Now take another breath and push our baby into the world."

She gritted her teeth, held on to her knees and pushed with all her might between screams. The bloody, wet baby slid into his hands. He stared in wonder at the precious life as his heart pounded against his ribs. He couldn't move or do anything else.

"Lay the baby on Lucky's stomach," Cadde said, "and be careful with the umbilical cord."

He gently laid the child on Lucky's chest. "We have a daughter, honey. A beautiful baby girl."

Lucky turned her head, kissing her daughter's forehead. "Kid, she's not breathing. She's not breathing! No!"

"Cadde!" Kid frantically glanced at his brother who was still on the phone with the hospital.

"Stick your finger in her mouth to clear the mucus."

He didn't hesitate, gently poking his finger in the tiny mouth to clean it. His hand shook and he prayed. *Please, please breathe, precious one.*

Everyone held their breath. First there was a whine and then a wail and it was the loveliest sound they'd ever heard.

"We're landing," Chance said. "Emergency crew is waiting."

Kid leaned over and rested his face against Lucky's.

"Look at her, Kid. Isn't she the most beautiful thing you've ever seen?"

He kissed her lips. "Almost."

Two hours later they sat in the neonatal unit watching their child through the glass of an incubator. "It's just a precaution," he assured Lucky. "She's fine. The doctor said she was just anxious to be born. He wants to keep her here for a few days."

She clutched his hand. "I was so afraid we were going to lose her."

"Me, too. I think I had a heart attack when she wasn't breathing."

"I think she's going to give us a lot of those in the years ahead."

"Mmm." He peered close at the gorgeous face. "I can't wait to get her out of here so I can hold her and carry her around."

"I can't wait for Daddy to see her."

"Chance is on his way to get him and Nettie."

She smiled. "It really does take a village for us to have a child."

"That's why when you go to school in the fall we'll have lots of babysitters. Mainly me who will probably not let anyone keep her."

She rubbed her face against him. "We have to give her a name."

"We've gone through every name in the alphabet, but I think I have the perfect one. I thought of it today when we were in that old house. My mother's name was Carol and yours was Rose. Let's call her Carol Rose. Carly for short. Of course, I'm calling her Precious."

She frowned.

"What?"

"Precious? And don't you dare say 'come on, Lucky.'"

He wrapped an arm around her. "I wouldn't dream of it. I'm happy. We can call her anything you want."

"You are such an…"

He kissed her and smiled into her eyes.

She smiled back. "Welcome to the world, Carol Rose Hardin—better known as Precious by her father." She stroked his face and everything was right in the universe.

* * * * *

HEART & HOME

Heartwarming romances where love can happen right when you least expect it.

COMING NEXT MONTH
AVAILABLE JANUARY 10, 2012

#1752 A HERO IN THE MAKING
North Star, Montana
Kay Stockham

#1753 HIS BROTHER'S KEEPER
Dawn Atkins

#1754 WHERE IT BEGAN
Together Again
Kathleen Pickering

#1755 UNDERCOVER COOK
Too Many Cooks?
Jeannie Watt

#1756 SOMETHING TO PROVE
Cathryn Parry

#1757 A SOLDIER'S SECRET
Suddenly a Parent
Linda Style

You can find more information on upcoming Harlequin® titles, free excerpts and more at www.HarlequinInsideRomance.com.

HSRCNM1211

REQUEST YOUR FREE BOOKS!

2 FREE NOVELS PLUS 2 FREE GIFTS!

Harlequin® SuperRomance®

Exciting, emotional, unexpected!

YES! Please send me 2 FREE Harlequin® Superromance® novels and my 2 FREE gifts (gifts are worth about $10). After receiving them, if I don't wish to receive any more books, I can return the shipping statement marked "cancel." If I don't cancel, I will receive 6 brand-new novels every month and be billed just $4.69 per book in the U.S. or $5.24 per book in Canada. That's a saving of at least 15% off the cover price! It's quite a bargain! Shipping and handling is just 50¢ per book in the U.S. and 75¢ per book in Canada.* I understand that accepting the 2 free books and gifts places me under no obligation to buy anything. I can always return a shipment and cancel at any time. Even if I never buy another book, the two free books and gifts are mine to keep forever.

135/336 HDN FC6T

Name (PLEASE PRINT)

Address Apt. #

City State/Prov. Zip/Postal Code

Signature (if under 18, a parent or guardian must sign)

Mail to the **Reader Service:**

IN U.S.A.: P.O. Box 1867, Buffalo, NY 14240-1867

IN CANADA: P.O. Box 609, Fort Erie, Ontario L2A 5X3

Not valid for current subscribers to Harlequin Superromance books.

Are you a current subscriber to Harlequin Superromance books and want to receive the larger-print edition? Call 1-800-873-8635 or visit www.ReaderService.com.

* Terms and prices subject to change without notice. Prices do not include applicable taxes. Sales tax applicable in N.Y. Canadian residents will be charged applicable taxes. Offer not valid in Quebec. This offer is limited to one order per household. All orders subject to credit approval. Credit or debit balances in a customer's account(s) may be offset by any other outstanding balance owed by or to the customer. Please allow 4 to 6 weeks for delivery. Offer available while quantities last.

Your Privacy—The Reader Service is committed to protecting your privacy. Our Privacy Policy is available online at www.ReaderService.com or upon request from the Reader Service.

We make a portion of our mailing list available to reputable third parties that offer products we believe may interest you. If you prefer that we not exchange your name with third parties, or if you wish to clarify or modify your communication preferences, please visit us at www.ReaderService.com/consumerschoice or write to us at Reader Service Preference Service, P.O. Box 9062, Buffalo, NY 14269. Include your complete name and address.

HSR11

SPECIAL EDITION

Life, Love and Family

Karen Templeton

introduces

The FORTUNES *of* TEXAS: Whirlwind Romance

When a tornado destroys Red Rock, Texas, Christina Hastings finds herself trapped in the rubble with telecommunications heir Scott Fortune. He's handsome, smart and everything Christina has learned to guard herself against. As they await rescue, an unlikely attraction forms between the two and Scott soon finds himself wanting to know about this mysterious beauty. But can he catch Christina before she runs away from her true feelings?

FORTUNE'S CINDERELLA

Available December 27th wherever books are sold!

www.Harlequin.com

SSE65643

Brittany Grayson survived a horrible ordeal at the hands of a serial killer known as The Professional... who's after her now?

Harlequin® Romantic Suspense presents a new installment in Carla Cassidy's reader-favorite miniseries, LAWMEN OF BLACK ROCK.

Enjoy a sneak peek of TOOL BELT DEFENDER.

Available January 2012 from Harlequin® Romantic Suspense.

"Brittany?" His voice was deep and pleasant and made her realize she'd been staring at him openmouthed through the screen door.

"Yes, I'm Brittany and you must be..." Her mind suddenly went blank.

"Alex. Alex Crawford, Chad's friend. You called him about a deck?"

As she unlocked the screen, she realized she wasn't quite ready yet to allow a stranger inside, especially a male stranger.

"Yes, I did. It's nice to meet you, Alex. Let's walk around back and I'll show you what I have in mind," she said. She frowned as she realized there was no car in her driveway. "Did you walk here?" she asked.

His eyes were a warm blue that stood out against his tanned face and was complemented by his slightly shaggy dark hair. "I live three doors up." He pointed up the street to the Walker home that had been on the market for a while.

"How long have you lived there?"

"I moved in about six weeks ago," he replied as they

walked around the side of the house.

That explained why she didn't know the Walkers had moved out and Mr. Hard Body had moved in. Six weeks ago she'd still been living at her brother Benjamin's house trying to heal from the trauma she'd lived through.

As they reached the backyard she motioned toward the broken brick patio just outside the back door. "What I'd like is a wooden deck big enough to hold a barbecue pit and an umbrella table and, of course, lots of people."

He nodded and pulled a tape measure from his tool belt. "An outdoor entertainment area," he said.

"Exactly," she replied and watched as he began to walk the site. The last thing Brittany had wanted to think about over the past eight months of her life was men. But looking at Alex Crawford definitely gave her a slight flutter of pure feminine pleasure.

Will Brittany be able to heal in the arms of Alex,
her hotter-than-sin handyman...or will a second
psychopath silence her forever? Find out in
TOOL BELT DEFENDER
Available January 2012
from Harlequin® Romantic Suspense
wherever books are sold.

Copyright © 2011 by Carla Cassidy

HRSEXP0112